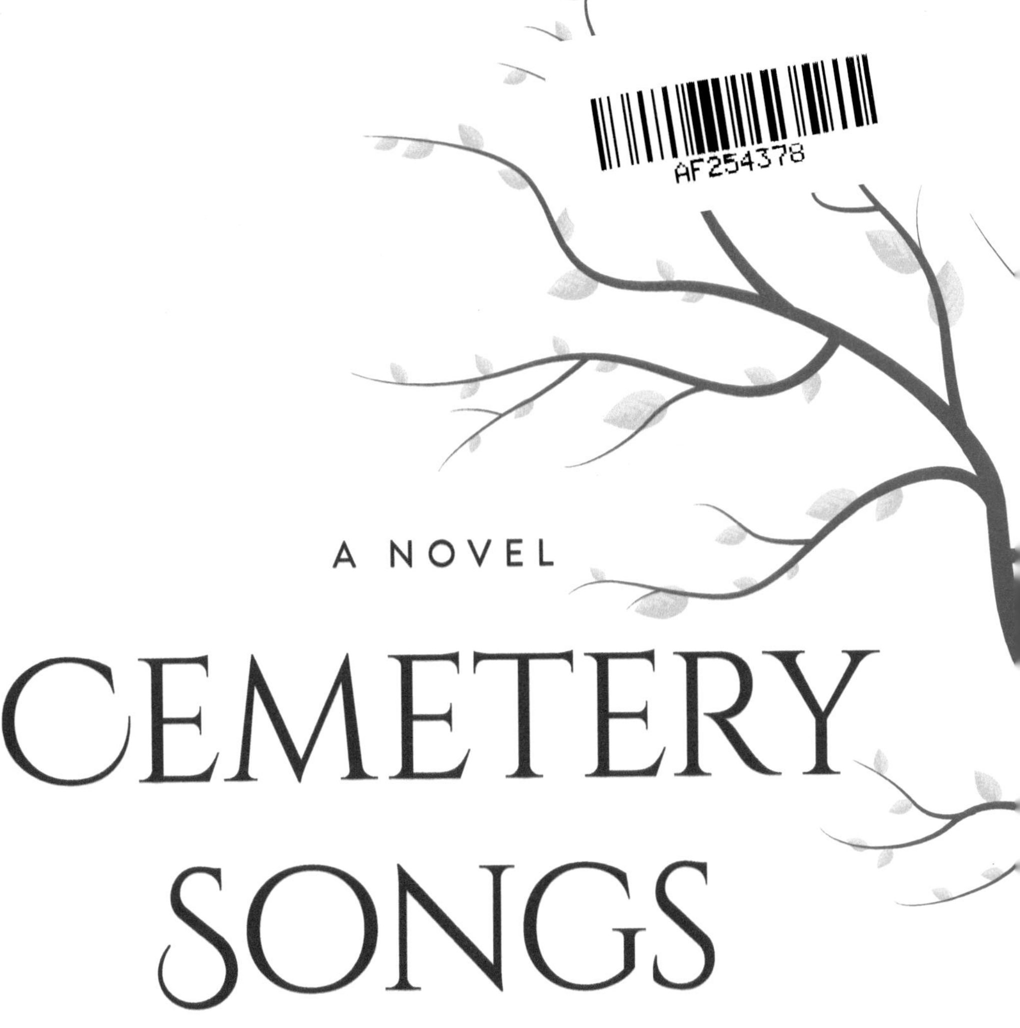

A NOVEL

CEMETERY SONGS

BY JULIE GILBERT

LAKESTONE PRESS
Saint Peter, MN

LAKESTONE PRESS

juliegilbertbooks.com

Design by Lisa Vega

Publisher's Cataloging-in-Publication Data provided by Five Rainbows Cataloging Services

Names: Gilbert, Julie, 1976- author.

Title: Cemetery songs / Julie Gilbert.

Description: Saint Peter, MN : Lakestone Press, 2020. | Summary: Transracial adoptee Polly Stone investigates the mystery of an abandoned Black settlement with the help of a ghost. | Audience: Grades 9-12.

Identifiers: LCCN 2020917319 (print) | ISBN 978-1-7356804-0-8 (paperback) | ISBN 978-1-7356804-1-5 (ebook)

Subjects: LCSH: Young adult fiction. | CYAC: Racially mixed people—Fiction. | Supernatural—Fiction. | Adoption—Fiction. | Detective and mystery fiction. | BISAC: YOUNG ADULT FICTION / Ghost Stories. | YOUNG ADULT FICTION / Mysteries & Detective Stories. | YOUNG ADULT FICTION / Family / Adoption. | YOUNG ADULT FICTION / Social Themes / Prejudice & Racism.

Classification: LCC PZ7.1.G55 Ce 2020 (print) | LCC PZ7.1.G55 (ebook) | DDC [Fic]—dc23.

For Jesse and Sam

AUTHOR'S NOTE

The inspiration for *Cemetery Songs* came one misty morning on a car ride through southeastern Minnesota. I drove past a rural cemetery and an image jumped into my head of a young woman walking peacefully among the stones. I wondered what would bring a teenager to an abandoned cemetery on a foggy day. The answer to those questions became *Cemetery Songs*.

Polly's exploration of her identity as a transracial adoptee is inspired by my experiences as a white adoptive parent raising children of color. I drew on situations I've encountered as a parent, as well as the questions and experiences of my own children. I do not speak for my kids, nor do I speak for other transracial adoptees, their families or birth families. Transracial adoption – like all adoption – is complex; this book represents some of my efforts to better understand and illuminate those complexities as I have experienced them.

The history of African Americans in Minnesota grounds the novel. I read everything I could find on the subject and spent several days exploring various collections at the Minnesota History Center. This book is not historical fiction, however. Rather, it is fiction that has been inspired by the historical record, especially by the gaps in what we know and the "what ifs" that have been lost to time. There is no Monroe, Minnesota, just as there is no Jessam Crossing. But these imaginary places are rooted in actual history.

At the end of the novel you'll find recommended readings to help you further explore transracial adoption and the Black experience in Minnesota. Any errors in facts or interpretation in the novel are solely mine.

Julie Gilbert
September 2020

CHAPTER

ONE

S he's down there," Billy says, his voice interrupting the night. It's the first thing he's said since we left his dusty truck to trudge among the dead buried at Bluff Hill Cemetery. The arc of his flashlight reflects off the headstones, drawing my eyes from the last light of day that stains the horizon. Granite erupts in fireworks, tiny sparkles glinting like a million cat eyes.

I trip on the gravel, the ruts that were first molded by spring's torrential rains and later baked by the sun that settled over Monroe, Minnesota, at the start of July. My knee slams the ground.

"You hurt?" Billy's voice is closer now, his flashlight narrowing to a perfect circle at my feet.

"No," I say, picking myself up before he can touch me. I brush off my shorts and shake out my legs like I do before I step onto the blocks at a swim meet. "I'm fine."

Billy watches me from under hooded eyes. Then he reaches into his pocket and pulls out a crumpled piece of paper.

"Figured you'd have that thing memorized by now," I say, trying to pretend my voice isn't shaking.

The flashlight tips and for an instant Billy's olive skin glows orange and monstrous red. His eyes are pits of tar. I take a step back, chastising myself

1

at the same time for being afraid. I've played this game at countless slumber parties. I know it's just a trick of the light.

"Yeah, well. Let's just get this over with."

He slips the paper back in his pocket and sets off along the path, his boots making a hollow sound as they thud against the ground. A backpack bounces against his broad shoulders. I hurry to catch up with him, the skin prickling between my shoulder blades. I can't shake the feeling that the cat eyes are real.

"You're not having second thoughts, are you?" I ask, squelching the hope rising in my chest. I tug on his arm to get him to stop. His skin is warm and I release him quickly.

"Polly, we're long past second thoughts. I must have been crazy to think this would work."

"You're the one who came up with this ridiculous plan in the first place!" I protest.

Billy's pacing tight circles and running his hand through his dark hair. "You're gonna have to think of another way to buy my silence," he says at last.

"You don't really believe that I can do it," I say. "You don't think I can hear what they're saying or that I can amplify their memories."

"Would *you* believe you?"

I prop my hands on my hips. "You seemed certain enough when you came to my house a few weeks ago. You told me everything I supposedly said in the woods that night."

The problem was, I didn't have any memory of what I'd said at the party last April or who might have heard. I was drunk. I don't remember blathering my secrets. Apparently I did, however, and Billy heard. He knew all the details, which meant he had learned the secret only one other person in the world knew: I could hear the final thoughts of the dead.

"Maybe I got it wrong," Billy says. I can feel his eyes on me in the dark. I debate what to do. I could pretend that whatever I said was nothing more than drunk delusion. Then I remember why we're here. Pretending Billy is wrong won't save me.

I don't remember much of the rest of that night, either. But Billy followed me after I left the party. He saw what I did at the school. And he took pictures. If those pictures get out, my future would be ruined. Billy won't give me the pictures unless I pay him, but I'm broke. In the end, my abilities to hear the dead are all I have to offer.

"You didn't get it wrong," I say.

There's a pause. It's freeing to admit my abilities to someone else. I'm reminded of when I told my ex-best friend Henrietta when we were eight. She thought it was cool and never doubted me. I have no idea what she thinks of it now. We haven't spoken in two years.

"Even if you can hear what they're saying, what are the odds you'll learn anything I can use to crack those security questions?" Billy says.

"You brought something from her house, right?" I ask, feeling a surge of determination. I march down the path with Billy at my heels. This is the first time in months I almost feel like myself.

"In the backpack."

"What'd you get?"

"Coffee mug. Couple of seashells that were sitting on her windowsill. I wrapped 'em up in an old sweatshirt that was on her bed."

"Fine. Keep your head down and stick close to me."

"Jesus, Polly, this isn't *Mission: Impossible*," Billy mutters as he follows me.

"You have any trouble getting into her house?"

"Nope. Went during the funeral yesterday. They'd left the back door open."

"Huh." A thought occurs to me. "Why didn't you just steal her bank card or grab some cash when you broke in?"

Billy huffs. "Don't you think I looked?"

Sweat trickles down my forehead and the curly ends of my ponytail brush the back of my neck. We skirt the edge of the security light and I catch another glimpse of his face. He looks like a jungle cat straining against its leash.

"You're afraid, aren't you?"

Billy's footsteps stumble but his voice is even. "I don't like cemeteries. Let's just do this."

I keep walking, my flip flops slapping against my heels. We don't say a word as we approach the gravesite, but the walk is not quiet for me.

Don't forget to feed the chickens, a woman's voice slides through the darkness. *Don't forget to feed the chickens,* she implores as we pass.

Goodbye, you sons of bitches! a man shouts to my left and I choke back a snort of laughter. Sometimes the dead are funny.

We reach an older section of the cemetery and I'm enveloped by the singsong lilt of Swedish. I've been around enough dead Swedish immigrants to pick out words and phrases.

"You're doing it now, aren't you? Listening to them?" Billy sounds wary.

"Old habit," I shrug. "Now where's Ms. Svenson?"

"There." Billy points to a mound of fresh soil midway down a row in the new section. The clouds covering the moon slide toward darker parts of the sky and in the dim light, I can see it.

"Okay, what do we know about her?" I ask when I'm standing over the grave. I nudge the dirt with my sandal. Grit creeps between my toes.

Billy switches on the flashlight and pulls the crumpled paper from his pocket again.

"Ida Mae Svenson, ninety-seven, died in her sleep at the Benedictine Living Center. Funeral was today, with memorials preferred to the Humane Society. Interment at Bluff Hill Cemetery immediately following the service. You want to see a picture?" he asks, thrusting the paper at me.

"I'll see her soon enough," I say, crouching next to the dirt. "What else?"

"Not much. Born in East Farmington, the youngest of eight. Married Carl here right after the war."

I glance toward where Billy is pointing. A flat stone spans the mound of dirt, bearing both their names.

"They having some kind of big reunion or something?" Billy asks.

"I told you, it doesn't work like that. I can hear echoes of their final thoughts. That's all. At least until I amplify them. And I'm not going to amplify Carl." Still, I cock my head and concentrate on the flat patch of earth just beyond Ida Mae's grave. "He's saying . . . he's saying, 'It's forty-three degrees in Albuquerque this morning.'"

"That was his last thought? What the hell does that mean?"

"I just report it, Billy. I don't interpret it." I lay my hand on the earth covering Ida Mae. Her voice is much louder. I stop and listen. "Ida Mae is saying, 'Now where did I put that thread?'"

"That's all?"

"That's all."

"Missing thread won't give me access to her bank account."

"That's why I had you go to her house," I say, irritation rising from a hot knot in my gut. "Now let me have the stuff."

He swings the backpack off his shoulder and into my hands. I ease the zipper open and start unwrapping the objects Billy brought.

"Carl died in 1985," I note. "She was a widow for almost three decades. Think she ever dated again?"

"Gross," Billy comments, returning to the obituary. "They had three children, all married. Eight grandkids. No, seven. One died."

"Huh," I murmur.

"What?"

"It's sad is all," I say. "Does it say how old the kid was?"

"Why? You gonna raid his grave next?"

I shoot to my feet and the seashells clatter to the ground.

"Listen to me, you asshole, I'm not a grave robber. And do I need to remind you that this is your crazy idea? If you're going to insult me, we can leave right now."

Billy takes a step toward me. "And how exactly will you buy seventeen grand worth of my silence?"

My breath catches in my throat as he towers over me. I take a step backward from the warmth radiating toward me, trying to ignore the scent of pine and sweat wafting from Billy's skin. I've saved exactly $342 from lifeguarding this year. The rest has gone to the mall and the college savings account my parents made me set up, even though I might never make it to college now that I'm flunking out of school.

I tuck that thought away. It's another secret I'm keeping.

"Fine," I say. "I'll do it. But stop pissing me off."

Billy holds up his hands and withdraws. I sink onto the grave, sitting cross-legged. It hasn't rained in weeks and blades of grass prick my thighs, sharp enough that I wonder if there will be scratches on my skin later. I line up the coffee cup next to the seashells and then drape the sweatshirt over my lap. I straighten my spine, imagining I am one of the Buddhist monks in the documentary about the Dalai Lama we watched in my world history class last spring.

"Am I supposed to do something?" Billy asks, and I jump. I've only ever amplified in front of Henrietta before.

"Just leave me alone and keep watch."

Billy moves away, leaning his hip against a nearby stone. I think about messing with him and telling him that he's sitting on top of devil worshippers planning on stealing his soul, but he wouldn't believe me. There may be devil worshippers in Monroe, but they wouldn't be buried in Bluff Hill under a marker carved with a tractor and a sewing machine.

I shut out thoughts of Billy and concentrate on the woman lying beneath my feet. I take a breath and when I exhale I discover I'm whispering an apology. Ida Mae doesn't respond except to repeat her inquiry about the thread.

I wrap my hands around her coffee mug and slide toward her mind.

I don't remember the first time I heard a dead person. It was just always something I could do. When I was four, my mom did a pottery series inspired by mid-1800s cemetery markers. She spent most of the summer in rural cemeteries, kneeling before stones with paper and charcoal. I ran wild in the long grass, the sun warm on my face, listening to the murmur of lost voices.

I was eight when I realized no one else could hear them. We were at my grandmother's funeral and I was laughing because Elmore Schabert (1917–1982) in the next plot over kept yelling, *FART!* at the top of his lungs. My dad had to take me aside and calm me down. I asked why he wasn't laughing and he sat unmoving as I explained what I had heard. When his face folded in an origami of concern, I amended my story and told him that of course I was imagining it.

It never seemed weird to me. It's always been a part of me, like my brown skin or the fact that I was adopted. But as I watched the worry emerge on my dad's face that morning, I knew that it was a secret I had to keep. Just like my skin and adoption story, hearing the dead made me different in my little world. Even at eight I knew not to draw attention to it.

It wasn't until seventh grade that I learned I could amplify the voices and tumble into the memories of the dead. Rory Donaldson had been diagnosed with leukemia in October that year. We organized bake sales and bowl-a-thons to raise money for his treatment. His friends shaved their heads when Rory's hair fell out. But not Billy, I remember. He was already lost in a haze of pot smoke by then. Rory was soon lost in a tangle of hospital tubes. He was in the ground by the next April.

It snowed hard that year, huge storms rolling off the plains to squelch any hopes of spring. On the day of Rory's funeral, his parents gave us each one of the hundreds of friendship bracelets Rory made in the hospital. I was clutching mine and snow was pelting my neck as I listened to Rory's final thought (*Swing and a miss*), when suddenly I was in his mind, watching an army of Pokémon figures advance on Barbie's Dream House beneath a shelf full of trophies. The scene shifted and I watched two Christmases and a pool party before I realized I was doing more than just hearing his final thoughts. Shocked, I dropped the bracelet and earned a few confused looks from my classmates.

I experimented again a few weeks later. The next time we visited my grandma's grave, I clutched a Little Mermaid beach towel she had brought me from Florida. While my parents watered geraniums and clipped the boxwoods, I gripped the towel and fell into her mind, past the sigh that had been her last thought. I saw Florida, the sandy beach tinged with sadness as she walked alone. I saw a young version of my mother fall off a bike and I saw my grandmother aim a BB gun at the pigeons on her roof. Then I saw my own face, velvet brown pressed against her white hand. It was weird.

I stopped visiting cemeteries a few years ago. I didn't renounce my abilities or anything, but I just drifted away. I had new friends, a boyfriend. When everything fell apart a few months ago, I started coming back. Mainly to the Sigrudsons behind my house. But a few times to Bluff Hill and some of the other cemeteries in town. This will be the first time I've amplified anyone in years, though.

Billy clears his throat behind me, the sound rumbling in his chest, and I realize I am floating on the current of Ida Mae's thoughts. I push my memories aside and tighten my grip on her coffee mug. I tuck the seashells between my palm and the cup. Their spiky horns dig into my flesh. I take a breath and let Ida Mae's words float over me and pull me under. It's as familiar to me as breathing.

A torrent of images rushes through my mind. I see white gardenias in a bridal bouquet and a scrap of pink afghan. I sail through feedsack dresses and curling irons. I am present at christenings and ice cream socials. Big band music echoes in my ears and I watch in dismay as President Kennedy's death is announced on the television. The later years contain cheap cardigans from Sears, grandkid artwork taped to the refrigerator, and one glorious, sun-soaked week in Palm Springs.

I grasp at details but they spin away, lost in the vortex of a fading mind.

Then, a picture of an orange tabby jumps into my head, a mangy creature that Carl pretended to hate but tolerated on behalf of the kids. The tabby poses on a table, bobbing as he attempts to jump to the Christmas tree, which is dripping in tinsel. There's a shout and a broom handle knocks the cat to the floor.

"Army," I say as the picture fades.

"Huh?" Billy asks.

"It was the name of their cat. They had a cat that tried to jump onto the Christmas tree one year. Carl almost killed it."

Billy scrawls in a notepad that he pulls out of his back pocket.

"Army, cat, okay. What else you got?"

"Not much," I say, although I tell him the name of the hotel in Palm Springs and a few other details. We already have the dates of anniversaries and birthdays from the obituary. Billy's plan is to use the details to answer security questions and break into bank accounts. He found lists of common security questions on the internet and I'm supposed to get as many details about first grade teachers and prom dates as possible. Billy hopes we stumble across a match or two when he tries to log into the newly dead's bank account. I don't like it, but I don't have much of a choice if I want to pay him off before he tells everyone what I've done.

"You need to do anything else?" I ask, suddenly anxious to leave.

"Nope, let's go."

The cat eyes on the gravestones follow us the whole way out, silently marking our passage.

The road to my house winds through the grassy meadows overlooking Monroe before climbing Brammer Bluff. Streetlights carpet the plain below us, cheap sequins on a discarded prom dress. The thick, inky ribbon of the Mississippi River hugs the miniature downtown, dividing us from the sleeping farmlands across the Wisconsin state line. Billy's muffler rattles as his truck bounces over the unpaved roads. I hold my armpits up to the vents, but the wisps of cool air are not strong enough to dry my shirt. We don't say anything.

Billy eases the truck to a stop underneath the massive cottonwood tree that marks the entrance to my driveway. The drive curves toward the house, blocking the truck from view. I've told Billy this but he turns off his lights anyway.

"You good?" he asks as I reach for the handle.

"I'm fine," I say, popping the door open. I'm about to slide to the ground when Billy's words stop me.

"We're not even." His hands grip the wheel. "Not yet."

"I never said we were," I reply after a long moment.

I lean against the cottonwood as Billy executes a perfect three-point turn and vanishes down the hill. Only then do I exhale the breath I'd been holding. I collapse against the rough bark. I'm tempted to stay here all night, sleeping underneath the thick branches, but mosquitoes start nipping my ankles and neck.

Images of the past few months spin through my mind: the party, the flames, the drive halfway across the country, all sparked by the phone call that destroyed the axis of my world.

"Not now," I tell my thoughts. I don't have the strength to go through them again right now. Instead I wander back to the house.

It is surprisingly easy to sneak out of my house, especially when my dad is away at his lab, like he is this month. A few hours ago I hugged my mom goodnight and waited until she trailed down the hall to her bedroom. Then I slid open my window and climbed onto the kitchen roof. The original farmhouse was built in the 1890s and has been expanded and renovated several times, mainly by my parents when they bought the place fourteen years ago. There are countless nooks, crannies, and conveniently placed footholds to help a girl sneak in and out, as long as she is careful to avoid the compost pile behind the kitchen.

I shimmy through my window and reattach the screen, then close the curtains and light a few candles on my bedside table. Soon the scent of pine and frankincense permeate the air. When I put the lighter down, my hand knocks something to the floor. I bend and retrieve a tiny black elephant figurine studded with rhinestones. I'd almost forgotten about it. Henrietta gave me the elephant two years ago after she came back from a mission trip to Thailand with her family. It was only a few weeks before we stopped being friends. I've meant to throw the elephant away countless times but I always hang onto it; a sign of my guilt and regret, I suppose. I return it to its place next to the candles.

I step over the squeaky pine board near the foot of the bed and turn on my iPod, filling the room with the brassy growl of Nina Simone. I undo my ponytail and shake down my hair. I should rinse it under water and slather it with conditioner before running a comb through it, but I'm too tired. I catch sight of my reflection in the mirror. I haven't been avoiding the mirror in the past four months, but this is the first time I've stopped and looked in a long time.

What I see surprises me. I'm Polly but I'm also different. My skin is its usual darker summer shade, thanks to my lifeguard job at the city pool. My hair is extra curly from the humidity, the dark strands jutting from my scalp. My face has always been lean but now it looks almost gaunt. I step back and pull my shirt over my head. My shoulders and upper arms are muscled. My breasts are small and round. I look into my eyes last, wondering if I inherited them from my birthmother. Did she ever stand in front of a mirror, wondering who the woman was looking back? I gaze for another moment, seeing a despair that wasn't there at the beginning of spring.

I flop on my back and gaze at the ceiling. There are two cracks, one near the window and one that branches over my bed. They look like rivers on a map of a fantasy kingdom. I've been watching for years to see if the two will ever meet. So far they haven't. June bugs bounce off the window screen. For a second I think about opening my history book and tackling the mountain of work that is crushing me. *You don't want to start a big project when you're tired,* my mind tells me. *You just need to find some big block of time where you can really concentrate on your work.*

"Maybe tomorrow," I murmur. I wrap my hair with a silk scarf, snuff the candles, and go to sleep.

CHAPTER

TWO

The next morning I stand in the shower until the water runs cold. At least my curls will be happy. When I get back to my room, my elbow bumps the books and notepads piled on top of my laptop. I jump to keep them from sliding to the floor, although I'm not sure why I bother. When I had my "reaction"—as Mom and Dad call it—last April, my parents sprang into action, asking the school to excuse me from classes for the rest of the year and give me extensions to finish the work by the end of the summer. There was a time when I wanted to finish the work. I've always been an A girl. I excel at everything I do, mainly because I'm smart and I work hard. But after a few days of being home from school, I lost all of my motivation. Every time I sat down to write an essay or make a timeline, I couldn't shake this thought: *Why bother?*

I feel terrible about it. My parents went out on a limb for me, and this is how I'm repaying them. But I can't quite make myself sit down and do my work. The few times I've tried, I've felt like a million ants are swarming over my skin, and if I sit still, I might die.

"Maybe later," I say to a battered copy of *Middlemarch* that's teetering on a tower of pre-calc and chemistry textbooks. I try to pretend I'm not lying.

I pull on some shorts and a tank and head downstairs. My mom has already poured me a bowl of granola and the pottery rasps on the counter as she pushes it toward me. Wisps of brown and gray escape her ponytail and her eyes have the distracted look she gets when she's in the middle of a piece. Her pale skin is just starting to wrinkle around her eyes. The observation startles me. When did my mom get old?

"Hey, Mom," I say, giving her a hug.

"Morning, sweetie," she says, kissing the top of my head. There's a thick pad of paper open on the counter next to her. She pulls a pencil from behind her ear, jots a few lines and stands back, squinting. I start eating. Mom jumps at the noise and starts attacking the paper with an eraser.

"Maybe . . ." she mutters.

"How's the sculpture going?"

"Oh, fine, fine," she says, pursing her lips. She tears out the page. I'm a little surprised to see her in the kitchen. Usually when she's this distracted, she forgets to eat.

"What's the piece about?"

"Fire," Mom says absently.

All of the muscles in my body contract. I take a deep breath. "Fire? Why?"

"Oh, I suppose the fire at the school got me thinking about it. How fire is destructive but also cleansing."

I can't think of anything more to say other than "Huh."

"There was an article in the paper the other day about how the new machine shed is almost complete."

"Do they know anything more about the fire itself?" I ask, trying to keep my voice level.

"The paper didn't say. I don't think they know much more," Mom says, never taking her eyes from her sketches. Sunlight spills through the window behind her.

I start to relax for real. All anyone knew was that an equipment shed at the high school caught fire on a Saturday evening in April. Someone lit the pile of wood the school was saving for the year-end bonfire. No one is sure if the arsonist meant to burn down the shed, too.

"Well that's good," I say, pushing back from the island. I check the rooster clock hanging over the stove. "I gotta go. My shift starts soon."

"What time will you be back, Pol?"

I drop my bowl into the sink with a clatter.

"Um, after work."

"Apollonia Stone, you're at the archives until noon and then at the pool until four. They're forecasting thunderstorms this afternoon, so if the pool closes early, I want you back here no more than a half hour later, working on your homework."

I wrinkle my nose when she uses my full name. She and Dad wanted to name me Madison, but my birthmom had already picked out the name Apollonia. My parents could have changed it, but they wanted to honor my birthmom's wishes, so I got stuck with the most unwieldy name in Monroe. Maybe the whole state.

"Yes, Mom."

"Will you finally have a draft of that essay to show me?"

"Um, sure," I lie.

"Your odometer is at 134,908. There shouldn't be more than thirty more miles on it by the end of the week." I must look surprised because my mom's face drops and she lays her hand on mine. Her fingers are cool and strong.

"Polly, it's for your own good. Your dad and I are trying to give you space within the limits we've set. We trust that you'll figure things out. But . . ."

"But you don't want me driving halfway to Arizona again."

"I don't want you frightening us again. Not like that."

My shoulders slump. "I know," I say, even as frustration bubbles to the surface. "Although . . ."

"Although what, sweetie?"

I pull my hand free. "I'm seventeen, Mom. I'll be out of the house next year. You can't control me forever."

This time my mom looks surprised. "We're not trying to control you. We're trying to keep you safe. It's what we've been trying to do your whole life."

I shouldn't say it but I do: "You're not trying to keep me safe from the world. You're trying to keep me safe from myself."

I see the hurt in her eyes and feel a shameful triumph knowing I'd put it there. For a moment I imagine slamming my palms against the counter and ranting that I had reasons for driving halfway to Arizona and would have been totally fine if they hadn't interfered. I swallow and my throat feels raw. It's muscle memory from the weeks where I actually threw those fits, screaming and raging at my parents.

"We're trying to help you get your head on straight," Mom continues. "Polly, your dad and I see our role as facilitating your journey to adulthood and—"

My frustration is full-fledged anger by now. We've been dancing around this fight for weeks.

"Mom, I don't want to hear it," I snap. My mom stops talking.

This is a first for her. She's always believed there isn't a problem that can't be solved by talking through it. It doesn't matter if my hamster died or if some awful stranger yelled the n-word at me out a car window (both things happened when I was twelve and both left me stunned), Mom will employ talk therapy. Even if her own heart is breaking from fear and worry. I know she's trying to help, but sometimes she talks so much that I can't hear my own thoughts. It's like she can't help herself. She has to run in to fix things instead of just letting them be.

I take a few deep breaths. The dripping faucet punctuates the rush of air.

"I should get your dad to fix that," Mom says, her eyes sliding to the sink. "He's back for a few days next week. The Weston-Hernandezes are going to Dijon for the rest of the month and your dad decided the lab could do without him for a little bit."

I clear my throat. "Well, that's good."

We are a frozen tableau in the sunny kitchen, *Mother and Daughter Engaged in Misunderstanding.*

"Polly," my mom starts.

"What?"

"I just . . . I just wish I could make things okay again."

Tears prick my eyes. "Like going back in time before my birthmom died?"

"Yes, like that," Mom says at last.

"I didn't know you felt like that," I whisper.

Mom makes the first move, coming over to wrap me in her arms. "Oh sweetie," she murmurs against my hair. "If I could, I would."

I relax against her, breathing in her familiar scent of rosemary and cedar. Maybe things will be okay between us, I think. But then Mom keeps talking.

"We can't go back. And I wish Althea hadn't died before you had a chance to meet her. Before we all had a chance to meet her." She sniffles and wipes at her nose as she pulls back from me. "I just wish I could make life easy for you. Remove all obstacles. Protect you forever. The world is not nice sometimes. Most of the time, I guess."

Oddly enough, her words make me feel worse. Not because I don't want her to protect me and keep me safe. But because I know it's impossible. I sigh and shake my head.

"Thanks, Mom," I murmur. I make a show of checking the clock again. "I have to go. Tasha's waiting for me."

"How's the archives work going?" Mom asks.

"Good," I say. "Some of it's boring but I kind of like other parts of it."

"And Tasha?" Mom asks, her eyebrows lifted in anticipation.

I turn away to roll my eyes. I know what she's asking. "She's a good role model," I say.

"Well, that's good," Mom says. I wonder if she's as relieved as I am that we're talking about normal things again.

I grab my stuff and walk past Mom on my way out the door. She catches my arm and gives it a squeeze. She looks like she's going to say something but changes her mind. I slide my arms around her neck and give her a quick hug.

"See you later, Mom."

The clock on the dashboard of my 1998 Buick hasn't worked in years, but a quick glance at my phone tells me I have a few minutes before I have to be at the archives. Before winding down the hill into town, I turn onto the gravel road that leads to the scenic overlook. I need a few minutes to think.

Monroe spreads before me as I scramble onto a picnic table near the parking lot. I'm alone, looking down from on high like an exhausted superhero at the end of a movie. Tiny gray and brown buildings dot the flat plain beneath the bluff. Railroad tracks hug the boundary between town and river. The river itself slides past town in several lazy channels interrupted by islands dotted with trees. A hot wind moves up the bluff, carrying the scent of mulch and honey.

I register little of this. My mind slides back to an evening three months ago when everything changed. The scene is like a movie, one I've watched so many times that I know it by heart. Sometimes the memory washes over me, while other times I notice something new, a detail I had forgotten. I rest my forehead on my knees and remember.

Thursday, April 16, 2015. My dad was home from a symposium and we were lingering at the table, the pearly evening light softening the windows. Our dining room is narrow and paneled in oak. There's a massive table and a built-in china hutch, which I always bang my hip against. So it's not the most comfortable room, but that night my family sat and chatted as the end of the vegetarian cassoulet congealed on our plates.

We were talking about college, like we often did. We had gone on a bunch of college tours already, the visit days geared toward enthusiastic and high-achieving juniors, like me. I already had an entire binder filled with colleges and their early application deadlines. The colleges I was considering were all elite private liberal arts colleges. Most of them were on the east coast, although there were a few on the west coast, too. I'd also planned to apply to Carleton, which was only an hour's drive from my house. That was to appease my parents; I wasn't planning on staying in Minnesota.

I knew I was "supposed" to go far away to college and get a great job in a big city and see my parents at most on holidays. This wasn't anything my parents had promoted, really. It was just something I knew I could and should do. This was what success looked like. Besides, my parents had talked about selling the house and moving to Minneapolis after I left for college. There would be nothing left for me in Monroe.

Will there be anything for you in Arizona?

Of all the details I remember from that evening, I remember that thought, because that's when the phone rang.

My mom took the call, all of us a little surprised to remember we still had a landline, especially one that jingled so loudly. Dad and I were quiet, trying to overhear her voice in the kitchen. All we could make out was a low murmur. Then mom carried the phone into the dining room. Her voice was hollow as she held the phone against her chest.

"Polly, the adoption agency wants to talk to you."

"What adoption agency?" I asked. "Why are they calling me?"

"I . . . the social worker wants to talk to you directly but - hang on a moment." She raised the phone to her face. "Can you call back in a few minutes? I want to tell my daughter the news first."

She hung up the phone and sat across the table, stretching her arms across the lace tablecloth to take my hands in hers. "Apollonia, there's no easy way to say this. But your birthmother has passed away."

Beside me, Dad let out an involuntary sigh and started rubbing my back between my shoulders. I remember feeling like I had been turned into a statue or a tree, like those women in the Greek myths we were studying in World Literature.

"What?" was all I could say.

"Your birthmother died," Mom repeated. "She was diagnosed a few months ago with stage four cancer."

"I . . . how . . . um, what?" I asked. I wasn't making much sense but I felt like I should say something, feel something. I felt frozen as the news tried to ram its way into my brain.

"The social worker knows more of the details, but I wanted you to hear the news from me. Polly, I'm so sorry." Mom's face was gray around the edges and her big blue eyes filled with tears. I couldn't figure out why she was so sad. She had barely met Althea.

The phone rang again. This time my mom answered it and passed it directly over to me.

"Hello?" I asked, pressing the phone against my ear.

"Hello? Apollonia? My name is Nancy and I'm the social worker at the agency your parents used during your adoption. Did they tell you what happened?"

"Yeah," I said. I don't remember too much more about my conversation with Nancy. My mom took the phone back after I let it slip from my hand. She learned that Althea had breast cancer that had gone undiagnosed until it had spread. "She had no options to go in for a mammogram," my mom told me later while we were still at the table, her own jaw gritted in anger. "I swear, this country and the way it treats women, especially poor women and women of color. I could just spit."

"Can we go to the funeral?" I asked, the question slipping from my mouth.

My mom looked like she was about to throw up, and that's when I knew.

"They already had the funeral."

"Yes. It just took awhile for the notice to get to the agency and for them to call us. But maybe we could arrange a trip to Arizona this summer? Visit her grave? We could show you the hospital where you were born, too, and the hotel where we stayed. Would you like that?"

I remember pushing her away and getting to my feet. "I need to go to my room."

I laid on my bed for hours, looking at the frozen rivers on my ceiling. My parents came by a few times to check on me. At one point Mom left peppermint tea on my bedside table. I let it get cold.

I still can't quite put how I felt into words. The best I can describe it is that it was like being on a glass bridge, a sturdy one that spanned a rocky valley thousands of feet below. For my entire life, I had been walking across that bridge, knowing I wouldn't fall even though I could see the rocks below.

When I learned that my birthmother had died, it was like the bridge had suddenly vanished and I hung in that breathless moment before free fall.

There was no birthdad to ask for answers, either. According to the adoption paperwork, he was a white guy who had told Althea he loved her and wanted to stay with her forever, but as soon as she got pregnant with me, he vanished. Althea chose not to disclose his identity.

That night I grabbed my keys and jumped into my car. I wasn't going to wait for a squishy family trip this summer. I needed answers now

Except I didn't get to Arizona. I was just outside of Wichita, Kansas when the cops pulled me over. My dad's college roommate is a Minnesota state trooper, and once my parents realized I had left town in the middle of the night, my dad called in a favor. The cop who pulled me over was nice enough, even though I'd gripped the wheel in terror as he approached the car, images of Michael Brown and Ferguson racing through my head. The cop said he couldn't force me to go home, but he'd be happy to escort me to the station where I could wait for my parents to fly in from Minneapolis. I knew I wasn't going to get any farther. I called my parents and then drove home, arriving a little after six that evening.

After my parents cried and hugged me, they grounded me for the rest of the year. In many ways, they were great. They were the ones who asked if I wanted to take some time off school. I think they thought it would be a week or two at most, but they didn't balk when I asked if I could stay home the rest of the year.

In their minds, that was the worst of it. I'd had a shock, I was grieving, and I was going to get back on track after taking a little time. They don't know the rest of it, though. They don't know I got drunk at a party a few weeks later and that I got the idea in my head that I needed to destroy the only connection I had to Althea, other than my DNA. They don't know I dragged my adoption paperwork and a can of gasoline out of the garage and took them to the school. They don't know the one secret that Billy is holding over my head: I'm the one who set the fire at the school.

CHAPTER

THREE

The Perrineville County Archives are located in the basement of the Monroe Public Library, which, according to my boss, Tasha Washington, is the second worst location for the archives on account of the leaky egress windows, the water pipes crisscrossing overhead, and the fact that the city never bothered to install climate control. Tasha says the only system that would be worse would be to store the cardboard boxes directly on the roof.

I started learning about water damage and mold and preservation when I began volunteering at the archives in May. My parents arranged it, telling me I needed to get out of the house. I'd rather work at the pool for longer hours since I'm not getting paid to be here, but I don't mind it. I'm not sure I want to be an archivist or anything, but it's kind of cool to learn about the history of the county. And to spend time with Tasha.

I pull into a free spot and crack the windows before I head toward the building. The library sits on the east side of Ash Lawn Park and overlooks a playground swarming with kids. The swings squeak just like they did when I was little. I pick out several brown faces among a sea of white. After a hundred and fifty years of lily-whiteness, Monroe is slowly changing. There's been a steady Hispanic population for nearly a decade, a handful of adopted kids like me, and even a few Somali families. I wonder what it would be like to be in kindergarten today and see some darker faces. I was the only brown kid in school until Chase Ryan moved to town in fifth grade. Our classmates thought our matching skin tones made us "exotic" (their insensitive word), which is probably the main reason Chase and I dated for two years in high school.

The other reason is that none of the white boys I liked ever asked me out. I had a lot of guy friends, and had major crushes on a few of them, but whenever I hinted about going out, they always stammered excuses, usually about how they mainly saw me as a friend. One of them even blurted something about how his parents wouldn't like it. I remember smiling through my shock and saying it was okay, as if I were the one who had to apologize.

Of course there was also Henrietta. Always Henrietta. She was the only African American kid in Monroe until me. Henrietta was homeschooled, so when we were together, it was as if we existed in our own realm, independent of Monroe and the rest of the world. We became friends after my mother befriended hers at the playground via an awkward conversation about hair care. Our mothers never really clicked, but Henrietta and I were like sisters parted at birth. For several years, I held onto the secret hope that she really was my biological sister somehow, another girl who had been placed for adoption by Althea. My mother found about it one day and told me gently that it wasn't true.

I jog up the library stairs. It's not yet ten but heat is already radiating off the stone, sliding up my legs and stroking my arms. I hold the doors open for an army of grim moms with strollers. They make a sharp left to catch the ramp that zigzags down the side of the building. A curly-haired toddler in the last stroller gazes at me with serious eyes. I give her a tiny grin and at the last moment her face breaks into a smile.

The doors swing shut behind me as I walk into the main hall. Rows of bookshelves march down the rooms on either side of the hall. The shelves are cheap, their metal sides dinged and scratched. They look weird next to the crown molding and wall sconces that date from a time when the library was the centerpiece of town. I catch a glimpse of the kids' section in the room behind the massive circulation desk. The walls are bright celery.

"The paint looks nice, Tessa," I call to the woman behind the desk.

"Thanks, Polly!" She wrinkles her nose, which causes her cherry-red glasses to tilt to one side. "Does it still smell like paint? I can't tell anymore."

"Kinda," I say, swinging around the side of the desk and clattering down the stairs to the archives. It's cooler down here and the ceilings are low. There's a door to the left that leads to the furnace and storage. I was only in there once with Tasha looking for additional shelving. I ended up with spider webs in my hair and Tasha scraped her calf on a rusty bolt. We abandoned the search so she could go to the hospital for a tetanus shot. The rest of the basement, which isn't large, belongs to the archives.

I drop my backpack on one of the long tables beneath the egress window. Three wobbly tables and a dusty printer make up the reading room. A low counter stretches across the area at the base of the stairs, separating the reading room from the administrative offices and storage rooms. When she gave me a tour the first day, Tasha laughed as she pointed out the cramped broom closet she uses as her office.

Marilyn Hanson sags against the corner of her desk behind the counter. The phone is pressed to her wide cheek and her fluffy gray hair waves as she speaks.

"Oh, that's terrible. That's just terrible, Sheila. Well, what do you expect when he does something as foolish as that? Honestly, that man has no more sense than the day you married him."

Marilyn keeps nodding, ignoring me as I drop into a plastic chair, the runners squeaking against the linoleum. One of the storage room doors opens and Tasha comes out. I wave and sit up straighter.

It's no secret that I idolize my boss. She dresses like she should be on the cover of Vogue. Today she's wearing wide-legged black slacks and a sleeveless white cowl-neck top. Her braids are pulled back from the side of her face and hang down her back. She's the only person besides my parents who calls me Apollonia, and they only do it when they're being serious. Tasha grins when she sees me.

I haven't told Tasha why my parents are making me volunteer at the archives. I've come close to telling her a few times, but I always chicken out. I'm afraid of seeing the same disappointment on her face that I see on my parents'.

"Well," Marilyn huffs, hanging up the phone. She swivels to face Tasha. "You'll never guess what happened."

"Sounds serious," Tasha says, reaching for a manila folder.

"That son-in-law of mine went waterskiing this weekend. Can you believe it? Waterskiing! That boy's not a spring chicken. The idiot got halfway across the lake when he fell and broke his leg!"

Tasha closes the folder and cradles it against her chest. "That is serious. Did they have to cast it?"

"He's at home now but my daughter's just beside herself. Their daycare is closed for the week and he was supposed to watch the kids," Marilyn prattles. Her breathing becomes lighter and faster, the shelf of her bosom heaving.

"You have some vacation time stored up, don't you?" Tasha asks, laying her hand on Marilyn's shoulder. "Why don't you take the week to be with your daughter?"

"Are you sure?" Marilyn asks. "I don't want to leave you in the lurch."

"You're not. We'll manage just fine, won't we, Apollonia?"

Marilyn starts and turns toward me. "Oh, Polly, I didn't even see you come in. How are you, dear? Did you hear about my idiot son-in-law?"

"Yeah. Too bad about his leg," I say, toeing the floor. "You should go be with them. I can help out around here."

Marilyn snaps into business mode, thumbing through the appointment book and catching Tasha up to date on the researchers who are coming in this week. Marilyn is efficient and organized, which is probably why Tasha hasn't fired her yet. If I had to work with Marilyn every day, I'd want to hide in the broom closet as much as possible.

"We'll be just fine, Marilyn. You take care of yourself," Tasha says fifteen minutes later after Marilyn has collected her insulated lunch bag and the white cardigan that hangs over the back of her chair.

"Thank you, Tasha," Marilyn says. "I'll keep you posted."

I'm surprised to see Tasha embrace her. Marilyn returns the hug before hoisting herself up the stairs.

"Doesn't she get on your nerves?" I ask once Marilyn is out of earshot. I wish I could take it back when I see Tasha frown. "I mean, she chatters on the phone all the time. That must get long."

"When I first got this job, Marilyn not only brought me enough casseroles to fill my freezer for a month, she gave me three quilts and an old parka, even though I'm from Chicago. I already had parkas and quilts of my own. She's a good person, Apollonia."

"I'm sorry," I say, shame cascading through my body. "I shouldn't have said that."

Tasha tips her head, her braids falling over one brown shoulder. "Do I wish she spent less time on the phone? Of course I do. And I'm sure I do things that annoy her, too, but that's life."

I nod and hug my elbows to my chest. "Sorry," I repeat.

Tasha gives a little snort. "It's fine. I didn't mean for this to turn into an After School Special."

"A what?"

"Nothing. It's from before your time," she grins, propping her hands on her hips. "Remind me, what have you been working on?"

"I've been processing the Holmberg collection," I say, rising to my feet and waving in the direction of the storage room. The Holmberg descendants are having a huge family reunion in August and Tasha's been helping them track down records about the family farm and their Swedish relatives. My job is to go through boxes of letters, farm receipts, and random paperwork and organize them into folders.

"You've done a good job with that but I think we can put that aside for now. The Holmbergs have almost everything they need."

"What do you want me to do instead?"

"What do you know about Fredrickson Annex?" Tasha asks, leaning against one of the long tables.

"What's Fredrickson Annex?"

"I guess that answers my question," she says with a laugh. I purse my lips. "You know where 61 makes that turn south of town right past the McDonald's?"

"Yeah."

"Fredrickson Annex is on the other side of the ridge. It's a plot of land roughly 2 square miles that the city annexed in the 1920s when Leland Fredrickson was mayor. Hence the name. From what I can piece together, it was just known as Monroe Township before that. There isn't much there, but the city has taken an interest in the space. It's mainly in a floodplain and too marshy to develop, but the city has been eyeing the ridge for senior housing."

"Okay," I say, struggling to see where this is going.

"Two things," she says, holding up one finger. "Before they can do anything, the city needs to figure out if the land is in private hands. They've asked me to help by sorting through old property records, some of which are at the courthouse and some of which might be hiding in the archives. Second," she says, holding up another finger. "They also need to make sure the land isn't historically significant. That's also where I come in."

"Significant how?"

"Well, you can't build on sacred sites, for example, so if it turned out to be a Native American burial ground, they couldn't build there."

"Is it?"

"Probably not, but there is an abandoned cemetery on the ridge, and I need your help mapping it."

I trip over my sandals and crash into the counter, knocking a mug of pencils to the ground.

"Shit," I mutter, cutting my thumb on a shard of ceramic.

"Here," Tasha says, shoving a wad of tissues into my hand. She disappears for a second and returns with a first aid kit. "Come with me. Last thing I need is to explain to my board why my best volunteer had to get stitches."

"It's not that bad," I say, sucking the base of my thumb. Hot blood fills my mouth, salty and sweet. Althea's blood, I think, as Tasha leads me to the sink in the tiny kitchen. She holds my hand in hers as the faucet runs, her skin several shades darker than mine. I wonder what it would have been like to grow up around hands like that.

"You okay?" Tasha asks after she's applied antibiotic ointment and a bandage to my thumb. Once we wipe up the blood it turns out the cut isn't deep.

"Yeah. Sorry about that."

"No problem. My fault for surprising you. Not a fan of cemeteries?"

I glance at her face, wondering if she knows my secret and is playing with me. Maybe she knows Billy and this is all an elaborate setup. I tell myself I'm being paranoid and that there's no way the elegant archivist would know a random high school dropout, even in a small town.

"No, cemeteries are fine. I like them, actually."

"Great," she says, breaking into a smile. "Then I suppose it's okay to tell you that legend has it that the cemetery is haunted."

She wiggles her eyebrows and I pretend to laugh, even as a chill steals down my spine. "Is it?"

Tasha sobers. "That's what Scott, the city manager told me. I think he was pulling my leg. I've been an archivist for several years now, and let me tell you that every single town has a cemetery or a crossroads or an old house that's supposedly haunted. It's part of the stories that towns tell themselves. I never believe the stories but I appreciate them."

"Cool," I say, for lack of anything better.

"The cemetery's on the ridge. I'll give you directions and we'll talk about how to map. Basically, you're just translating what you see in the cemetery onto paper. I was out there briefly the other day and there are only a handful of graves, so I don't think it will take you too long. You'll end up with a hand-drawn map of the cemetery, so we know who's buried where and can start investigating the names."

"Sounds okay," I say.

"I think you'll like it. It'll get you out of the basement, at least."

"I like it here."

"And I like having you here. I'll still need some help with the Holmbergs as it gets closer to August, but this way you get to be outside a bit."

I don't bother reminding her about my job at the pool, where I'm outside all the time. We spend the next half hour going over Tasha's instructions. I must start frowning at some point.

"What is it?"

"If there's already a cemetery on the ridge, doesn't that mean the city can't build there anyway?"

"They know about the cemetery already. It complicates things but they're still going ahead with preliminary plans. Cemeteries can be moved, after all, especially ones as small and untended as this one."

"That doesn't seem fair."

"When is life ever fair?" she replies. She's making a joke but I also catch a note of sadness in her voice. She hides it quickly, handing me a backpack containing a notebook, several pencils, and written instructions. "Come back in a few days and let me know how it's going."

"I will," I say, waving goodbye and climbing the stairs to the main entrance. I brace myself as I emerge from the cool subterranean gloom of the archives into the bright humid air of the outside world.

CHAPTER

FOUR

My stomach growls as I drive to the pool for my shift, so I stop at Russ's Village Market. I wander the aisles, tossing a box of rice crackers and some apples into my basket.

There's only one lane open, and I groan inwardly when I see that the checkout girl is one of my classmates. Nyssa doesn't say anything at first but midway through scanning my groceries, she picks up the box of crackers and studies it. Her fingernails are coated in chipped blue polish.

"These for Darcy's party?" she asks, snapping her gum. Her white-blonde hair is pulled back from her face. A few ragged strands dyed magenta hang around her pointy ears.

"What party?" I ask. As soon as I see the feral gleam in Nyssa's eyes, I kick myself. Rookie mistake.

Nyssa leans in like she smells blood. "Her big houseboat party. The one she throws every year."

"Oh yeah, that party."

"You didn't know about the party," Nyssa says, chomping her gum.

"I know about the party," I say in a bored voice. "I'm just not going." These things are both true. I really had forgotten about the party and I didn't feel like going anyway. Also I'm not sure Darcy ever officially invited me.

Nyssa chews on this information for a moment, bobbing her head as the skinny bag boy at the end of the lane picks at his cuticles. "What'd you do to piss off Darcy?"

"I didn't do anything to piss her off. I just talked to her a few days ago and I'm seeing her at work in a few minutes. If I ever get out of the store, that is."

"Days? You haven't talked to her for days?" Nyssa's eyeballs look like they're going to pop out of their sockets.

I glare at Nyssa. "That's what I said." She has a point, although I'd never tell her. A few months ago, Darcy and I used to text all the time. Now, after Arizona and everything else that happened, I really only talk to Darcy at the pool. Huh. I hadn't even really noticed.

"Maybe you're not invited."

I shove my credit card into the card reader. "I'm invited."

"She's mad at you. She told me so."

I fix Nyssa with a hard stare. "Darcy Sanderson came into Russ's for the sole purpose of finding you to tell you that she's mad at me. Her best friend." I try to ignore the voice in my head that tells me I've been a shitty best friend lately.

Nyssa flushes and shoves the box of crackers down the belt toward the bag boy. "She came in with Hannah. They were in my line and talking about it."

"Whatever."

"I heard that Darcy said she's done with friends who lie to her and ignore her. She said she doesn't want friends who are trouble and who aren't there for her."

"And you're one hundred percent sure she was talking about me." Again, I ignore the voice that tells me Nyssa is probably right, that Darcy was talking about me.

"Who else?"

"If this is true, it's news to me," I say, gesturing at the stalled credit card reader. "Look, are you gonna let me pay for these groceries or not?"

"Jesus, sorry," Nyssa says, pushing some buttons. A line is forming behind me. "You don't have to be so sassy."

"What did you say?" I ask between gritted teeth, a familiar knot clenching in my stomach.

Nyssa's eyes widen at my tone. She knows she said something wrong. "I just said not to get so pushy."

"No, you didn't say pushy. You said sassy."

"So?"

"As in sassy Black woman? Stereotype much?"

Nyssa's eyes narrow. "Are you saying I'm a racist or something? Jesus, Polly, I don't even think of you as Black."

And there it is, the qualification that I've heard so often during my life, including inside my own mind.

"Well I am Black, asshole," I say, grabbing the bag. The bag boy starts to protest that he'll take it to my car for me but I ignore him. I practically knock Nyssa down as I swing the bag from the counter and march out the doors.

It's started to rain, thick pellets smacking the pavement and making the parking lot smell like the inside of an oven. I race to my car and stuff the groceries behind the seat. Thunder rumbles overhead and lightning jabs the sky.

The squall goes through by the time I reach the pool.

"We'll have a delayed start to make sure we're free of lightning," Ms. Bulland calls as I storm into the locker room. Ms. Bulland is both the pool manager and my swim coach. I've known her for years.

"Fine," I grunt over my shoulder.

The locker room is empty. I drop onto a bench and shove a few crackers into my mouth. They turn to sawdust and I shove the box to the back of my locker.

I remember how proud I was when I first got this locker two years ago. I'd sailed through all my lifeguard training, and I liked the work. But the locker was my crowning achievement because it was right next to Darcy Sanderson's.

Darcy was always one of the popular girls. Ever since first grade when her parents put in the below-ground pool. I was always in the middle of the social pack; notable because of my skin color, but never elevated to the in crowd. I told myself I didn't mind, but a part of me always envied the cool kids, with their parties and flirting and the vintage bags they found at upscale thrift stores.

Then came the mess at Darcy's houseboat party two years ago, which killed my friendship with Henrietta and initiated my rise as one of the cool kids. At the time, I had wanted to be one of the cool kids more than anything. I wanted to be popular and admired and accepted. It worked. Now Darcy and I are best friends who share clothes, makeup, and gossip.

But when have you ever talked about anything real?

The thought surprises me as it snakes through my mind. I may have had more substantive conversations with Billy Meyer than I've ever had with Darcy. A thought emerges from the cage where I've trapped it: *I made the wrong choice.*

I shove the thought back into its cage.

⚬

Half an hour later, I'm in my lifeguard chair, watching the sunlight spark over the water. The pool is empty except for one guy swimming laps across the short edge. This is the sweet spot, the break between morning lessons and open swim.

"Hey, Pol," Chase says, sauntering over to my chair. His eyes are level with my bare legs. I sigh. Chase started working at the pool this summer. I was surprised he was motivated enough to complete the training, but if I'm correctly interpreting the way Chase Ryan has been looking at Darcy, he has an ulterior motive.

"Hey, Chase," I say, rubbing sunscreen on my calves. After dating for almost two years, Chase and I broke up at the beginning of junior year. Looking back, I'm not sure we had much in common. Whenever I tried talking about being biracial, he'd stick his tongue in my mouth. To be fair, that's what happened whenever I wanted to talk about anything other than basketball. We broke up after Chase spent last summer in Georgia with his grandparents and accidentally (so he claimed) sent me a picture of himself with some scantily clad girls. I wallowed for a few weeks and then woke up one morning feeling relief that I didn't have to deal with his shit anymore.

"You doing anything after this?"

"Gotta get home," I say, adjusting the umbrella. "Still grounded."

"Yeah, that's right," Chase says, and I get the sense that he hasn't forgotten. "You think it'll be busy today?"

I glance at the pool, where the lap guy switches from a dull front crawl to an uninspired breaststroke. "It's supposed to be ninety today, so yeah, I think it'll be busy."

"Might storm again, though."

"Yeah," I say, wondering if Chase was always this scintillating a conversationalist.

"We used to have a good time together, didn't we, Pol?" Something brushes my calf and I realize his fingers are on my skin.

"What're you doing, Chase?"

"Nothin'. Could be more, if you want."

"I thought you were interested in Darcy."

"Yeah, she's sweet."

"And me?"

He pauses. "You're sweet, too."

"Huh."

Darcy strides on deck, her blond hair pulled back in a ponytail. She's shorter than I am, with stubby legs and arms, but her eyes are bright green and she has a sparkle that draws people to her. Including Chase, whose eyes track her movements. His hand falls from my leg.

"Hey, Polly!" she calls. Does her voice sound too bright as she approaches? "You want to hang out after work?"

"Can't," I say, shaking my head.

"Your parents still being weird?" Darcy asks. Chase unfolds as she approaches, tilting his body so that he leans over her ever so slightly. Darcy's eyes flit to him and then up to me. I purse my lips and shrug. Darcy winks at me.

"Yeah, you know," I say. I didn't tell my friends about Althea's death or my near-escape to Arizona. My parents said I could tell people whatever I wanted, so I spun a tale about being sick with mono and having to miss school. Then I told them I was grounded because I partied too soon after recovering. It's lame but apparently I'm a good enough liar because no one's questioned my story. Maybe they don't really care to dig deeper. Or they don't know me well enough to know it's a lie.

The only person I wanted to tell about Althea was Henrietta, but I doubt she'd see me.

"Tomorrow's my day off," Darcy says. "Maybe we could hang out?"

"Can't," I say. "I'm doing stuff for the archives."

"What kind of stuff?"

I'm a little surprised Darcy is asking. When I told her about my volunteer position at the beginning of the summer, she wrinkled her nose and said it sounded boring.

"I'm doing some work in a cemetery," I say.

"A cemetery?" Her face goes pale and she and Chase exchange a look. "Oh."

"Yeah. Why?"

Darcy pastes a fake smile on her face. Chase stares at me.

"It's just creepy is all," Darcy says. She keeps talking before I can answer. "You're not going to miss the houseboat party though, are you? It's Thursday." She rests her arms on the base of the chair and arches her back, giving Chase a better view of her body.

"I . . . um, did you tell me about it?"

"Yeah I did," she said, her face wrinkling. "The group text."

That explains it. I had stopped paying attention to group texts. I guess Nyssa was wrong and Darcy didn't forget to invite me. For a moment I felt elated. I hadn't been forgotten. But then I pictured being at the party and suddenly I felt exhausted. "I don't know if I can make it."

Darcy hesitates for a split second. "Oh. Okay." Is it my imagination, or does she look disappointed?

There's an uncomfortable silence.

"I'll have to ask my mom," I finally say, although I can imagine what Mom's response will be. She might let me go if I show her the pages and pages of essays and math problems I've finished. Too bad I haven't done any of it.

"I'm free after work if you want to hang, Darce," Chase drawls.

"I don't recall asking you," Darcy laughs.

"I'm still coming to the party, right?" Chase says, a little too fast.

"We'll see," Darcy says. She does a little pirouette and heads to the chair on the other side of the pool. She waves at the guy swimming laps. He's probably my dad's age but he perks up when he sees her leaning over him. She says something and gestures at the clock. The guy says something in return, his eyes glued to her ass as she climbs into her chair. After a moment, he gets out of the pool and saunters toward the locker rooms, adjusting his trunks under his gut.

"So. A cemetery," Chase says.

"What about it?" I ask, my voice flat.

"You spend a lot of time in cemeteries lately?"

A chill steals down my spine despite the heat radiating off the pool deck. There is something in Chase's voice I do not like. "Why do you want to know?"

"Just that you talking about cemeteries reminds me about what you said last spring. At the party."

I don't say anything.

"You don't remember? You were pretty wasted that night. Sayin' all kinds of stupid shit."

"I don't know what you're talking about, Chase," I whisper, horror growing as snippets of memories come floating back.

"Really? It was last April. We were in the clearing behind Darcy's house."

I freeze. Billy hadn't been the only one to hear my confession. He'd told me he was lying behind a log, getting high, when he heard my voice. He could see my hair haloed in the moonlight but nothing else. He said he thought I was talking to myself. I clung to that belief and assumed no one else had heard, since no one said anything. But now it seems Chase knows my secret.

"I have to go," I say, dropping the sunscreen bottle as I clamber down my chair.

"Why are you freaking out?" Chase asks. He looks momentarily concerned. Then his face changes as he sees my panic. "Holy fuck, you really believe it, don't you?" he rasps as I stumble across the deck to the locker room.

"Hey, what's going on?" Darcy calls from her perch. "Pol, you okay?"

"Leave me alone!" I cry.

"What the fuck," Chase hisses, grabbing my arm.

"I was wasted," I say, shaking my arm free. "Don't believe whatever you heard."

Chase's eyebrow quirks. "Don't believe what I heard? Oh believe, me, I don't. Darcy's another story, though."

"What do you mean?"

Chase's eyes bore into mine even as he raises his voice and shouts across the pool. "Hey, Darcy! Polly wants to know if we think she's crazy because she says she can hear dead people."

The world stops for a second. The water stops sloshing against the side of the pool. The breath freezes in my body. Even the hornet hovering around the eaves halts in midair.

"Shut up!" I say as the world floods over me again.

I hear feet slapping on the concrete and Darcy is beside us. "Quiet, you two. You're going to have Ms. Bulland out here." She won't meet my eye.

"Darcy. Were you in the clearing that night?"

"Um, yeah," she says, her eyes not meeting mine.

"What did I say?" I ask. Maybe there's a chance my friends only heard part of my secret. Maybe it was so garbled that they thought it was nonsense.

"Oh, well, you were really drunk," she begins.

"What did I say?" I demand.

She takes my hands and leads me to a lounge chair, urging me to sit. She perches on the chair next to mine, still holding my hands. "Polly, you were obviously under a lot of stress that night after being sick with mono and all. And then you were talking about hearing voices and stuff. I figured it was just the whiskey. But then Chase . . ."

"But then Chase what?" I ask. Chase, standing a few feet away from us, snorts.

"Chase remembered that you used to spend a lot of time in that cemetery behind your house. And that it was a little creepy."

I feel another arrow pierce my chest as Darcy describes my Sigrudsons, my special family, as creepy.

"So I googled some stuff and it's really bad if you are hearing voices," Darcy continues. "Like really bad."

I take a breath. "That party was months ago. Why didn't you say anything about this earlier?"

"You didn't mention anything more about it and like I said, I thought it was just because you were drunk and being weird."

"Weird," I say. "Is that what you think of me? I'm now your weird, biracial friend?"

"Ugh, forget about it!" Darcy exclaims, dropping my hand. "It has nothing to do with being biracial. Why are you even bringing it up?"

I shrug.

"You've been weird ever since that party in the woods," she continues. "Before that, even. You barely call me anymore. You don't return my texts. I don't even know what's going on with you." She pauses, folding her arms over her chest. "I'm worried about you."

For a second I think it will be fine, that I can forget about the past few months and go back to being popular Polly, Darcy's best friend.

But then Darcy keeps talking. "I just want you to be normal."

"Normal," I repeat, the word stale in my mouth.

A hot breeze stirs the treetops outside the fence. The rustling sounds like dozens of ghostly prom dresses on a marble staircase.

"Well, maybe I'm not normal," I say at last. "And I go to cemeteries because I like them."

Both Darcy and Chase look at me like I'm something the cat coughed up.

"Do you . . . do you like going to cemeteries because you can hear voices?" Darcy says.

My eyelids drift shut and I know when I open them my world will be forever altered. "I can't hear voices," I lie. "But that doesn't make it weird for me to hang out in cemeteries."

"Well, that's your choice," Darcy says. "I'd say that maybe we shouldn't hang out anymore, but you barely want to see me now."

"Whatever." Her words sting but I am too tired to care.

Chase is more direct. "Fine. Be a stupid bitch."

The fear that has been coalescing inside of me explodes in rage. "Are you fucking kidding me? Fuck you, Chase. And fuck you too, Darcy."

"Polly, get a fucking grip," Chase is saying, although I can't hear him as I march toward him, my finger jabbing his chest.

"Stop it, Polly," Darcy says, holding onto my arm.

"Everything okay here?" another voice calls. It's the guy who was swimming laps. He comes out of the locker room, a towel around his waist.

"Get the fuck out of here!" I shout, switching targets.

"Watch your mouth, girl," he says, shock and disgust on his face.

"Polly, Polly, listen to me," Darcy is saying, tugging on both of my hands now. There are more footsteps on the deck and the voice of my boss.

"Polly, staff room. Now," Ms. Bulland is saying, her hands on my shoulders.

"Crazy bitch," someone mutters as I walk away from the glittering pool. I'm not sure if it's Chase or the old guy who is talking. I suppose it could be Darcy.

Five minutes later, I'm sitting in a broken lawn chair in the staff lounge, a beach towel around my shoulders. Ms. Bulland is sitting across the table.

"Polly, do you want to tell me what's going on?"

I shrug and pick some lint off my bathing suit.

"Honest to God, Polly, you remind me of my five-year-old," Ms. Bulland says. "He's hit that stage where he's fine until you tell him no. Or until you do something he doesn't want you to do. Or he has to eat his peas. You know what I'm saying?"

"No."

"I don't either," Ms. Bulland sighs, pushing her hands through her short hair. "The point is, your behavior has been erratic, to say the least. It's not just today. You've been late to shifts, you've left early, and sometimes you've been downright rude to the swimmers."

"Sometimes they've been downright rude to me," I protest, although I can think of only one time when I told off a kid for running and he stuck his tongue out at me. If I recall, I returned the gesture.

"I don't want to hear it," she says, raising a hand. I wonder what her son does at this point in the lecture. "I'm taking you off the schedule."

"What?" I demand, snapping to attention.

"You heard me. I'm placing you on unpaid leave for the next two weeks."

"But I need this job," I protest. "I'm saving up for college!" Although mainly I'm diverting as much as I can into a fund to pay back Billy.

"I need a lifeguard I can rely on. You're not that lifeguard right now. You got me? I'm not going to fire you outright, but this is your only chance. In order to return, you need to show me that you're not going to go off the deep end again. So take two weeks and reflect on your behavior and show me you can return to the pool."

"You're giving me a time out."

She searches my face, no doubt trying to tell if I'm being sarcastic or not. I try to look reproachful.

"You want my honest opinion, Polly?"

"No."

"Well, you're going to get it. I don't mean this as a criticism of Darcy or Chase. They're fine kids, but I liked you better when you were hanging out with Henrietta."

Her words thud into my chest like bullets in the westerns my dad watches on television sometimes. I stand, clutching the towel.

"You want me to check in with you in two weeks, then?"

"Call me after a week," she says. "And Polly, I'm going to have to tell your parents."

"I know," I say, not bothering to change into my clothes when I leave.

CHAPTER

FIVE

My tires screech as I pull out of the pool parking lot, eliciting frowns and a few gestures from the parents herding their children through the gates. I turn left onto Dolly Madison Avenue and hear horns blaring as I race up the hill. Ten minutes later I'm pulling into the garage and storming into the house.

Mom's already on the phone, her voice trailing down the hall from her studio. "She did what? . . . Oh, I see . . . Yes . . . Yes . . . Well, believe me—" Her voice gets cut off as she gets another earful from whom I can only imagine is Ms. Bulland.

I can't deal with this right now.

I drop my car keys in the dish on the hall table and head through our cozy living room to the big kitchen. I grab an apple from the pottery bowl on the counter, tucking it under my chin as I swap my flip flops for an old pair of running shoes in the mudroom. I find clean shorts and a shirt in the dryer. I should be wearing riding boots and jeans but I don't feel like going upstairs. After the day I've had, all I want is to see my special family.

The yard is dusty as I race to the barn. There's a faint breeze and it's slightly cooler here than it was in town. The chickens squawk and scatter but I ignore them as I walk into the cool barn. Astrid is waiting for me. She butts her head

45

against my chest as I scratch the white blaze between her eyes. I grab her gear and croon softly to her as I adjust the bridle and check the stirrups, although I'm the only one who rides her so they're always set to the right length.

"Let's head into the hills, girl," I say once I'm mounted in the saddle. I flick the reins and we start plodding along one of the trails behind the barn. The entire bluff is protected land. There are a series of footpaths that crisscross it, and even a trailhead on the south side, but almost no one comes this far north, so I've always thought of the area as my own private kingdom.

Mine and Henrietta's.

Henrietta and I spent entire summers in these woods playing pirates and cowboys and ebony princesses. One year we had an elaborate war between our two kingdoms, a conflict instigated by our duplicitous and devious fictional husbands. By the end of the summer, we'd had them beheaded and united our kingdoms in sisterly love. I still remember sunlight splashing on Henrietta's dark face, her brown eyes filled with mischief and affection, as she took my hand and kissed it.

We come to the trail fork and I nudge Astrid to the left. When we get to the small, fenced cemetery, I slide from Astrid's back and tie her reins around a branch. I push open the rusted gate and survey the seven headstones. I can't remember the last time I was here, so I'm surprised to see that the plot looks neat and tidy. Brambles have grown around Oleg's stone and the forsythia I planted a few years ago swamps Caspar's marker, but someone has been through this spring to sweep up the leaves and trim the grass. I wonder if it was my dad.

"Hey, Sigrudsons," I call as I lightly touch each stone. There are a few that are simple markers laid into the earth and I toe those with my shoe. "Long time no see."

I settle into the hollow next to Oleg's grave and lean back against the stone, which is warm through my thin shirt. Oleg's voice is low and grumbly as he reassures me in quiet Swedish. According to his stone, Oleg died when he was forty-eight, but I picture him as a grandfatherly seventy-year-old, a gray beard curling down his chin and a twinkle in his eye as he whittles a toy top in front of the fireplace.

His wife, Pethra, babbles underneath a hickory tree, her words sounding like water tumbling over a stone creek bed. I always picture her in an apron and carrying a warm pie. Five of their seven children surround them. Three died in infancy and one was killed in a farm accident when he was eight. Albert, the only adult son buried here, outlived the rest of the family by twenty years. I have no idea what happened to the two who aren't buried here. Tasha helped me find information about the Sigrudsons in old church records when I started volunteering at the archives in June. We didn't find much, but I know the Sigrudsons lived in my house and Oleg worked in the lumber mill.

"I got in a huge fight with Darcy today," I tell them. "I yelled at her. I yelled at Chase too, but he deserved it." I pause. "Darcy didn't deserve it. They overheard me blathering my secret last spring. About being a death singer."

This is the term for what I am. A death singer.

There are a few hundred of us on the online forum I found after stumbling onto a Facebook page that made vague mention of death singing. There was an email address to contact for more information. Once I finally heard back, I had to fill out a long application and then do two separate phone interviews before they were convinced I was legit. Then I got an invitation to the private website.

I pull my phone out of my pocket. Ever since they installed the cell tower on top of Brammer Bluff, I've been able to get reception here. It might spoil the view of the bluff, but you can't beat the convenience.

I log in wondering, not for the first time, what it was like to be a death singer before the internet. The skill tends to run in families, so some death singers at least had the comfort of relatives. But others weren't so lucky. From what I've read in the About Us section, it wasn't uncommon for death singers to go crazy or to be branded—and sometimes burned—as witches. I'm still not sure if I like being called a death singer, but the term has been around longer than me. I've never felt like I'm doing anything that comes close to singing to the dead. But it's nice to feel like I'm not alone.

I scroll through the conversation threads, reading the updates in one of the amplification threads. Ilikethenight52 reports that she has completed a record of her grandfather's World War II service memories and also learned about his secret vice of horehound candy. I snort, wondering if she misheard his thoughts on that one. B47821 describes how he discovered that a grave of a Civil War soldier in his town has been mislabeled. He's looking for advice on ways to alert the cemetery association to fix the issue. Most death singers are also amateur historians, but no one's found a way around the problem of how to share our findings with the larger world. People always want proof and that's the one thing we can't immediately provide.

I keep scrolling. Icebreaker wants us to review a draft of the death singers' code of ethics. I flip past that message. I haven't followed the conversation closely, but I'm sure whatever I'm doing with Billy is breaking all kinds of ethical codes.

"Henrietta knew I was a death singer. She never thought it was weird, either," I say to the Sigrudsons. "Darcy thinks it's awful. Not that she believes me. But she thinks it's awful I'm not normal."

I stretch out my legs, brushing the tip of Benedict's grave. He lived for three days, longer than two of his siblings. I place my hand on his stone, hearing what might be the sigh of a final breath, but it might also be the wind in the treetops. This is how it usually is with babies. Maybe a breath, maybe a gurgle, but nothing more. Older children are rough, especially if they know they're dying. In a few cemeteries, there are paths I follow to avoid hearing the sound of dying children calling for their mothers, fear and desperation choking their voices.

Despite the heat, I feel a chill as I remember the corner in God's Acre where a murdered fourteen-year-old is buried. *What are you doing, Mr. Wilkinson?* he asks, again and again, his voice confused. I didn't understand what was happening until I looked him up in the newspaper, scrolling through the microfilm until I found the story of a boy shot by his neighbor for no apparent reason.

I shake my head and remind myself that the dead aren't talking to me any more than they're talking to anybody.

I lay back on the ground, acorns poking into my back, oak branches sweeping overhead. Only then do I let the memories of the end of my friendship with Henrietta flood my mind.

Every summer Darcy throws a massive, two-day party, the same one she's throwing later this week. The party starts mid-morning on her parents' houseboat, which Darcy's dad takes fifteen miles upstream to Farmington. They dock at an island and Mr. Sanderson takes a motorboat to the Holiday Inn Express so he can legitimately claim he has no knowledge of the drinking that starts as soon as he leaves. They sail back the next morning and the party continues at the Sanderson pool in the housing development on the edge of town.

Two years ago, I managed to wrangle an invitation for me and Henrietta. It was all part of my plan to become one of the popular kids. Henrietta didn't want to go. She was always uncomfortable with the cooler kids, but I promised to stick with her. I suppose a part of me hoped I could drag Henrietta closer to the cool kids as I made my own social rise. I kept my end of the bargain for the first couple of hours as the houseboat slowly rocked up the river, eating hot dogs with her in a corner of the upper deck. I was wearing a green and white polka-dot bikini, my stomach flat and my legs strong. Henrietta wore a one-piece swimsuit underneath her t-shirt and shorts, but as far as I know, she never took off her clothes.

"You know I don't want boys looking at me like that," she said, a little too loudly. Darcy's friends Hannah and Beth were standing nearby. Both of them looked her up and down with barely disguised sneers. They rolled their eyes and laughed. They looked at me and I found myself rolling my eyes, too.

They noticed, but so did Henrietta. She flounced off and I barely saw her for the rest of the party. That was the night Chase Ryan started paying attention to me. It started with him watching me as evening crept across the river and ended with awkward fumbling underneath a blanket on the semi-abandoned back deck. I stopped him when he started untying my bikini top.

"C'mon, baby," he'd panted in my ear but I squirmed away from him. He reached for me halfheartedly, his beer breath hot on my neck, but I pushed his hands away and went to sleep by myself in a chaise lounge on the upper deck.

It wasn't until we got back to the boat launch the next morning that I realized Henrietta was missing. I asked everyone on board but no one had seen her since the previous afternoon. I was a mess, confused by Chase's touch, lack of sleep, and too many wine coolers. I threw a fit until Mr. Sanderson agreed to drive me back upstream.

"She's probably fine," he said, but his tanned face looked white around the edges after he realized Henrietta wasn't on the houseboat. Losing a fifteen-year-old girl wouldn't look good for a guy planning to run for county commissioner.

I found her on the island, cold and shivering underneath a thin blanket she had found at an abandoned campsite. She had wandered away during the night, anxious to escape the party and my rejection. She didn't say anything, but her eyes were filled with accusation and hurt.

"I missed the boat," was all she said, shaking in my arms.

We had a big audience by the time we returned. The sheriff's department was questioning Darcy and a few others as we pulled up to the dock with Henrietta still trembling in my arms. She burst into tears when she saw everyone.

"I'm so embarrassed," she kept wailing against my shoulder.

"Well, you should be," I snapped. "Stop being such a baby!" I felt awful immediately. I shouldn't have said it. And I absolutely shouldn't have said it so loud. I knew I should have felt compassion for her but instead I felt irritated. I was the one with the friend who couldn't keep it together on a freaking high school boat party, after all.

"Polly," a voice called through the crowd. I remember feeling shock as Darcy approached me. She glanced at me and then at Henrietta. "The sheriff wants to talk to you," she said to Henrietta. Then her eyes flitted back to me. "Some of us are going back to my house for sandwiches. You want to come?"

It was the moment of truth. Pick Henrietta or pick Darcy.

To my shame, I picked Darcy.

I thought I was being coy. "Let me have my mom drop Henrietta off first," I remember saying to Darcy, who tilted her head and smiled in approval.

"See you soon."

I steered Henrietta to my mom's car, trying not to notice how stiff Henrietta's shoulders were.

"What a freak," someone said behind us. I was pretty sure it was Hannah. Everyone laughed, which made Henrietta cry harder. To this day I wish I had turned around and told them all to shut the fuck up, but I was angry at her, too.

We had a huge fight that night after I got back from Darcy's house. Lunch had turned into shopping at the Freehold Mall, and by the time Darcy's mom dropped me off at home, I was calm enough to talk to my best friend. In all honesty, the guilt made me drag out my bike and ride to her house.

"You embarrassed me," Henrietta had said. "The Polly I know would never have done that." She sat in a corner of the sofa, her hands folded in her lap.

"What about you?" I shot back. "You embarrassed me!"

"I don't know you anymore," Henrietta replied, never raising her voice. "What kind of friend does that?"

"I said I was sorry!"

"You'll stop hanging out with those people?"

"I'm not going to do that. They like me and they've accepted me."

Her brow furrowed. I could hear her mother moving around the kitchen, the soft clatter of pans and the flare of the gas burners.

"They're not very nice people," she said.

"No, but at least they're fun!" I yelled. The kitchen noises stopped. Henrietta looked like I'd slapped her.

"What do you mean?" she asked, her face going ashen as her eyes finally met mine.

"All I wanted to do was hang out with some new people and have fun. And you had to go and ruin it!"

Henrietta's eyes filled with tears, which made me angry. "Are you saying I'm not fun?"

"Look, I'm tired of playing dolls and hanging out in the woods."

"That's not all I want to do," Henrietta gasped.

"Really? You went to a freaking party and you freaked out. So no, you're not any fun."

"Polly, enough," Henrietta's mother said, appearing in the doorway. "I think you should go."

I glared at Henrietta, who had tears streaming down her face.

"You should go," she said, repeating her mother's words.

"Fine," I'd grumbled. "Call me when you grow up."

She never called me. Although to be fair, I never called her, either. Now whenever I see Henrietta around town, she looks the other way. She has her own small group of homeschool friends, and it's almost like we never knew each other. Sometimes I'm even able to ignore the ache in my gut whenever I see her.

"What do you think I should do, Pethra?" I ask, hoping not for the first time that Pethra Sigrudson would break her Swedish litany, switch to English and give me some advice.

"No such luck," I say to the cemetery when there's no response. "You know, for a bunch of dead people you have surprisingly little to say."

I sigh and push myself up, brushing leaves out of my hair. I glance around for Astrid but she's gone.

"Damn it," I say, scrambling to my feet. I thought I had secured her reins to the oak tree, but apparently she worked her way loose.

"Damn it, Apollonia," I repeat as I march down the trail whistling for my horse. Astrid can't get too lost in these woods, but there are ravines that plunge down to the river. I shake my head to rid it of an image of Astrid lying on her side, her front legs broken, me running for the vet as she screams in pain.

The path takes me up the ridge and I scramble up the rocky terrain. Even though she is old and slow, Astrid likes to climb paths that she should leave for a younger horse. It hasn't rained in weeks so I can't check for hoof prints. The path narrows ahead and I am about to turn back when I see a break in the under-brush. Some of the branches are bent at awkward angles and the breaks are new.

"Honestly, Astrid," I complain, striking out through the woods. I've had Astrid ever since I was a kid. My dad bought her for me after we took a trip to Dubai and I saw the ponies racing across the desert. I begged him for one of those fleet-footed animals and got Astrid instead. She's the least likely horse to race under the hot desert sun.

"Stop crying, Pol," I say, wiping tears from my face. "She'll be fine. And if she's not, you have no one to blame but yourself."

I walk south for ten minutes, branches tugging at my hair until I pull it back with a band I find in my shorts pocket. I stumble once and skin my knee on a boulder. I'm about to turn back when I hear a familiar nicker up ahead. Relieved, I burst through the trees and find Astrid munching on a shrub.

"There you are, you silly girl," I say. The words catch in my throat when I realize that somehow, this old horse is my only friend. A sob tears from my throat and soon I'm collapsed against my horse, crying like I'll never stop.

My mother is furious with me by the time I slouch through the door twenty minutes later. My parents pride themselves on not yelling, on being the kind of parents who sit you down and talk you through the consequences of your actions and why those actions may or may not be harmful to others. Even as a little kid I only remember my parents raising their voices when I got too close to the edge of the bluff or reached for the stove.

Mom sticks with that policy even now, but the lines around her mouth are white and her voice is constrained.

"You were supposed to be home right after your shift."

"Technically, I was—" I start to explain, telling her about taking Astrid for a ride, but my words evaporate as my mom raises her hand.

"I don't want to hear it, Polly. I asked you to come home right after your shift. I didn't expect to get a phone call from your supervisor telling me you'd been put on probation."

I dip my head, embarrassed. The red velvet sofa sags underneath me. Mom drops into the chair across from me.

"How's your schoolwork, Apollonia?"

I shrug and fidget, surprised by the turn of the conversation. "Fine."

Mom leans forward and captures my hands across the wide ebony coffee table. "Polly. I saw the books on your desk."

I sit up and jerk my hands free. "You went into my room?"

Mom sighs and shakes her head. "I wasn't trying to snoop. But after I got the phone call from Ms. Bulland, I started to wonder how your work was going. You haven't wanted to show me anything. Now I know why."

"It's all on my computer," I say. She doesn't know the password and she's not savvy enough to hack my laptop. "I've gotten a lot of work done," I lie.

"Then why don't you go get your computer and let me see your *Middlemarch* essay."

My phone buzzes and my fingers itch to check it. A part of my heart imagines that it's Henrietta, hoping we could hang out. Another part, the part I don't want to deal with right now, hopes it's Billy checking in.

"It's a rough draft," I say. "It's not ready. It might squelch my creativity if I show it to you now."

Humor lights Mom's eyes. She talks all the time about having to close the door to her studio until her pieces are ready to be seen and critiqued. Otherwise it will squelch her creativity.

"I'm sorry, Mom," I say.

"What are you sorry for?"

"I'm sorry I yelled at that guy at the pool. I'm sorry I ran away for a couple of hours today and didn't face up to the consequences of my actions. I should have come and talked to you the instant I came back from the pool. I'm sorry you had to find out from Ms. Bulland what happened."

This pacifies her a little. "Thank you, Polly." She takes my hand again. "What concerns me, however, is that you were yelling at that man in the first place. Can you tell me what happened?"

I pick at the red velvet cushion. I don't have a good answer. Chase Ryan's face drifts into my head. I squeeze my eyes shut for a moment and shake my head.

"Polly? What is it? Did the man say something offensive?" My mom is about to launch into full-on momma bear mode. While I love how she's willing to fight for me, the last thing I need is for her to call Ms. Bulland and accuse the pool patrons of being racist, so I say the first thing that comes into my mind.

"Chase is flirting with Darcy," I blurt. "They were both there on deck. He's into her and it was weirding me out. I think I took it out on that guy."

There is some truth to this. It's not like I was ever in love with Chase and I don't want him back, but I'm also not entirely sure I want Darcy to have him, either. It makes me feel like Chase was only using me to get to her.

Mom accepts the explanation. Finally, a teenage problem she can solve.

"Oh, love. Life's like that sometimes. You know, before I met your father, I was dating this photographer. It was never very serious, but sometimes I could imagine a future with him. Then he got interested in one of my friends. Sheila was her name." Mom frowns and chews on the end of her ponytail. "No, it wasn't Sheila. It was Debbie. Was it? Let's see, it would have been 1984 . . ."

"Great story, Mom," I say. This is what we say when Mom's stories start to veer into tangents, like they often do. If she's in a good mood, which she usually is, she laughs at herself. She smiles and gives my shoulder a squeeze.

"Are we good?" I ask.

"You're already grounded. I'm tempted to take that phone away, but I know what it's like to be young and have a broken heart. We need to address your schoolwork, though."

"End of the week," I say. "I'll show you a draft of the essay."

Mom's shoulders relax. "Okay, sweetie. I trust you."

Mom heads back to the studio and I dash upstairs, half believing that this time I'll actually do my work.

CHAPTER
SIX

The next morning I'm standing in a meadow holding a clipboard. Fredrickson Annex sprawls before me, a wide field ringed by a marsh of waving cattails. A fortress of sturdy trees shelters us from the Mississippi River and the highway. The long dry grass crackles with grasshoppers. The sky arches blue overhead and the thick humidity hints at thunderstorms to come. The wind brings the scent of heat and dust.

"You couldn't have mapped a more recent cemetery?" Billy asks, hovering over my left shoulder.

"Just doing my job. Besides, the big cemeteries have records. This one doesn't," I say, fiddling with the compass Tasha had tucked into the backpack. I squint at the coordinates she wrote in the notebook.

"You have any idea how to use that thing?"

"Um, nope," I say. Billy holds out his hand and I drop the compass into it. I try not to notice how strong his fingers are or that I'm wondering how they might feel wrapped around my waist. I give my head a shake. I wasn't planning on coming here with Billy, but he was waiting for me in front of the archives this morning. He texted me last night but I didn't answer. I couldn't quite deal with another visit to Bluff Hill and a newly dead person. But when I told him this morning that I was going to a cemetery, he came with me.

57

To tell the truth, I didn't mind the company. Fredrickson Annex isn't far from Monroe, but it feels remote.

We'd parked on a turnoff from Highway 61 and hiked one of the wetland trails to get here. The trail took us over a rise and deposited us in a wide hollow that stretches about a hundred yards to the west before it meets the bluffs. More hills guard the Annex from the northeast, cutting it off from Monroe. No wonder no one knows much about this place. I can hear the distant whoosh of trucks on the highway but otherwise there's no sign of anyone.

"Why do you even need a compass?" Billy asks, glancing at the coordinates. "Can't you just wander around until you hear them?"

"I told you already, they get quieter the older they get. If the cemetery dates from the 1860s, they're practically dead."

Billy snorts and walks a few steps to the east.

"You know what I mean. I can't hear them anymore. It's like the first time my parents took me to Europe. Dead people are everywhere. We even ate in a café in London that was in an old crypt."

"Gross."

"It was peaceful. I couldn't hear anyone."

"I didn't mean the crypt. I meant the fact that your parents took you to Europe."

"Yeah, my parents took me to Europe. So what?"

"Must be nice, is all," Billy says as he paces, his eyes on the compass.

"Fuck you, Billy."

He lifts his eyebrows at me, his words a low taunt. "Those are naughty words coming from Little Miss Perfect."

I storm across the grass and jab him in the chest. "If you've got something to say to me, you better just damn well say it. You got it?"

Crickets chirp and a bee drones past my ear. For a second Billy's head dips and I get the wild sense for one instant that he's going to kiss me. His lips firm and he points behind me.

"The southeast corner is over there," he says.

The sun peeks out from behind a cloud. I blink, pulling my sunglasses down over my eyes. I sling my backpack over one shoulder and march to the place he indicated.

"Why'd you come out here with me? I told you we wouldn't get any useful information," I say, setting the backpack at my feet and withdrawing a folder stamped with "Perrineville County Archives" across the front.

"Just protecting my investment."

"Your investment?" I ask, anger growing inside.

"Uh huh."

"Are you talking about me?"

"Yeah, so?"

"You realize how that sounds, don't you?" I say, glaring at him. "Like you own me, or something?"

The confusion in Billy's eyes clears, only to be replaced by shock. "Jesus, Polly, I didn't mean that."

"What did you mean, then?" I ask as I click the lead on my mechanical pencil and mark a spot on the graph paper Tasha gave me.

"I meant that the stuff you told me about that lady—"

"Her name was Ida Mae."

"Ida Mae, whatever, was right. I got into her bank account. You found enough right answers to the security questions. She used that cat's name for a few of them."

"How much did you take?" I ask, my voice flat.

"A few thousand. Didn't want to draw too much attention."

"She died a week ago and you just withdrew a few thousand dollars from her bank account. Someone's going to notice, Billy."

"Yeah, well, we'll cross that bridge when we come to it."

"That's your grand plan?" I say, letting the folder fall to the ground. "You'll cross that bridge when you come to it? This is what I'm risking my reputation for? What I'm risking jail time for?"

"You're already risking jail time because of the fire," he growls. "Or did you forget?"

My eyes drop. "I didn't forget, Billy."

"Then don't worry about what I'm doing. You just keep giving me information and I don't tell the cops you're the one who committed arson. I still have the photos," he said, wagging his cell phone. "Remember?"

I sigh and pick up the papers that fell out of the folder.

"I'm going to map now. Give me a little privacy."

"Not a problem," Billy says. I turn my attention back to the grid as he wanders away, but I have a hard time concentrating.

My mind flitters to when Billy set up our criminal activity. I still don't remember much about the party or spilling my secrets. I do remember sleeping fitfully for a few hours on a couch in Darcy's family room and waking at 4am with a grim determination to put the past behind me. When I sobered up some more, I drove home and gathered all the adoption paperwork. Billy told me he followed me in his truck to make sure I got home safe. He followed me again when I left a few minutes later. I drove over to the school and parked near the machine shed, where the custodians had been stockpiling crates and kindling for the end-of-year bonfire. I had a can of lighter fluid on the front seat that I'd stolen from the garage.

It turns out that I hadn't dragged the pile of wood far enough from the building, so after the paperwork went up in a whoosh that singed my eyebrows, the shed caught on fire. I went tearing back to my car and sped into the night, clutching a blanket to my chest. It was the blanket Althea wrapped me in before she handed me to my parents. I had planned on tossing it onto the fire but it was somehow still in my hands. You can clearly see the blanket in the pictures Billy took. You can also see my face in two of the shots.

Billy texted me the first picture a few days later and told me we had to meet. I ignored him at first. The picture was blurry and I was pretending to be tough, even though I was paralyzed by fear. He showed up at school a few times, loitering around the parking lot at the end of the day. People murmured about him, wondering why the dropout was back at school. I was the only one who knew why. I avoided him, ducking low and jockeying my way through the parking lot to my car.

Then he showed up on my doorstep.

I was sleeping on the old beige couch on the screen porch. It was cool that day, even for spring in Minnesota, and I had drawn a thin afghan over me. I was drifting in and out of consciousness as the wind rustled the leaves outside. I've always slept like that, tucked as far beneath the covers as possible. My mom used to say I looked like a woolly brown caterpillar and she'd call me her little bug. In my dream, I was riding my horse, circling round and round our riding ring, spinning in circles. Astrid's harness squeaked. Then I heard another squeak.

It was the second squeak that jolted me awake. It was the sound of a hiking boot on the porch steps. I sat up, recoiling when I saw Billy glowering at me from the other side of the screen door.

"What're you doing here?" I asked, pushing hair out of my face.

"You're avoiding me," he said through the screen.

"I barely know who you are," I said, lying back down, hoping my bluff would dissuade him and that he couldn't see my heart pounding through the blanket. I'd been jittery for days, imagining everyone could sense the guilt radiating off me. Rumors had circulated widely, fanned by the school's terse statement that the fire appeared to be arson and was under investigation.

"You know who I am," was all he said, his voice sliding through the porch like a stream of black ink in a pool of water.

I sat up again, dislodging the blanket. "What do you want?"

He watched me, his fingers curled around the handle of the door. "Information."

"What kind of information?"

There was a clatter in the kitchen: my mom dropping a mixing bowl in the sink.

"What was that?" Billy asked.

"My mom."

"What's she gonna think if she sees me here?"

I sighed and swung my legs over the side of the couch. I didn't tell him that my mom would probably take one look at Billy's dark hair and brooding face and want to sculpt him. "Let's go outside."

He pushed the door open and I had to step past him to get to the side yard. My body whispered past his and a wave of awareness spread through my limbs. Alarmed, I pushed the feeling aside as I walked down the trail to the paddock, Billy silent behind me. I braced my hands against the white fence, staring at the emerald grass in front of me. Billy leaned next to me. A wind rustled the leaves and carried the scent of lilac. It was almost a perfect moment, except that I was already in a heap of trouble and standing next to someone who wanted to get me into more.

"Is it true?" he finally asked.

"Is what true?"

"That you can hear dead people."

I paused for a moment and then faked a laugh, the kind I'd seen on the soap operas my grandma used to watch. "What are you talking about?" I even pressed my wrist to my forehead and gave my head a shake, hoping someone would hand me my Daytime Emmy right now and get me out of this conversation.

Billy didn't buy it. He caught my wrist as it floated down. His fingers were warm on my skin.

"I overheard you. At the party. You were drunk. And you wouldn't shut up about it. Then I found the death singers online. The secret website."

I stared at him. "How did you even . . . that's not possible."

"I'm good with computers, Polly." He dropped my wrist. "Are you going to keep denying it or not?" Then he told me how he followed me to the high school and took those pictures. "If you can hear the dead, you can help me."

"Help you how?"

"Money," he said. "I need money. You'll get answers to security questions, I'll break into their accounts, and then I won't have to turn you in for arson. Now, are you going to help me or not?"

———※———

I shake my head to forget the conversation and turn my attention to the folder. According to the information Tasha gave me, there's a cluster of marked graves near the top of the hill. I sling my backpack over my shoulder and start climbing. The hill is steep and even though I'm in shape from swimming, I'm a little out of breath by the time I reach the top. The broken teeth of grave markers poke out from the ground to my right, but a glimpse of blue through the trees draws me past them. I push through a tangle of brambles on top of the hill and find myself overlooking teeming wetlands stretching their long fingers to the waters of the Mississippi.

I love this river, the vast, silent sheet of water that is always moving and changing. It starts as a trickle in northern Minnesota but quickly broadens to a natural phenomenon that neatly splits the country in two. Growing up in a river town means we read a lot of dead white guys who were in love with the river. I didn't mind so much. I'm in love with the river, too. There are several channels near Monroe where it's shallow enough to swim. Every Fourth of July we watch fireworks explode over the water and eat cotton candy at Riverside Park. I've spent hours and hours exploring the banks while Mom harvests clay, returning with thick mud between my toes.

From our house on top of Brammer Bluff, you can see a tiny part of the river after the leaves fall in autumn, but nothing like this. For a second I forget I'm in a cemetery and I imagine building a house on this spot, with huge windows overlooking the river and a gate outside to keep everyone else away. No wonder the city wants to build here.

The river also always makes me think of Henrietta. She used to come with us on those clay trips, eager to escape her dour house and hours of prayer. When we were old enough we'd beg my mom to drop us at the beach where we'd preen in our two-piece suits, arching our backs to make our flat chests look womanly. Well, I'd preen and Henrietta would sit with a towel around her shoulders, flicking sand at me once she loosened up.

I frown, realizing how often I've thought about her in the past few days. I usually don't let myself think about her.

Farewell, my darling, a voice whispers, making me jump. Farewell, my darling, the voice repeats. The dead don't usually surprise me like that. I suppose I've been thinking about Tasha saying the cemetery is apparently haunted. I turn away from the river and approach the collection of tiny stones. The voice, a raspy baritone, hums beneath a worn stone marked with the initials XMP. There's no date. The rest of the stones spread before me. I wander through the small graveyard, picking up a few phrases and a sigh or two. Several of the graves are already quiet.

"Good a place as any," I say, and plop down beneath a huge cottonwood tree. A few sticks poke at my shorts and I brush them away before I start sketching. The cemetery is peaceful and quiet and I find myself relaxing. After I've made an initial drawing of the plot, I set up a grid and start walking through the stones in the first grid section, writing down what I find. Most of the stones only have initials, but a few have full names and some dates. There are a couple I can't read at all because the writing has worn away. I take photos of all the stones and make notations on the map.

I glance down the hill. Billy stands halfway up the bluff opposite me, arms folded across his chest, sunlight shining on his glossy dark hair. He stares at a spot to the west, where the bluffs ease to form the rest of the valley that belonged to Fredrickson Annex. For an instant I indulge in a romance novel fantasy, casting Billy as the strong, brooding stranger protecting the spunky heroine as we explore this strange new world.

"Yeah, right," I mutter, sketching lines on my graph paper.

After a while I lay my notebook on the grass near the XMP grave and wander back to the trees on top of the hill. The sun is bearable here, trickling through the branches and warming the back of my neck. A faint breeze carries the scent of moss and swamp, an earthy smell that lodges in the back of my throat. I pull out my phone, trying to decide what I could say to Henrietta in a text message that would make her want to see me again. Probably nothing. Sadness blooms in my chest and I blink back tears. I'm wiping my eyes on the edge of my tank top when I hear another scrap of song as a shadow flitters across my notebook.

In the light of evening, you've come to say goodbye.

It turns out that lots of people die thinking about songs. I've heard everything from hymns to nursery rhymes to Bruce Springsteen. One man in the Jesus Lives! Evangelical Cemetery probably died listening to television, fading away during an Ajax commercial. I don't recognize the melody but I pause to listen, waiting for the lyrics to loop. The music stops. This is a little unusual. Not all of the dead repeat their final thoughts at the same rate; some take a little pause every now and then, but usually they pick up again right away. I wait, my breath in my throat. A few seconds later, the song starts again from the beginning and I relax. Nothing out of the ordinary here.

"Nothing out of the ordinary other than your ability to hear the dead, Apollonia," I tell myself. "And talking to yourself out loud." I dart a glance down the hill. Billy is a speck on the opposite hillside, too far away to hear me talk or even see my lips move.

I fumble in my pocket for a hair band and pull my mass of curls off my neck. Sweat trickles down my back. That's as good a sign as any that it's time to pack up and show my work to Tasha. I'm heading back to the tree where I left my backpack, listening to the song fading.

I stand and watch as you start to sigh. I'd give anything, oh anything, to kiss you goodbye.

I trip over my backpack as the smooth baritone continues. The hair on the back of my neck stands up. Okay, I don't remember hearing that line before. The dead usually speak no more than a phrase or two. I turn back in the direction of the smooth voice. Another shadow flickers in the corner of my eye. I catch my breath, willing it to be a trick of the light and nothing more.

Farewell, my love. Someday we will return. Ha. That's a good one.

I halt, horrified, as the voice switches from singing to talking.

Although if I was going to return, I suppose there are worse places to be. Sure would be nice to see the river, though.

My knees buckle and I fall to the ground, scraping my hands. My head spins and fear chokes my throat. In front of me is a small flat stone inscribed with a name: Harrison J. Card. Below it are two dates: Nov. 26, 1907–Oct. 5, 1924. There's something else written beneath the dates but the words are obscured by matted grass. I reach out a trembling finger to brush it away. "He that is without sin among you, let him first cast a stone."

I clear my throat.

A visitor, how nice, the voice says. *Can't remember the last time anyone came by. I wonder who's there.*

The words flow from my lips, urgent and inevitable. "It's me."

There's a pause and I wait to see if the world will tip on its axis. I hear nothing but the hot wind in the oaks. A bird chirps nearby. I wonder if I've been hallucinating. I only had a small bowl of cereal for breakfast. Or maybe the heat has gotten to my head. I sigh and pull my hand away. I'm just turning away when I hear it.

Hello?

A chill races through me. I kneel in the dry grass.

"Hello?" I say, my voice trembling.

You can hear me?

I can't pinpoint where the voice is coming from. It's both beneath the ground and above me, but when I look, nothing is there. "Yes. And you can hear me." I pinch myself a few times to make sure I'm awake. It hurts, so I'm either really good at dreaming or this is actually happening.

I guess so. Do I know you?

I almost don't answer. This is crazy. I'm having a conversation with a dead guy.

You still there?

"Yeah, I'm still here," I say, my voice raspy. "Are you?"

A shadow under the cottonwood tree shudders and I shiver.

Is this your first time talking to a ghost? The voice is low. I'm on my feet now, but when I look into the shadows, I don't see anything. Not at first. But then my eyes catch on a flicker of movement, a flash of brightness that could be sunlight dancing in someone's eyes.

"Is that what you are? A ghost?"

I won't hurt you, if that's what you're asking. And as far as being a ghost, I'm not really sure. I . . . I'm dead. I know that.

"Seems like that would make you a ghost." My voice is shaky with nervous laughter. If I wasn't already a death singer, I'd be tearing out of here as fast as I could run. I hate ghosts and scary stuff like that.

Ghost feels like the closest thing to a description of what I am. But no one's ever been able to hear me before. Or talk to me.

"I can see you," I say, inching forward to the tree. The shadow I'm watching pulls back a bit, moving out of synch with the other shadows cast by the leaves.

You can see me?

"Is that you by the tree?"

The shadow shifts again, stills. I walk closer, even though my heart is pounding in my chest and I feel like my legs are going to collapse. Carefully, slowly, I lower myself to the ground beneath the tree, my back against the trunk. There, out of the corner of my eye, a form emerges. It is fairly indistinct, but I can make out a shape that might be someone's head.

"So . . . you're dead," I say, not sure exactly how to go about making small talk with a ghost.

I'm dead, he says, and now I can hear laughter in his voice. *And you can hear me. And see me?*

"A little. If I sit like this and don't look directly at you. I get a sense of your presence. Can you see me?"

I know I'm looking at an African goddess, skin the color of dry leaves, eyes like cinnamon and a halo of gorgeous, nappy hair. That sound like you?

I choke on crazed laughter. "Are you flirting with me?"

Maybe, the ghost says. *I can't help it if I'm charming.*

"You're Harrison?" I ask, remembering the name I read on the marker, the one with the boy who was my age when he died.

Yes, ma'am. And who do I have the pleasure of addressing?

"Apollonia Stone," I say, surprising myself. I almost never use my full name.

Apollonia?

"I usually go by Polly."

I suppose you'd have to, he says with a laugh. The shadow shifts, almost as if Harrison has propped his elbows on his knees. *What's the date today?*

"It's July fifteenth, 2015."

Huh. I guess I lost a few years there. Why'd your parents name you Apollonia? he asks before I have a chance to ask him about his cryptic comment about time.

"They didn't. My birthmom did."

Your what?

"My birthmom. I was adopted. Did they have adoption in the 1920s?"

Harrison laughs. It's strange not being able to look directly at him when he speaks. *I know what adoption is, Apollonia.*

"My birthmom wanted me to have a strong name."

It doesn't get any stronger than Apollonia.

"Apollo was one of the gods. God of the sun and a bunch of other stuff, like music, poetry, and medicine." I'm rambling now, my mind unable to fully grasp that I'm talking to a ghost about my adoption story.

We had Greek mythology back in my day, too, Harrison comments.

"Oh. Yeah. Of course."

This is an odd experience for both of us.

"Yes and no."

No?

"I can hear dead people," I start to explain. "Death singer, that's the name for what I am. Before this, I've only ever heard anyone's final thoughts and I certainly couldn't see them before. And I've never had anyone who could hold a conversation."

Really? You are something special, aren't you?

"No," I say, the word blasting from my mouth like a shot.

Then maybe I'm the special one, he says after a pause, skating smoothly over my words. *Although I'm curious what makes me special in this case.*

"I don't know. Do you remember much about your life?"

If I could describe the movement of Harrison's shadow, it looked like he shrugged his shoulders. *Not really. I have a lot of memories from being dead, but I only have a few images from my life. A sponge cake cooling on a checkered tablecloth. The feel of someone's shoulder underneath my head as I'm being carried. A scrap or two of melody.*

"Sounds like the kind of memories kids have."

I suppose so.

"What about your family? Friends?"

Again, a few images. A voice or two. But I don't remember names or faces. I don't know how many siblings I had or what my mom looked like.

"That's sad," I say, even as a wave of emotion hits me in the chest. It's similar to me and my birth family.

I remember the river most of all.

"Yeah?"

Sunlight sparkling on the currents. The feel of sand beneath my toes. His voice warms with the memories.

"I like the river, too," I blurt. "That still doesn't answer the question of what makes you different from the rest of the dead. Maybe it has something to do with how you died?"

There's a pause before Harrison's voice flows toward me. *I don't remember how I died.*

"Oh. So have you . . . have you just been trapped here all this time?" I ask, twisting a strand of grass around my thumb. I'm not sure I want to hear the answer.

Trapped isn't the word I'd use. It's like being on the river. Sometimes you get caught up in a current and everything moves swiftly. Other times you float in a back channel, half asleep, and you wake up to realize most of the day is gone. I missed most of the 2000s, for example.

"So you haven't just been wandering here for ninety years, thinking about your life."

No, he says with a laugh. *Although I can't wander far. I can get to the bottom of the hill on a good day. Can't get past the vines behind us to see the river, though.*

I risk a glimpse at Harrison. Is it my imagination, or does he look more substantial? I can almost make out what looks like a trimmed Afro and a glint of teeth.

"Wait, Harrison, are you Black?"

We didn't call it that back in those days but yes, I'm Black, just like yourself.

"I'm biracial," I say on autopilot.

You're bi-what?

"Biracial. My birthmom was Black and my birthdad was white."

There's a long pause. *And that's okay? A Black lady and a white man?*

"Yeah, for the most part. Some people are jerks about it, but it's not illegal."

Good to know, good to know. Are things getting better?

I know what he's asking. I think back to what I know about the time period where Harrison was alive, which isn't much. "Better than in the past, I guess. In some ways. Civil rights and all. But then Black men get shot by the police and no one is held accountable."

So not much has changed. There's a pause and it feels like Harrison is watching me closely. *Do people still call you . . . ?*

And then he says the ugliest word I know. I fold over as if I've been punched in the gut. It's a word I've heard from time to time. Too often, although even hearing it once is too much. The last time was when I was fourteen. Henrietta and I were at the mall in Rochester. We'd just gotten makeovers at the

Clinique counter and overheard one of the sales ladies say she was due for a break, "once she finished with the two little n—s." I'd sat in shock while Henrietta took my hand and led me out of the store. I cried all the way home.

"Like you said, not everything's changed."

We sit in silence for awhile, listening to the breeze in the trees.

So what brings you to Jessam Crossing? Harrison asks at last.

"Jessam Crossing? What's that?"

I see a gesture like an arm flung wide. *Jessam Crossing is the name of this bit of land.*

"It is? Tasha called it Fredrickson Annex."

I don't know what they call it now, but I do know that it was called Jessam Crossing at one point.

I narrow my eyes. "How do you know that if you don't remember much more about your life than a sponge cake?"

Harrison's laugh is low. *Touché. Well, I am buried here, and my soul has a sacred connection with this space, something you can never fully appreciate until the hour of death approaches, oh naive one. Let me tell you the wisdom of the dead, although be warned that it could cost you your soul.*

It takes me a moment to realize he's messing with me, right about the time he doubles over in laughter.

"So did you make up Jessam Crossing, too?" I ask when his laughter has subsided.

Nah, this place is called Jessam Crossing. I heard a couple of conversations awhile back and someone used the term 'Jessam Crossing' and I felt something click into place deep inside. Recognition, I guess.

"Hm, okay," I say, jotting down Jessam Crossing in my notebook. I'll have to tell Tasha about it, although I'm not sure how I'll explain how I know. My mind circles back to an earlier part of my conversation with Harrison.

"Do you mind it? Being dead and stuck here?"

It's better than the alternative, I guess.

"What do you mean?"

Harrison's voice grows quiet. *What if all that waits on the other side is nothing? I may be stuck on this patch of ground, but at least I'm me. At least I'm still here.*

I have nothing to add to this. He's right—there might be nothing after death. At least this way he gets to stick around for a bit. I'm about to ask him more when Billy shouts my name, saving me from further contemplation. I glance down the hill to see him striding across the meadow.

You got a friend here?

"That's Billy."

He your daddy?

"No, my dad's in New Jersey for work," I say, scrambling to my feet.

I meant your sweetheart.

"Oh! No. No, he's definitely not my sweetheart. Look, I gotta go."

You'll come back and visit me?

"Yes," I say. "I promise." I know deep down that as weird as this is, I will come back.

I sling the backpack over my shoulders and trip down the hill toward Billy. Scraps of the song Harrison was singing float toward me. He's singing much louder than he was earlier.

See you later, Apollonia, he calls after me.

"What's up?" I ask Billy, coming to a breathless halt before him. He glances over my shoulder.

"Why are you out of breath?"

"No reason. Did you need something?"

"Yeah, I gotta get back to town," he says, gesturing with his phone. "My uncle . . ." his voice trails off.

"You want a ride?"

"I can walk," he says, gesturing to the hills behind us.

"It's like three miles back to Monroe, plus you have to get over the hills. Let's just go back to my car. I'm done here anyway."

"Fine." Billy nods, following me down the dirt path. "Don't you have to work at the pool anyway?"

"Um, no," I say, surprised he remembered my other job. "I got banned," I say, the words slipping out.

"Banned?" he asks, a flicker of surprise crossing his face. "How come?"

"A . . . a misunderstanding," I sputter. "So what does your uncle want?" We've reached my car. The door handles are hot and the steering wheel sizzles beneath my palms.

"Same old shit," Billy says. He tips his head against the back of the seat and closes his eyes. I glance once more at the cemetery on the hillside, then shift the car into reverse, turn it around, and drive us back to Monroe.

CHAPTER

SEVEN

Two days later, I sit in the lot in front of the library, staring at the steering wheel. I'm still in shock. Did I really talk with a ghost? I've tried to ignore it ever since I got home. I've spent the past few days doing chores around the house and still neglecting my schoolwork. I did text Tasha that the place might have been known as Jessam Crossing at one point, if that would help with her research, but otherwise I've been pretending the place doesn't exist.

I can't get Harrison out of my head, however. I need answers.

With shaking hands, I pull out my phone and check the death singers forum. I do a couple of searches to see if anyone's talked about having a conversation with any of their subjects. No luck. I start a new thread: Sungoddess98 wants to know if anyone's ever had a back and forth conversation with a ghost. I refresh the screen a few times after posting, but no one's written back after four minutes. I shouldn't be surprised. Oddly enough, the death singer community tends not to believe in ghosts, which always cracks me up, seeing as we can hear the dead. Maybe someone knows more than they're saying.

"Apollonia, what a nice surprise," Tasha says as I stumble down the steps to the archives. She's wearing a sleeveless turquoise blouse and wide-legged tan trousers. Her braids are loose and fall over her shoulders. I've always wanted to try braids, but the nearest salon is over an hour away and between work and swim practice, I never had time to go. Maybe I should see if I could go with Tasha sometime.

"As you can see, Marilyn is still gone," Tasha says, sweeping her arm to indicate the piles of papers stacked on the counter behind the desk. "I can't quite figure out her filing system, but I'm pretty sure we haven't reneged on any bills. At least not yet. I figure if the lights go off it's time to take a vacation. Anyway, I wanted to talk to you about the cemetery. How's the mapping going?"

Images of Harrison's grave flash before my eyes but I shove them away.

"It's good. I made some notes, took a few pictures, and started the grid." I unzip my backpack and start pulling out my materials. The phone rings. It's an old-fashioned one with a dial and a cord connecting the handset to the base. I thought it was an antique the first time I saw it, but Tasha said there wasn't room in the budget to upgrade to a cordless phone. The old phone still works fine and Tasha said visitors get a kick out of it.

"Let me get that," she says. I wander past the counter and head toward the first table, where several cartons are lined up in a row. I'm surprised to see the first one is marked Jessam Crossing.

"We have open hours on Thursday afternoon," Tasha is explaining on the phone, "although I'm here most days and we certainly could schedule an appointment for a time that works for both of us."

There's a sound of paper flipping.

"Friday at ten is just fine. I'd be happy to pull some records ahead of time. Tell me more about what you're researching."

There's another pause and I lift the corner of the box. There are two folders and an old book inside.

"Perfect. We should be able to help," Tasha says. The phone clatters as she hangs up. I drop the lid.

"I see you found my research," Tasha says to me. "You were right, by the way. I'm glad you texted me. The place *was* known as Jessam Crossing, in addition to being called Monroe Township, before it was annexed by the city. That was really important information to discover. How did you find it?"

This is the question I have been dreading ever since I texted her a few days ago. "Um, I saw it on a headstone, I think? So what did you find?"

Tasha gives me an odd look but I can also tell she's anxious to show me what's in the boxes. "After you sent me the name, I did some digging. I found these in storage in the basement of the city utility building."

"There's archives stuff in the utility building?"

Tasha comes over to the table. "Unfortunately, there's stuff everywhere. About half the collection is actually in the archives, but they seem to have run out of room about two decades ago. So some things are in the utility building, some are in the attic of city hall, and I suspect there are a few random boxes stored at various houses in town. I'm trying to get a sense of how large the collection is and then write a grant proposal to renovate this space. Of course, if the collection is as large as I suspect, I may need to be looking for a new spot all together. Only don't tell the city manager that yet," she finishes with a grin. "Go ahead," she says, nodding at the box.

I lift the first folder out of the box.

"Now, I've already gone through some of these records, but I thought it would be interesting for you to look through the items, and then we can talk about your impressions," she says.

"Um, okay." This isn't the first time Tasha has tried to get me to think like an archivist.

"Take a peek and see what you think. I've got to sort through some invoices. I'll just be at the desk."

I glance overhead at the egress windows and the light filtering through their heavy black bars. I suppose it's better than having no windows at all.

"You want me to wear gloves?" I call to Tasha.

"Nah, you're fine," she says, her eyes glinting at me from over the top of the counter.

"I'm supposed to find something in these boxes, aren't I?"

"Like I said, I have some theories. I want to hear yours, too."

"Okay," I say.

Tasha starts typing and the sound punctures the silence in the basement. I pick up the book, which is a faded gray and has the word "Records" stamped across the front. It smells like all kinds of mold. I crack open the cover and read the inscription.

"Ebenezer Baptist Church, Jessam Crossing, Minnesota. 1867—"

There's a list of names down the side of the first page, along with a few other notations. It's hard to read the spidery script and I end up squinting. From what I can tell, the book contains a mishmash of information about the church, including a list of members and some occasional notes about attendance at Sunday services. I flip through the pages and find more of the same. The last dates recorded are in the 1880s.

"There was a church at Jessam Crossing," I comment with surprise. I suppose it makes sense. There's a cemetery, so maybe there was a church nearby.

"Uh huh," Tasha says, nodding in such an encouraging way that I know she wants me to make some other kind of connection. "Keep reading."

The first manila folder contains a single torn page, its edges ripped. Like the church records, there's a list of names down one side. On the other side, there are numbers.

"What's this?"

Tasha comes over to the table. "Look at what's underneath the names."

I peer at the faded writing. There are notations about eggs, nails, and thread.

"This is from a store?"

"I think so. The page is most likely torn from a store ledger, where they would have kept track of people's accounts. I found it tucked between the pages of the church records book."

"So there was a store at Jessam Crossing." For some reason I feel the hair rise on my arms. Instead of an empty marshy field, I'm starting to imagine a shadowy outline of buildings taking shape. My mind adds a few roads, a couple of houses, and a smiling young man waving at me from a porch with a view of the river.

Tasha frowns and chews the inside of her cheek. "Maybe. We have to recognize the limitations of this record. It's a single page torn from a ledger." She points at the corner, where there's a tiny notation. "What does that say?"

I squint. "Um, JC General?"

"That's what I got, too. Other than that, there's no date and no store name. We have no way of knowing if it's tied directly to Jessam Crossing, except that the page ended up in church record. It's possible it has been misfiled."

"Can't we check the names on the ledger against the names in the church book?"

Tasha grins at me like I've told her it's Christmas morning. "Yes, we can do just that. It still might not tell us much, but at least we can establish a connection between the ledger and the church. Although to be honest, we still haven't tied the church to Jessam Crossing either."

"But it says Jessam Crossing in the church book."

"Someone might argue that it's not conclusive proof that the church was actually in Jessam Crossing. But buildings leave records, too. If there was a church there, they probably built it out of wood. If we're lucky, they might have used a stone foundation, which can be uncovered. It takes a lot of equipment that we don't have, but the state historical society might be able to help out if we get a solid lead on Jessam Crossing having historical value."

"But if there's a church, a cemetery, and maybe a store, doesn't it mean that people lived there?"

"Probably," Tasha says. "I stayed late last night and looked through a few microfilm rolls from the dates mentioned in these records. The *Monroe Morning Call* mentions the settlement a few times in passing. There's nothing specific, just a few references to the place. With the bluffs and the wetlands in the way, it's not surprising that the towns didn't have much contact."

"Okay," I say slowly. I'm still not sure what exactly I'm supposed to see. Tasha seems like she's waiting for me to make a startling discovery.

"Well, there is one more clipping you need to see." She nudges the second folder across the table.

I pull the folder toward me and flip it open. It contains one yellowed newspaper clipping, its edges ragged. I skim it and then go back to read it again more slowly. The hairs on my neck rise just like they did when I first heard Harrison. After I've read the clipping a third time, I raise my eyes to Tasha, who's watching me with a mixture of excitement and something else. It takes a moment before I recognize a hint of sadness in her gaze.

"Jessam Crossing was a Black colony?"

Tasha props her hands on her hips and skims the newspaper article with me. She's starting to smile again. "Yes. Exactly. It looks like Jessam Crossing might have been a colony for Blacks after the Civil War."

"Whoa," I say.

"Whoa indeed," Tasha replies, grinning. "This is huge."

Fifteen minutes later we've put the records away and are sitting in Tasha's windowless office. I'm cradling a mug of tea in my hands. I'm not really a tea drinker but taking the mug seemed like the polite thing to do. It's some kind of herbal blend and tastes like licorice and roses. I wrinkle my nose.

Tasha sits behind the massive wood desk that's been crammed into the tiny room. I'm settled in the rocking chair in the corner with a purple afghan over my legs. It gets cold in the basement.

"So you think that there was a Black colony in Jessam Crossing," I say, still trying to wrap my mind around what Tasha's telling me. I think about my new friend and wonder if Harrison lived in an all-Black town.

"The clip you just read from the *Monroe Morning Call* references Jessam Crossing and its inhabitants," she says, tapping her polished fingernails on a photocopy of the newspaper article. She doesn't bother reading it to me. I've read it about ten more times since she showed it to me. The article is short, a few lines mentioning the "encroachment on our land and freedoms" and then says something about the "the blight of the Negro colony to our South, in a hollow known as Jessam Crossing." The language makes my skin crawl.

"I've never even heard of anything like a Black colony."

"It wouldn't have been the only one. Ever heard of Dearfield, Colorado? Or Boley, Oklahoma? There's also Fort Mose in Florida, which was an all-Black settlement before the United States became a country. After the Civil War, there were plans for a few settlements throughout Minnesota, too."

"How do you know all this?" I ask.

"I did my thesis on Blacks in rural Minnesota in the nineteenth century," she says. "There may have been a Black colony planned in Todd County, but the evidence is inconclusive. There was also a guy named Thomas Montgomery, who was an officer in the Sixty-Seventh US Colored Infantry. He was approached by a land agent to set up a farming settlement for his soldiers near St. Peter. But nothing came of that, either. It's possible that someone like Thomas Montgomery planned something similar at Jessam Crossing. And if Jessam Crossing was a planned colony, it would be hugely significant."

"I just never thought there were many Black people in Minnesota, especially right after the Civil War."

Tasha laughs. "That's a sad and yet common misconception."

"But why Minnesota?"

"Blacks have been here as long as European explorers and settlers. There was George Bonga, who was a fur trader and a translator. He was Black and

Ojibwe. There's a township named after him. And there were enslaved people at Fort Snelling. You knew that, right?"

"Um . . ."

"You know the Dred Scott case? The one that said African Americans couldn't claim citizenship?"

"I've heard of it," I say, my voice trailing off. I know the names but I don't know any of the details.

"Dred Scott and his wife, Harriet, were slaves living with their master at Fort Snelling. Scott claimed that since slavery was illegal in Minnesota, he and Harriet should be granted freedom. The case went to the Supreme Court in 1857, where they decided African Americans had no claim to citizenship or freedom."

"I do remember that one now," I say, my mind drifting to the uncomfortable few weeks in middle school when we learned about slavery. Everyone stared at their desks and cast awkward glances at me. I usually sat with my head ducked and played with my hair. Chase usually skipped those days. One time during gym Ronnie Babcock trapped me in a corner, looped a jump rope around my wrists and said he was taking me to the auction to see what kind of price he'd get. I kicked him hard in the shins and ran away, too ashamed to tell the teacher on him, even though I knew what Ronnie did was wrong.

"After the Civil War, some Blacks came North with returning soldiers," Tasha was saying. "Under the Homestead Act, former slaves and Black veterans could file for land. Minnesota seemed like it provided some opportunities. It wasn't easy. There was a lot of opposition, too."

"'The blight of the Negro colony,'" I quote from the clipping.

"Lots of racism. Lots of competition for resources. That's part of the history, too. And the present."

"So what happens next? With Jessam Crossing, I mean?" I take a sip of my tea.

"I still need to do some more digging to see if I can find anything else about Jessam Crossing. I'm hoping to find more in our archives, although the records are a mess. Since I've been working on this grant, I'm starting to realize how messed up they are," she laughs. "There were four different volunteer archivists in the past thirty years alone, plus countless other hands helping out. Everyone seems to have used their own version of record keeping, so who knows what's in every box."

"I can help look."

"That would be great! I've been meaning to ask, which grave mentioned Jessam Crossing?"

Tea sloshes in my mug. "Um, I forget which one it was. I saw it right before I was leaving. Sorry."

"That's fine. Next time you're out there, though, snap a picture for me. We might learn more if we know whose stone mentions the town. Also check to see if any other ones do, too."

"Okay," I squirm, not sure how to get out of this one.

"There are some online sources we can use to do the research, too, like federal and state census records. I might have you start with those once we have more names from the cemetery, so I'd like you to keep working on the cemetery."

"Sure. I can do the mapping in the mornings and be over here in the afternoon to work on the census whatevers."

"You sure you have enough time for that? What about your job at the pool?"

My voice trails off. "I'm taking a little break from it for now." I shift in my chair, twisting the mug in my hands.

Tasha fixes me with a level gaze but I don't meet her eyes. "Is everything okay, Apollonia?"

"Um, yeah. Well, I had a strange thing happen at the grocery store the other day," I say. Suddenly I find myself telling her about the encounter with Nyssa.

"I see," Tasha says when I finish. I squirm in my chair again, the tea mug lukewarm against my skin. Tasha sighs. "People suck."

A burst of laughter explodes from me. I'm horrified for a moment and then Tasha lets out a guffaw and soon we're laughing until we're crying. "Oh, Polly," Tasha says after she's caught her breath. "I'm sorry, but it's true." She hands me a Kleenex and I wipe my eyes. "How often does that kind of thing happen to you? Those clueless, horrible comments?"

"Lots. People are always asking if they can touch my hair."

Tasha rolls her eyes. "Same. What else?"

"Well, people stare a lot when I'm with my family, although that's more of an adoption thing."

"It's a race thing, too."

"Yeah, and sometimes strangers ask dumb questions, like where I'm from. Or they tell me how exotic I look or they say, 'So, what are you?'"

Tasha smiles. "What do you say?"

I shrug. "Usually I say, 'I'm a person,' or something like that. Seems nicer than telling them to fuck off." I clap my hand over my mouth but Tasha just laughs.

"My office isn't a swear-free zone," she says.

I smile. "How about you?"

"Let's see, I get a lot of strangers telling me they voted for President Obama. Or saying it's a post-racial world now. And people like to go out of their way to tell me I don't talk Black. Or sometimes they'll say how articulate I am. This happens at conferences a lot. One time I was giving a presentation and I went to introduce myself to the white man who was moderating the session. He started telling me where I should leave the pitchers of water before he realized I wasn't working in catering."

"People do suck," I say. For a second I feel such kinship with Tasha that I almost tell her my secret, that I can hear dead people, and that one of them started talking back to me. I want to tell her about Billy and the fire and how I'm afraid I've messed up my life beyond repair.

Instead I chicken out.

"I should get going," I say. I set down my mug. "My mom needs me at home."

"Oh, okay," Tasha says. "Well, good job with the mapping, Apollonia. See you tomorrow."

"See you tomorrow," I say, jogging up the archives stairs. As I leave, I think about the lost Black colonies and all of the stuff Tasha and I just discussed. I feel an unbearable weight and sadness settle on my shoulders.

What's the point?

It's only when I dash down the sidewalk in front of the library that I run straight into Henrietta. My hands pull back to my sides even though they want to slide around her waist and give her a hug.

"Henrietta, hey," I say, breathless.

She's wearing long olive pants and a pink striped t-shirt. Her hair is scraped back in a ponytail, the edges starting to turn in the humidity. She peers at me from behind blue-framed glasses. Henrietta was never interested in fashion but she's starting to rock a geek chic look. I wonder if it's intentional.

"Hi, Polly," she says, clearing her throat.

"How are you?"

Her full lips press together in a tight line. "Fine."

"What are you up to?"

"I'm heading to the library."

"Oh? I was just there. I work in the archives."

"I know."

I feel an unaccountable release of tension in my chest. "You do? You should come by sometime. And do you know Tasha? The archivist? She's African American, too."

"I saw her picture in the paper."

"You'd like her a lot. I'm helping her with some cool projects that you'd like. Hey, have you ever heard about Jessam Crossing? It's the spot that's now called Fredrickson Annex. Sometimes they called it Monroe Township," I babble. "Anyway, Tasha and I just figured out some really amazing stuff about it and I'm doing some work in the cemetery for it."

I almost tell her about Harrison, but Henrietta's eyes slide away when I mention cemeteries.

"You still . . . um, do that? Listen to them."

"Well, yeah," I say, feeling a defensiveness rise within me.

"Oh."

"It's not something you outgrow."

"I thought maybe you'd lost interest. With all your new friends and everything." She pushes her glasses up her nose and doesn't look at me.

"No. Well, maybe a little. I got more interested in it after my birthmom died."

This time she does look at me, her eyes growing wide behind her lenses. "She died? When?"

"March."

"I'm sorry, I didn't know."

"No one knows. Besides my parents, I mean. I . . . I didn't tell anyone."

"Not even your new friends."

"You're the only one I wanted to tell."

She adjusts the messenger bag over her shoulder. I think she's about to say something more about my birthmom but her gaze drops and she shakes her head. "I need to get going. I'm meeting some friends."

"Oh. Okay. It was good to see you, Hen."

She's already halfway up the library steps, marching with the precision of a marionette, and soon she's swallowed up by the front doors.

I watch her go, knowing I have no one but myself to blame.

CHAPTER

EIGHT

Once I'm back in the car, I check my phone. There are several messages on my thread.

"Sungoddess98, what exactly are you asking about?" ISeezDemons asked an hour ago.

"Ghosts aren't real!!!" DontGiveaDamb had replied almost immediately.

"Hm, I think maybe there's more that she's not telling us?" DeathBarbie84 said. "Maybe you can fill us in? I'd like to hear more!"

I roll the phone in my hands, trying to decide what I should say. They've always been supportive the other times I've posted questions or made comments. But suddenly I get the sense that I'm in uncharted waters. My gut tells me not to raise an alarm.

"Thought I heard something weird in a cemetery the other day," I write, "but I think I was hearing a radio or people talking from a nearby campsite." The lie slides easily from my fingers. "Sorry for the concern!! Thanks!!!"

I stop and erase a few exclamation points before I post the message. If I leave now, I'll have time to visit Harrison again before Mom expects me at home. Maybe I can get more answers from him.

I'm about to toss my phone on the passenger seat when it buzzes. It's from a private number. *I read your description in the forums, as well as your hasty and clumsy redaction. What you describe is extremely dangerous.*

A chill goes through my body as I read the message again.

My phone buzzes again.

Please contact me right away.

Chills run up and down my spine, even though it's ninety-six degrees outside. My fingers hover over the screen and I type a return message: *Who is this?*

The phone buzzes almost immediately, the message much shorter. *Alatar. From Death Singers.*

How did you get my number?

Membership form.

How did you access it?

I have my methods.

I stare at the phone for a few minutes. When I asked to join the forum, I talked with two separate people on the phone. One was a woman named Mary who lived in the Pacific Northwest, screen name Ereshkigal (a Babylonian death goddess—I looked it up). The other was a man in Halifax named Colin, whose screen name is Merlin. I don't remember anyone named Alatar. The death singers aren't particularly secretive with each other when discussing our abilities and experiences, but we don't like to share too much personal information, even with each other. There's a spot on the forums where you can initiate a process to meet others in person, but it involves direct messaging personal information and I've never done it.

The phone buzzes again. *I don't know where you live and I didn't mean to frighten you.*

Too late, I shoot back. I'm rewarded, oddly enough, with a smiley face. I drop the phone on the seat.

When I reach the intersection of Martha Washington Street and Dolly Madison Avenue, I stop. I'd been planning on turning left and going down to Highway 61 to Jessam Crossing, but Alatar's message unnerved me.

A car honks behind me. I flip the blinker and turn right. Up the bluff toward home.

After I park the car in the garage, I run up the stairs, calling a quick hello to my mom.

"You home already?" she asks, poking her head out of her studio.

"I finished up at the archives early. I'm just going to do some homework," I say, leaning over the railing.

Mom's face breaks into a smile. "Good idea, Polly. Dinner later? I made falafel."

"Yeah, sure."

Mom disappears into the studio and I run up the steps.

When I get to my room, I march to my desk, push the books out of the way, and turn on my MacBook. It's been a long time and it takes a while to load the page. The internet is slow in the country.

I click on my profile. Like most of my fellow death singers, my profile is sparse. I uploaded a picture of a prairie flower instead of a picture of me and for location I listed "Flyover Country." Taking a deep breath, I search for Alatar's profile.

All it shows is a drawing of a wizard with a long white beard wearing a sky blue cloak. For location it says, "Elsewhere and Everywhere."

I stare at the screen for fifteen minutes until I finally send my reply.

I'm just looking for information.

The response comes almost immediately: *Liar.*

"Fuck you, Alatar," I whisper, tossing my phone on the bedside table. I don't write back.

I take Astrid for a long ride. Once she's back in the barn, I lie on my bed for a few hours, doing nothing more than listening to the house settle and the cicadas whine outside my window. I suppose I could attack the pile of homework on my desk, but I don't even know where to start. I sigh. Maybe I'll just repeat junior year after all. I try to picture what that would look like, starting the year again in the same place I was last fall, watching my friends graduate next spring and start their lives while I repeat junior year over and over. But I can't imagine ever progressing beyond where I am right now, and I sure as hell am not in the same place I was last year.

My phone buzzes. Billy's name flashes on the screen. I ignore the burst of energy I feel in my stomach when I see that he's texting me.

It's probably for a job, Polly, I tell myself.

I'm right. Billy's text is terse: *11pm tonight.*

I don't bother texting back. The phone jumps in my hand for a second time. I feel relief when I see my dad's face flash across the screen.

"How's it going, Polly-Wolly?"

"Hey, Dad." I let the nickname slide. "How're you?"

"I'm fine. The lab's closing for a little bit next week. Ramona's going to France with Peter, so I thought I'd sneak away, too. I'm looking forward to seeing you."

"Me, too, Dad."

There's an awkward silence on the line. I sit cross-legged on the patchwork quilt underneath the eaves.

"She told you, didn't she, Dad?"

My dad sighs. "Of course she did, Pol. You know we're worried about you."

"I know."

"Mom said she wasn't going to give you any more consequences for running out on her the other day. To be honest, I'm not sure what more we can do to you except take your car away."

"You guys gonna do that?"

"If I was home, I'd insist on it, Polly. But with your mom's schedule it makes more sense for you to be able to drive yourself to the archives and the pool. Well, not the pool anymore."

"I'm just suspended for a few weeks."

"You'll be spending more time at the archives, then." It's not a question.

"I don't mind," I say.

"You and Tasha have a good relationship, don't you?"

"Yeah, I like her. We have good conversations about being Black." My parents are always happy to hear whenever I've taken an interest in my racial identity. I know they think they've never done enough to help me figure out what it means for me to be biracial. They're probably right, although they didn't have a lot of resources in Monroe. They talked about moving to the Cities once and finding a more diverse community, but it never panned out.

"Good, good." My dad sighs again, a rushing noise through the phone. I take the receiver away from my ear for a second and miss his next words.

" . . . just love you so much and don't want to see you like this," he is say-ing. "You have so much potential."

"Dad, it's okay," I say, interrupting him before he can start crying. Before I can start crying, too. He gives a little laugh.

"I know, sweetie. Look, we'll talk more when I get home, okay?"

"Okay, Dad."

"And you'll finish some of your homework?"

Now it's my turn to exhale. "Sure, Dad. Love you."

"Love you too, little frog."

That's the nickname I hate. I wrinkle my nose as I hang up. My mom is hovering in the doorway.

"You okay, sweetheart?"

"I'm fine, Mom."

The light from the hallway glints in her hair. There's more silver than I remember.

"Your dad and I love you so much and we just want you to be happy," she says. I halt her words with a wave of my hand and an arm around her waist as I approach the door. My parents can't help but wind their love around me like bubble wrap.

"I'm fine," I repeat.

She nods against my shoulder. "Dinner's ready."

"Sounds good," I say, and I follow her to the kitchen.

I decide to forget everything happening outside of the kitchen, so dinner passes in a comfortable hour. We don't talk about much in particular, but it's nice to sit with Mom around the table. Soon I'm back in my room, watching the numbers march to eleven. Still no message from Alatar.

"Fine, be that way," I mutter to my phone.

———

At 10:40 I pull on a black t-shirt and shorts. My mom went to bed a little while ago but I'm still cautious as I jimmy open the screen and slide out the window. In a few moments I'm safely on the ground, cutting through the paddock on my way to meet Billy.

"Hey," he says as I slide into the cab of his truck.

"Hey," I reply, buckling my seatbelt. For a second I have an overwhelming urge to tell Billy about Alatar, but suddenly I feel bone weary and the only thing I want is to be quiet. Fortunately Billy is not much of a talker.

The truck bounces over gravel as we head west, away from the river.

"Where are we going?" I ask eventually as town falls away behind us. He tosses a newspaper in my lap.

"Obituary's in there."

"Does this thing turn on?" I ask, fumbling for the dome light.

"Only when you open the door."

"Are we playing truth or dare now?" I ask, surprising both of us with the flirtatious tone in my voice.

"Don't—" Billy yelps as my hand sneaks to the handle. I'm not really going to open the door, but I barely touch it when the truck hits a rut and the door pops open. Gravel races past my eyes. I scream as the brakes whine. My arm gets tangled in the seatbelt and I slide down the seat toward the opening. My feet scramble for a foothold against the floorboards but my sandals slip and for a second I am airborne, about to tumble headfirst out of a moving vehicle.

I'm saved when the truck rattles to a halt on the opposite side of the road.

"I didn't mean . . ." I'm babbling, scarcely noticing Billy's arm flung across my torso, his voice low in my ear, although I can't make out what he's saying. Eventually my breathing slows and I'm aware that we're sitting at the edge of a dark wood, Billy's arm pressed against my body, his hand curved over my hip. His fingers are warm. We sit for a second too long.

"You okay?" he asks after a moment, loosening his arm.

"Yeah," I nod. "I really didn't mean—"

"The handle's a bit sensitive. Should have warned you."

"S'okay," I say. My heart pounds in my chest and I still feel like I'm falling, even though the truck is motionless. I'm gradually aware that my leg feels warm. I look down to see Billy's hand resting on my knee. His touch is reassuring, anchoring me to this world, and I'm glad for the contact.

"You sure you're okay?" he asks.

"I'm fine."

He glances at his hand on my leg before removing it. The headlights bob as the truck rolls up the hill. We clear the top of the bluff and drive in silence for a few minutes, the darkness punctuated by an occasional yard light in a clearing of trees. The trees thin and soon we are driving through fields.

"You farm, right?" I ask Billy.

He looks at me out of the corner of his eye. "My uncle has a farm," he says at last.

"Oh?"

"I help him some. Almost time to detassel the corn."

"Sounds fun," I say. My mind is looping footage of gravel racing past my face.

"It's the opposite of fun."

"Yeah, I don't actually know what it is," I confess, drawing a laugh from Billy, who starts describing detasseling. Apparently, it's hot and dirty work that involves removing the tassel at the top of the corn and has something to do with pollination control. I think.

"Are you going to keep farming?" I ask after a while.

Billy stares at me. The moon hovering over the fields turns his face ghostly silver. "You don't know?"

"Know what?"

"About the farm."

"I think we've established that I know nothing about farming, Billy."

"Not farming in general. The farm. My uncle's farm. It's supposed to be my farm but my dad lost it years ago."

"What?"

Billy sighs. "My dad and my uncle were drinking and playing cards. My dad got really drunk, drunker than usual, and gambled the farm away."

"Holy crap. I thought that was just something that happened in movies."

"They went to court but my dad actually managed to do something right when he lost the farm. Had the whole deal notarized and everything. He had no legal grounds to get it back."

"Is that why we're doing this? You're trying to buy the farm back?"

"I don't want the fucking farm," Billy growls. "Turns out my uncle's almost as bad a farmer as my dad. The land's hardly worth anything. I want to get the fuck out of Monroe."

"Where do you want to go?" I ask, feeling unaccountably sad even as I resonate with his words. I want to get the fuck out of Monroe, too.

"Seattle, maybe. Or up to Alaska. Work on a fishing boat." He sighs and slumps over the wheel. "I need the money to pay off my dad's debts. He died last year. Creditors keep calling."

"Oh. I'm sorry."

"Don't be. He was an asshole. The world's better off without him."

I must look shocked because Billy keeps talking. "I'm not secretly grieving or anything. He was a jerk. Gone for half my life, knocked my mom around . . ." Billy's voice trails off and he shakes his head. "The world's better off," he repeats.

"What about your mom?" I ask. Billy's hands clench on the steering wheel and then I remember. "She died, didn't she," I say. I dimly remember my mom and dad talking about it a few years ago.

"Cancer," he says.

"Oh," I say, thinking this is something we have in common. "I'm sorry."

Billy grunts something that might have been thanks.

"So stealing from the dead is your plan," I press.

"You got any better ideas?"

"College?" I say, the word squeaking in my throat.

"College costs money," Billy snorts. "Plus I dropped out of high school three years ago. I've got no prospects, Polly."

"What about getting your GED?"

"Who's going to tutor me? You?"

The breath catches in my throat. "It was just an idea," I mumble.

We ride the rest of the way in silence until we reach the cemetery, which is set behind a wide lawn. There's a plaque and a bell standing near the road. There's just enough light from the moon to read that the bell belonged to the parish of St. Nicholas, which stood on this site for fifty-seven years before being torn down in 1976.

"People are still being buried out here even though the church was torn down almost forty years ago?" I ask as I follow Billy across the lawn. A duffle bag is slung over his shoulder. I stumble as my heel falls into a divot.

"Badger holes," he says, glancing over his shoulder. "Watch your step."

He strides to the cemetery and steps over the low chain fence strung around the perimeter.

"What if someone comes by?" I ask, looking back at his truck, which is parked right off the highway.

"If anyone came by, they wouldn't know what we're doing. Or they'd think . . ."

"They'd think what?"

"They'd think we were out here screwing," he says.

"Oh," I reply, glad it's dark and he can't see how red my face has gone.

We stop in front of a marker that's been split in two. My feet sink into soft earth. Billy fumbles with something in his hand and then a flashlight beam cuts through the night.

The grave belongs to Arnold Weber. There's only a birth date—March 25, 1952—and a blank spot for the death date. They must not have carved it yet. There's a mound of dirt over his grave, bedecked by a wreath of decaying flowers. A frilly cross in a bed of flowers is carved into the corner of his stone, along with some words.

"Consider the lilies of the field, how they grow; they toil not, neither do they spin," Billy says, the beam of the flashlight resting on the flowers, which I now see are the trumpets of Easter lilies.

"Huh?"

"Jesus telling his disciplines not to worry about earthly concerns. It's from Matthew."

It is too dark for Billy to see the expression on my face but he must infer it from my silence.

"My grandmother was religious," he says. "I'm not."

"Obviously."

"What's that supposed to mean?"

My hands fly uselessly into the air before dropping to my side. "We're out here stealing secrets from the dead. It's hardly the Christian thing to do, even if you're doing it to get out of debt."

"What about you, Miss Straight As?"

I fold my arms over my chest. "Call me by my name or don't say anything at all."

In the light of the flashlight, I see Billy's mouth quirk. I feel an unwelcome flutter in my stomach at the sight of that grin. The memory of his hand is warm on my knee. I scowl.

"All right, then, Apollonia," he says, drawing out all syllables of my name. "Are you a Christian or not?"

"Why do you care?"

"Just making conversation."

He starts unzipping the duffle bag.

"I wasn't raised in the church," I start explaining. "My parents are atheists."

"And you?"

I can't see what he's pulling out of the bag.

"I have no idea," I say, rubbing the back of my calf with the toe of my worn shoe.

Billy stops what he's doing and looks at me over his shoulder.

"You're kidding, right? You talk to the dead. You must have some theory about religion."

"I told you, I don't really talk to the dead. They make broadcasts and I pick them up. That's all." I push away thoughts of Harrison.

"So how do you explain that? If there's a final broadcast, as you call it, doesn't it mean that there's something after death?"

"Maybe. It could also be that what I'm hearing are the final echoes of life. Sometimes I think that our minds are like fields of energy, and when we die, the energy lingers. I told you that the sounds fade after a hundred years or so. Or maybe it's like how stars die. Their light lingers even after they're gone."

"Huh. So you think that once we die, that's it. Nothing."

"Would it be so bad? Just nothing?"

"No," he says, and I wonder if he's thinking about his mom. "What do you think?"

"I don't know," I say, even as a blade of sorrow cuts my heart. If there really is nothing after death, I will never meet my birthmom. I suck in a breath to stop from crying. "You about ready?"

"Sure," Billy says, sitting back on his heels. He swings the flashlight to illuminate his handiwork. There is a series of objects arranged around the perimeter of the grave. Nearest me is a chipped coffee mug with the Monroe city logo on it. Next to that there's a single golf glove and a pile of golf tees. A worn dog leash curls in the corner, nestled against a plastic water dish. At the foot of the grave there's a stack of magazines. As I approach I see the curve of a breast and a ripple of wind-blown hair.

"*Playboy?* Really?"

"Old Arnie had quite a collection. Thought I might help myself to a few."

I shake my head and get settled at Arnold's headstone. "Why does his name sound familiar?"

"Obituary says he was the city comptroller, whatever the hell that means."

"Handles the finances," I say.

"Really?" Billy says, interest catching in his voice.

"I won't help you steal from the city, Billy," I warn. "There's no way to do that without getting caught."

Billy holds up his hands. "I know, I know. Just exploring my options."

"He's the guy who died at his desk, isn't he?" I ask, the pieces clicking into place. "Like two weeks ago or something." My mom mentioned it over dinner the other night, the city employee who'd been physically fit but plagued with anger management issues. Apparently he died in the middle of a conversation.

"Yeah, that's him. You know him?"

"No, but I'm about to."

I wrap my hands around the mug, drawing in a few deep, clean breaths and turning my attention to Arnold Weber, sliding into his mind, or whatever's left of it.

He died during an argument, I learn. The paper said it was an aneurysm. *What the hell, Scott?* was his final thought. I wonder briefly about Scott, escaping a fight through death. I hold the mug tighter and images start to appear in my mind. I see the inside of an office paneled in wood and carpeted in gray. There's an industrial desk dominating the small space, buttressed by several filing cabinets. Two nature prints are on the wall, both showing a large buck in various degrees of noticing the hunter poised nearby. The hunter holds a shotgun in one print and a bow and arrow in the other. A clock ticks on the desk and I see that it's golf-themed and inscribed with the word "Pinehurst."

A wave of memories rushes through me as I amplify Arnold further. I see a woman's blonde hair shot gray at the temples, her eyes tired and distant. I see the same woman in a photograph, younger, her eyes wary but hopeful beneath the veil of her wedding dress. I see a parade of children and I see Arnold and the woman standing near this very spot on a cold, October day, watching as a tiny coffin is laid into the ground.

There are more memories. Christmas morning, Halloween night. Endless meetings and workshops where the phrases "organic synergy" and "workflow analysis" rattle around sterile conference tables. There's a cruise in the Bahamas where everyone got sick and another to Alaska where they saw whales. I see countless golf greens and even a wave of tears as Arnold stands on the first tee of St. Andrew. As I release the mug, there's one last image of Arnold as a college student, skipping over the art class that tugs at his pen and reluctantly signing up for an accounting class instead.

I can feel myself return to the surface, can hear Arnold's voice yelling at Scott in my mind. Before I break through into consciousness, I hear the words "Jessam Crossing" and a voice says, "She can't use what she can't find." Then I'm back in my own body, crouching over a mound of earth as bats swoop overhead.

Billy is studying me, the *Playboy* discarded at his side.

"How long was I gone?" I ask.

"About thirty minutes. You okay?"

"Yeah."

"What did you learn?" he asks, sweeping the items back into the duffle bag.

"Lots." I shake my head. "Lots of images and memories. More than with Ida Mae. I'm not sure where to start."

"I can ask you the security questions when I find them," Billy says, his voice low. "Only if you want. I'll keep your name out of it, I promise—"

"Might be easier," I interrupt. I clamber to my feet and we start walking back to the truck. I take a final glimpse at the Weber plot, the tiny white stone belonging to Doreen Ann, the little baby who lived for a day before she took her last breath and they laid her in the ground.

It hits me that Arnold knew something about Jessam Crossing. I'd almost forgotten. I wonder if the person they were talking about was Tasha. I'm concentrating so hard on trying to recall other snippets of the conversation that I step on another badger hole and stumble to my knees.

"I gotcha," Billy says, bending down. His hands slide from behind me to cup my elbows and leverage me to my feet. When I'm standing again, I've got my back to him. We're not touching, other than his hands at my elbows, but I can sense him, his entire body towering over me, sheltering me. It's electric. I swallow and feel my breath speed up. He moves a hair closer to me, his chest against my back, his legs brushing mine. He's so much taller than me but I feel tall and strong standing here like this. His head dips and I can feel his breath on my neck.

"Polly—" he says, just as a bat swoops overhead, breaking the spell. I jump and take a few steps toward the truck.

"I should get home," I say. I put my hand over my throat to conceal the rapid flutter of my heart, even though I know he can't see it in the dark anyway.

"Let's go," he says at last, his voice gravelly. We go back to the truck and don't talk the rest of the way home.

CHAPTER

NINE

I show up for work at the archives the next morning unable to shake the uneasy feeling that I need to tell Tasha what I heard at Arnold Weber's grave. I want to tell her about Harrison, too, but I can't figure out a way to tell her about either of these things.

"Ready for some census work?" Tasha asks, her smile wide. She laughs when she catches sight of my face. "It's not as bad as it sounds. We'll start with 1870, since it was the first census to gather detailed information on Blacks." She jiggles the mouse on the ancient desktop computer and pulls out the chair, gesturing me to sit.

Within a few minutes I'm looking at a scanned ledger book, the spidery handwriting difficult to read. Tasha zooms in and points out a line. We're studying a record for a woman named Eliza Robinson, born in North Carolina in 1848 or 1849. She lived with her four siblings and her mother in Minnesota at the time of the census. Her mother was a housekeeper. Eliza and her family are listed as Black. Tears prick my eyes and I sniffle loudly, hoping Tasha thinks I'm just coming down with a summer cold.

Her hand comes to my shoulder and gives it a squeeze. She knows what I'm thinking. "Pretty amazing, isn't it, to see these Black families in Minnesota? And look."

Her finger points to the top of the scanned page. I squint to make out the words.

"Monroe Township?"

"Jessam Crossing doesn't appear as a place name in this census or any of the next ones. Only Monroe Township, at least until the land was annexed in the 1920s. What this tells us is that there was a difference between Monroe and Monroe Township. If you look at records from families we know lived in Monroe, it just says Monroe. It's slight but it tells us that some people lived close to Monroe but not close enough to be considered part of the town itself."

"Wait, so you've already looked at all the census records?"

"I searched for all the Black residents who lived in Perrineville County. The other interesting thing I discovered is that most of the older residents of Monroe Township were born elsewhere, primarily in the South. What does that tell us?"

"Um," I search my brain. "I'm not sure?"

"Migration. Movement. That there must have been a reason a lot of Black families from the Deep South picked up and came to Minnesota. To Monroe in particular. It suggests they might have been recruited to be a part of the colony."

"Wow. Wait, recruited by who? That Thomas Montgomery guy you mentioned?"

Tasha shrugs. "Maybe. Another officer who wanted to provide for his soldiers once the war was over. We may never know. Or maybe the answers are buried in a box somewhere. Anyway, now that we've got names from the cemetery, I'm going to search for them, see if we can establish links between the families."

I cast a doubtful eye at the screen and its spidery handwriting.

"Fortunately there's a search function and typewritten transcripts," Tasha says, clicking on a few links. "Much easier to read than the books themselves.

I just wanted you to see what the original record looked like, first. We'll also use what you find to track down property records. It's in the city's best interest—and ours—to know who owns what. Problem is, those records might be hard to locate, if they even still exist."

"You need me to do anything with those?"

"Wading through historic property records is not for the faint of heart," she grins. "I want you to keep at the census records for a bit this morning and maybe head back to the cemetery this afternoon. I don't want you to go cross-eyed."

We go over what I'm looking for in more detail, mainly what I'm supposed to record. The rest of the morning passes faster than I would have expected if someone had told me what I was going to be doing ahead of time. My stomach growls at 11:30 and I show Tasha what I've done so far. I've confirmed that sixteen people from the cemetery lived in Monroe Township in 1870.

"This is really good work, Apollonia. Really good."

"Thanks."

I wander to the tables as Tasha pages through the rest of my notes.

"What about people who are in unmarked graves?" I ask, pretending to study the cracks in the wall.

"Do you think there are unmarked graves in Jessam Crossing?"

"Um, maybe?"

"It's highly possible. It looks like the oldest stone you recorded has a death date of 1900, except for the one from 1924. That's a little odd, to have such a gap." I hold my breath, waiting to hear what she has to say about Harrison's grave. "You haven't mapped the whole thing yet, right?"

"I'll do more this afternoon."

"Well, maybe there are other ones between 1900 and 1924. Anyway, to answer your question. If there was a settlement at Jessam Crossing in the 1860s or 1870s, and if they were using that site as a cemetery, there would likely be unmarked graves. Or at least graves that were once marked but not anymore."

"Can they be identified somehow?"

Tasha lays the folder on the desk. "There are ways of locating graves, usually using radar, although it requires special equipment. It costs money, of course. But it might be something to consider as this site unfolds. I like seeing the research bug in you, Polly."

"Yeah, well," I say by way of avoiding the statement. My mind flashes back to last night. "Is there anything weird about the city's interest in Jessam Crossing?"

"Weird how?" Tasha fixes me with a sharp look.

I want to kick myself for blurting out my question. "I just know that sometimes people can get pretty worked up about development projects. And, um, how important it is to do things according to code. Like when my parents redid the basement, they had to get all of these permits but then it turned out that there was no way they could do the stairs to code, because of how the house was built. So they had to do some work that was technically illegal," I blather, knowing I sound like an idiot. "Anyway, it made me wonder about the city, is all, you know. Corruption and all that. Not that Monroe is corrupt but, you know."

Tasha looks intensely at me. Then she drops her head to the side and frowns. "Have you heard something, Polly? About the city and their plans for Jessam Crossing?"

"What? Oh, no, I haven't heard anything. Nothing at all. Why?"

Tasha is still frowning but her eyes have slid over my shoulder. "No reason." She glances at the clock on the wall. "You up for a field trip? I'm in the mood to see Jessam Crossing."

I'm not sure what to say. If I go to Jessam Crossing with Tasha, she might ask me to show her the headstone that had Jessam Crossing on it. The one I made up.

Tasha takes my silence as a yes. "Let's eat first - on me - and then go see our discovery."

"Great," I say weakly. I guess I'll figure it out when we get there.

———

Tasha takes me to lunch at The Price You Pay Diner. Over pancakes, she tells me about her family and growing up in Chicago. She asks me what I'm interested in at school and I tell her about the clubs and sports I used to do before I quit everything this spring, although I don't tell her this last part. We get a few looks from the other customers—all of them white. Maybe they're not looking at us because of our skin but I doubt it. Even with the increased diversity in town, I still get different looks than my white friends. I used to stare right back but today I take Tasha's lead and ignore them. She stops and chats with a few people she knows on our way out the door, though, answering their questions about an upcoming genealogy workshop at the archives.

Then we're off to Jessam Crossing in Tasha's VW Bug. We park in the same turnout where I parked with Billy and then hike to the Crossing. It's hot today, even more humid than yesterday. By the time we clear the ridge my shirt is sticking to my back and I have to pull my hair back into a fluffy ponytail.

I feel a sense of familiarity as I walk into Jessam Crossing with Tasha. For a moment I imagine what it would be like if we were sisters, or even good friends, and we lived in an all-Black town. I'm suddenly surprised that walking into Jessam Crossing feels like walking home, at least for a brief second.

"Where would you build your house if you were building here?" Tasha asks, raising an arm to her forehead to shield her eyes from the sun.

"Um, I guess I'd put it over there near the trees," I say, pointing at a pretty little dip in the flat section of Jessam Crossing.

"Let's check it out," Tasha says, striding through the knee-high grass. "What do you think of it now?" she asks once we're standing in the spot.

I look at the trees arching overhead and the grassy plain stretching before me. "Hey, we can see the river from here," I say, pointing to the glimpse of dark blue shimmering in a gap between the rushes on the opposite site of the plain.

"What do you know about river floods?" Tasha asks.

"Well, there was the big one in 1993 before I was born, then the one a few years ago."

"Uh huh. And what do you know about the lock and dam system?"

"Not much. We took a field trip to one of the locks and dams in second grade, but I don't remember much. Why?"

"This whole area is a floodplain. Before the lock and dam system was built, Monroe flooded much more often than now. Jessam Crossing sits even lower than Monroe, so . . ."

"So it flooded a lot."

"Yes. There's a long tradition of Black people getting the less-than-desirable land."

I turn around, seeing the land with new eyes. "So if you wanted to build anything, you would want to build on the ridge. But they put the cemetery there."

"It's a big ridge, large enough that the city is considering senior housing."

"So the whole town was up there?"

"Possibly. Or some of it might have been down here to start if they hadn't learned much about the flood patterns yet."

"What about farming?" I ask, thinking about my conversation with Billy the night before. I start to flush thinking about Billy and I duck my head, hoping it just looks like the heat is getting to me.

"What about it?" Tasha says with a smile that is meant to encourage me.

"They needed food. So could you farm down here?"

"Probably not. It's practically wetlands," she says, pointing at the spot where the grass transitions to rushes. "You could maybe have gardens but not fields big enough to support a community. But they did have the store, so it stands to reason they had money to buy food."

"So jobs and stuff?"

"Yes. My hunch is that once it turned out that the land couldn't support agriculture, many of them took jobs in Monroe. I think we'll find as we go through the federal censuses that we'll see a lot of people who worked as housecleaners and the like."

"Huh," I say. "So would everyone who lived here be in those censuses?"

"Most likely. Why?"

"No reason," I say, deliberately keeping my eyes from the cemetery. "So what happens next?"

"We keep at it. You finish mapping the cemetery and we'll do some more research. I am going to take the names you find and start exploring property records. I'll keep digging through the archives, too. I'd love to find any kind of documentation that suggests when the town started and when it folded." She turns and looks at me, her smile bright. "Let's wander."

For the next half hour we walk the parcel of land. Tasha points out things I wouldn't have noticed, like how there's no access to the river except through the marshes and how the railroad tracks are on the opposite side of the high-way.

"You could have put tracks through here, even with the marshland," Tasha comments at one point.

"Who wants to live near the tracks, though?"

"Commerce. It was hugely important to be near the tracks once the rail-roads took off in the 1880s. If the tracks went through Jessam Crossing, you'd get economic growth. There are lots of towns that fade once the railroad passes them by. Kind of like small towns today that get bypassed by the highway sys-tem. It's probably why Jessam Crossing faded."

"Yeah?"

"I was looking at some old maps. The railroad tracks make a weird turn a mile out of town. My guess is that the town fathers set up the tracks to bypass the Black colony." She shrugs. "It's hard for a town to thrive if it's been cut off from a major form of income."

"The area's pretty small, though," I say, pointing at the woods encroaching the field. "Would tracks even fit?"

"Monroe looked like this back in the day, too. Woods can be cleared. If the railroad came through here, Jessam Crossing would have had a future."

"Maybe we should go back to the archives and check it out?" My motives aren't pure. I want to get Tasha out of Jessam Crossing before she wants to see the cemetery.

Tasha looks up the hill past my shoulder. I have to stifle an impulse to see if she's staring at the outline of a ghost. "Wait, before we go, can you show me the grave that says Jessam Crossing?"

"I . . . um, I don't remember which one it is and I have to get home because my mom wants me back so maybe next time?"

"Ok," she says. "Maybe next time."

"Yeah, next time," I say, following her to her car on shaking legs and try not to think of what I'll say the next time she asks.

"Sounds good. Let's get back to town."

I'm relieved. Even an afternoon looking at old census records is better than having to lie more to Tasha.

———

Harrison is singing when I approach his grave later that afternoon. I decided to swing past to see him after I left the archives, since I didn't get to talk to him this morning. I settle next to his plot, trying to take shelter in the shadow of the cottonwood tree. It doesn't help much. The wind is like a furnace. I swat away a whirring grasshopper and listen.

I can hear singing, a smooth voice crooning a pretty jazz song about dancing and heaven.

"Harrison?" I call as I approach the tree.

Apollonia Stone, as I live and breathe.

I have a feeling again of a presence. A shadow materializes near me. This time it's easier to see how it takes the shape of a boy. "Ha ha. What were you singing?"

Something that was popular in the Forties.

"Now tell me how you know songs from 1940 if you died in 1924?"

The same way I know James Brown and Nirvana. Kids have been coming out here for years to smoke and drink and have sex. Sometimes they bring music with them. They used to sing but then they'd start bringing radios and whatever else you all have.

"It's weird that you know Nirvana."

Is it? I always thought the name was appealing for a dead guy. I wouldn't mind reaching nirvana.

"So you really don't remember anything concrete about your life?"

No. It's just like I told you. A few glimpses, but that's all.

I rip a strand of grass from the ground, its brittle edges crumbling between my fingertips. "What if I could find out a few things about you?"

I can feel his eyes on me. *What kind of things?*

"Well, like about your family and where you were born. Maybe if you had a job or something. Stuff from census data."

Census data. And you could learn about me.

"We're investigating everybody who's buried in the graveyard, so I'm going to find out things about you anyway. Do you . . . do you want me to tell you what I find?"

How about you see what you can find and then you ask me again.

"Deal," I say, shifting my legs so I'm resting on one hip. I run my hand over the grass, letting the tips prickle my palm. Billy flashes though my mind and for a moment I wonder what it would be like to run my fingers through his thick, silky hair. I sit up and shove the image from my head. This time I can almost see Harrison's expression in his eyes. He's watching me like he knows something.

"I know we've been through this before, but why do you think you're here and not somewhere else?" I ask Harrison. "Every other dead person I've ever heard only repeats their final thoughts. But not you."

Harrison lets out a low whistle and shakes his head. *Isn't that the question. I really don't know.*

"Do you have any kind of unfinished business or anything?"

Probably, but who doesn't?

"I still think it might have something to do with how you died," I say. It hits me that Harrison died when he was seventeen, the same age as me. "People don't tend to die when they're teenagers."

I did. His voice is suddenly tight.

I only know a few kids who died. There was Rory, the first person I ever amplified. And two summers ago Phoebe Harstead's older brother Ryan drowned in the river after a boating accident. It was terrible but unusual. Of course in 1924, there were more chances to die from accidents and diseases.

"What's the last thing you remember?"

You're persistent, aren't you? he mutters.

"You don't have to answer my questions."

I know, but if you go, I'll be lonely again. He makes a sound that reminds me of a throat clearing, like he's decided not to avoid my questions. *In terms of what I remember, you're better off asking about the first thing I remember. After I died.*

"Which was?"

Awareness that my body was in a box.

I stiffen. For a moment I imagine myself stuffed in a box, deep underground, left to suffocate. I draw a few deep breaths and tilt my head back to look at the sky arching overhead.

"That sounds horrible," I finally say.

It was. Then I realized I was aware of the space around the box. I could feel the worms and beetles scurrying through the earth. Then I heard the birds, calling above me. Then the wind rustling in the trees.

"And then?"

Then I fell asleep for a while. When I was aware again, there were some kids smoking underneath the tree and talking about Germany and war. But this time I was able to expand my awareness. I guess that's why I became able to leave the box, as it were, and wander the cemetery a bit. Since then I've been aware off and on, although I still think I go to sleep now and then.

"Huh," I say.

Harrison somehow knows what I'm unable to ask. *Hey, darlin', I'm the lucky one. You said everyone else in this cemetery is dead and gone. I'm dead, but I'm not gone.*

"But you might be here forever," I point out. "Long after everyone else is gone. Climate change could knock us all out, or make the river flood. Or maybe we'd all get destroyed in a nuclear war, but you'd still be here."

Harrison is silent for a moment and when he speaks, his voice is grim. *Well, when you put it like that . . .*

"You'd still stay?" I ask.

Wouldn't you?

It's a question I don't want to answer. No one wants to die, but at least Harrison is still himself. My mind flits to the cemetery in Arizona that I've pictured often but never seen, the voice that echoes there.

"Are you going to go to sleep again soon, do you think?" I ask, changing the subject.

Not when I have a pretty girl like you to talk to. The flirtatious tone is back.

"Ha." The cemetery is blocked from the highway by the bluff and the trees, but I can still hear shades of cars and trucks whooshing past on the other side of the hill.

What?

"There may be others like you, you know," I say. "There's this guy named Alatar—"

Alatar?

"It's not his real name," I say. "But he's a death singer, like me. He says that what's happening with you is rare. And that I should be careful."

Huh. What do you know about this Alatar? Harrison frowns.

"Not much. He said he cofounded the death singers group on Facebook. Do you know what Facebook is?" I ask after a pause.

Not really.

"It's kind of like a place that lots of people can see through their computers—um, through machines that we all have. Or phones, in some cases. Wait, here let me show you."

He lets me stumble through a few more minutes of explanation before we agree that his understanding of the finer points of web design isn't essential.

So this Alatar might know more about others like me. Interesting.

"Yeah," I say.

What?

"He's creeping me out a little bit. I don't like how he found me. But then again, he hasn't written back in a while." This much is true. I've checked my phone multiple times, but nothing from Alatar, not since he called me a liar. Maybe he decided I was lying about the whole thing and I'll never hear from him again.

You tell me if he contacts you. And I'd feel better if you had someone else protecting you.

"Protecting me? I can take care of myself, thank you very much."

Has it changed so much, then? That a young woman can go off by herself without any fear of being attacked?

"No," I say. "It'd be better if men stopped attacking and raping women."

Fair point. What about that man you were with the other day? The one you said wasn't your sweetheart.

"Who, Billy? He's not my boyfriend."

What is he, then?

"He's just this guy I'm helping," I say, wondering how much Harrison can detect from my voice.

Like you're helping me.

"Yeah, I guess."

Does he have your back in case this Alatar shows up?

I am tired of talking about Alatar, so I ask Harrison the other question that has been bugging me. "Do you know anything about the history of Jessam Crossing? Like how it might have been an all-Black colony?" I gaze at where the hill slopes down to the flat area.

Well, Harrison said slowly, *I know that's the name of this place. I've heard a few people mention it from time to time. Hikers who walk through or people visiting their ancestors. But I don't know more than that.*

"Tasha—my boss—said that if this was an all-Black colony, it would be significant. Like historically significant. She found a few items in the archives that provide some hints but nothing more."

Might explain why I'm here. Maybe Jessam Crossing was my home.

"Maybe, although it seems like the Crossing vanished before you were born. At least after you had died."

Oh.

"Did any of the visitors ever say anything more? Or anybody who wants to develop it or anything?"

Not that I can remember. Wait, there were two men once who came out and were talking about the cemetery. Sounded like they wanted to move it.

"Do you remember when this was?"

Wish I knew, but as you know, my concept of time is somewhat . . . unreliable.

"Was one of them named Scott? Or Arnold Weber?"

Not sure I ever heard their names. The shadow shifts a little, as if Harrison is shrugging his shoulders. A chill goes through me. Sometimes I forget I'm talking to a ghost.

"Maybe they talked about covering something up? Or they knew something about the Crossing but wanted to keep it quiet?"

I only remember two voices talking about how the cemetery would have to be moved. Can't say I'm in favor of moving the cemetery, by the way.

"Why do you think you're buried here? There aren't any other Cards nearby."

No? Hm.

"There might have been a church," I continue. "Ebenezer Baptist. That sound familiar?"

There's a pause and then Harrison coughs. *Sorry, doll. Why is it so important to find out about Jessam Crossing?*

"It's a mystery, Harrison. And maybe it was your home. Don't you want to find out more?" I am painfully aware that I am echoing Tasha's enthusiasm. But why do I get the feeling Harrison is hiding something from me?

Maybe the past should be the past. Focus on the future instead. The past is done and gone.

He has a point. After all, isn't that what I wanted to do when I burned my adoption papers? Forget about the past?

"You're no help," I grumble. I get to my feet and pull out my graph paper.

For the next hour, I chart the cemetery and chat with Harrison. We talk about music and some of the news he's missed from the past few decades. Sometimes he lapses into song. By the time I've finished for the day, I've marked the perimeter of the cemetery on the grid and mapped every stone. I've also transcribed any visible inscription on a separate sheet of paper. There are over two dozen marked graves. From the whispers I hear beneath my feet, I know there are at least a few more. I can make out only a few words from these graves. It's mostly sighs and murmurs that might be the wind through the leaves. They're fading and I'm the only one who can note that they were ever here.

I wonder if Harrison will fade away. The thought makes me sad.

"Bye, Harrison," I call.

See you later, gorgeous, he says, and the sound of him singing follows me down the hill.

CHAPTER
TEN

When I wake up, I can't get out of bed. It's not like I'm sick or anything. My legs just don't want to move. Neither do my arms or the rest of my body. The river cracks on my ceiling haven't moved at all, but there's something flashing on them. I'm confused until I realize it's my phone. My Facebook app is lighting up like it's the Fourth of July. In the instant before I check my notifications I remember it is Thursday and the day of Darcy's houseboat party.

Not that it matters. I'm not going.

I'm about to turn the phone off, but there's a text from Darcy: *Sorry about Monday. The boat leaves at 10. Maybe see you?*

I picture strolling onto the dock a few hours from now. The looks I'd get from my classmates. The falsely cheerful greeting from Darcy. I remember how she looked at me at the pool, when she thought I was crazy. Has she told anyone else?

"Thanks but no thanks," I say to the phone.

I roll onto my back and look at the ceiling, the view that I've had ever since I was a child. The feeling I've identified as homesickness fills me and I indulge it by letting my mind latch onto the childhood I might have had if I'd stayed with Althea.

I try not to think about Alternate Polly very often. She looks like me but she's shorter, for some reason. She lives in a trailer in Tucson, or a cramped apartment in Phoenix. She lies on a mattress, poring over outdated textbooks while people who look like her make dinner from cans and leave for their second jobs. Sometimes a dark hand lands on her hair, a gesture accompanied by a tired smile.

Other times Alternate Polly is the one standing over the stove, making rice and beans as bunches of cousins dance through the kitchen. The house is small but cozy. The sisters have jobs and Alternate Polly is heading to college in the fall. Alternate Polly's mom sits on the sofa, her feet up, watching the news. She smiles when Polly brings her a bowl of stew.

I wasn't supposed to be Apollonia Madison Stone. If my birthmom had chosen to parent me, I might have been one of these Alternate Pollys. Or maybe another one entirely. What's really weird is that I wasn't supposed to be adopted by my parents. My birthmom had selected a different family, who were ready to raise me. They had to pull out of the adoption weeks before I was born. Some kind of medical emergency, my mom said, although she didn't know more details. My parents were next on the list and so I came to Minnesota. When I was young I pretended that the failed family lived in Paris or Madagascar or Australia, and I would have had a glamorous, extraordinary life with them, free of pain and sadness.

I have always been a shooting star, a moon without a planet. The moment my birthmom signed the adoption paperwork I was both a particle and a wave. I went home with the Stones, but in some ways, I could have gone home with anyone. I could be anywhere right now.

But now here I am, lying in my bed, wondering how I can help a dead guy and about to fail high school. Life is strange.

My phone buzzes. I feel a wave of excitement as I see the number flash across the screen.

"Hello?" I say, hearing the surprise in my voice.

"You free today?" Billy asks, his voice gravelly, as if he has a cold.

"Um, yeah. I'm not up to another cemetery visit, though."

"Not that."

"What were you thinking, then?"

"A surprise."

"What kind of surprise?"

"Nothing bad. Do you trust me or what?"

"No," I say, but there's a trace of humor in my voice. "I'm at home right now."

"Pick you up by the cottonwood tree in fifteen?"

"Sure."

"Good deal. Oh, and bring your swimsuit."

The line goes dead. Bring my swimsuit? I swing out of bed and start rummaging through my drawers I contemplate my fire-engine red bikini for a moment, then set it aside in favor of a modest two-piece. I shove a few towels and a swim cap into a bag and sprint down the stairs.

"I'm off to the archives, Mom!" I yell.

"Okay, honey," she says from her studio. She pokes her head out the door. "When will you be home?"

"Um, four?"

She gives me a quick hug, which I return. "Have a good day."

"You too, Mom."

I grab a granola bar and an orange from the kitchen and in a few minutes I'm down at the cottonwood tree. I only feel a tiny bit bad for lying to my mom. Anyway, if there's time, I'll go to the archives for a few hours this afternoon. Billy's truck rumbles up to me. "Where're we going?" I ask as I clamber into the front seat.

"You'll see," he says, swinging the truck back down the bluff. "You got your suit?"

"Yeah."

We don't say much as we wind down the bluff. It's a gorgeous day, despite the heat, the kind of day I know I should savor to remember during those long, awful days of winter. I am always cold except on days like today. My parents say it's because I was born in the desert. Anytime the temp drops below sixty-five degrees, I want to put on a jacket.

Billy drives to the traffic light on Margaret Taylor Street and turns right onto 61.

"So we're not going to the community pool," I comment. Nor are we going to the launch for Darcy's party, I realize with relief.

"I thought you were banned from the pool."

"Well, yeah. Banned from working there, at least. We never got to the details of whether or not I could still use it."

"What did happen?" Billy asks, turning on the radio. Blake Shelton singing about honeysuckle and bees. I settle back against the seat and watch the river valley unfold.

"I got mad at one of the swimmers. Yelled at him."

"What'd he do?"

"He, um, interrupted a conversation between me and Darcy and Chase."

"Chase? You still hanging out with that asshole?"

"You don't like Chase?" I ask. I think Chase is an asshole too, and I feel relief that since I'm no longer his girlfriend, I don't have to defend him.

"He never passed," Billy says, leaning back against the seat as if this explains everything.

"He never passed? What does that mean?"

"When we played basketball in gym class. Chase would never pass."

"That's why you don't like him?" I ask, amused.

Billy shoots a hard look at me. "It means he's selfish and self-centered."

"Oh," I say. "Well, that's true."

"So what did he do at the pool?" Billy asks.

Telling Billy is easier than I thought. "He and Darcy were in the woods that night."

"Really?"

"Apparently they were in the clearing, too. Turns out they also overheard my ramblings about hearing the dead."

"Do they believe you?"

"They think I'm nuts."

"Huh," he says. Then, "You're better off without them."

I don't say anything, even though I know he's right.

"They gonna tell anyone about what you can do?" he asks.

"I don't know. I'm just hoping they don't blackmail me." I say it lightly, but my words send a look of frustration over Billy's face.

"Polly, look—" he starts, but I interrupt him.

"It's okay," I say. "Let's not talk about it today."

"I want to explain—" he tries again, but I shake my head and lay my hand on his thigh.

"Really, let's not worry about it today."

Billy relaxes under my touch and nods reluctantly. I remove my hand and roll the window down, letting the wind tangle my hair, even though I'll pay for it later. Billy grunts and turns down the air conditioning, not that the air conditioning really works anyway.

"You're getting dust all over the truck."

I raise an eyebrow and run my finger over the torn upholstery. "How would you even tell?"

"You're not making fun of my truck now, are you?" he asks. A slow smile spreads across his face. My stomach does a slow flip.

"I'd never make fun of a man and his truck," I say.

"You and Chase went out together for a while," Billy says.

"Almost two years."

"Why'd you break up?"

"Turns out we didn't have much in common."

"Why were you going out in the first place?"

"Usual reasons," I shrug, which makes Billy laugh and me blush. "I didn't mean sex. Well, not right away at least."

This makes Billy laugh harder and soon I'm joining him.

"We were both the brown kids. I think that's what brought us together," I explain. "Wasn't enough to keep us together."

Billy glances over at me, a bemused expression on his face. "That's funny. I don't think of you—"

"As Black," I interrupt, folding my hands on my lap.

"As shallow," he finishes.

"Oh," I say, surprised.

"You're not the kind of person who would be in a relationship with someone because of looks."

"It was more than just looks," I explain. "There weren't many Black people in Monroe when we were kids. Still aren't a ton, although it's getting better. It was nice to be with someone who had the same color skin, who understood some of the subtle racism we got. And none of the white boys asked me out."

"Then they were idiots," Billy mumbles under his breath, so quickly that I think I misheard him. "I get that being biracial brought you together," he continues. "Didn't keep you together, though."

"Nope. Chase never really wanted to talk about racism."

"You did?"

"I was looking for someone who understood."

We drive in silence for a few more minutes, past Ash Lawn Park where hordes of kids are running relay races. I think about what I just said to Billy. I did have people who understood when I was growing up, but only a few.

Henrietta and I talked about our experiences, one of her uncles giving us a reading list about systemic racism and white privilege one summer when he was visiting from college. My parents read a lot of Black writers, making sure we talked about race and racism on a regular basis. But then Henrietta and I fell apart and my parents didn't fully understand what was like to walk around in my skin. And Chase probably understood but never wanted to discuss it.

"It was fun to be with someone cool," I add as we start heading south on 61.

"You like the basketball players, huh?"

"There was only one basketball player," I say with a grin.

We pass the McDonald's. Jessam Crossing is on our right, but I can't see it behind the hills.

"There a lot of racism in Monroe?"

"There's racism everywhere. They're not burning crosses on my lawn or anything, at least not yet. But some people will always think I am less than because of the color of my skin." I toy with the upholstery. "Chase got stopped by the cops three times last year. Once he was going seven miles over the limit. He said his dad has told him for years about how to deal with the cops. Be super polite and not make any sudden moves and make sure they see your hands are empty. Otherwise you might get shot."

"Yeah," Billy comments, slowing to turn the truck down an unmarked gravel road a few miles south of the Jessam Crossing turnoff. The road starts climbing back into the hills. "All the Black Lives Matter stuff."

"Don't tell me you're one of those 'all lives matter' people?" I ask, feeling my anger rise.

Billy must sense my mood. "Calm down. I'm not."

"Good," I say. I can't let it drop, though. "Of course everyone's lives are important. But it erases the fact that Black lives have mattered far less to American society for almost four hundred years."

Billy glances over at me, his eyes honest and open. "Polly, I'm agreeing with you."

"Oh, okay."

We drive the rest of the way in comfortable silence. I'm so used to having to explain to Darcy why saying "all lives matter" is racist that it's a strange—but welcome—feeling not to have to do so now. I relax against the seat of the truck. The road is worn and we bounce over the washboard surface. I can feel the vibrations in my thighs.

"We going to the reservoir?" I call over the rattle of the truck. There's a humming noise coming from the engine as Billy accelerates over the gravel. The back of the truck fishtails slightly and Billy corrects the movement by taking his foot off the gas and turning the steering wheel into the slide.

"It's like driving on ice," I say. I have to repeat myself over the noise of the road but Billy nods.

"Yeah. You been here before?" he asks, the truck coming to a standstill on a bare patch of ground that serves as a parking lot.

"Never." I open the door and slide to the ground. The reservoir is huge, cradled between two hills. The water is blue and coruscates under a slight breeze. A heron stands in the reeds to the left. I can see across to the other side but the lake is irregular and I'm not sure what's around the bend to my right.

"Your parents never took you out here? I thought you had the perfect childhood. Minus all the racism crap."

"It was hardly perfect," I say over my shoulder.

"What, you only got thirty-four presents every Christmas?" His voice is teasing.

"And only thirty for my birthdays."

"Why didn't you ever come out here? I thought most kids did."

"We have a swimming pool."

"Figures."

"What's that supposed to mean?" I don't know him well enough to know if he's teasing or resentful.

"It means it figures that you'd have a swimming pool and a renovated house and a horse."

I start to get angry. "You through insulting me? Or maybe you should take me home."

Billy sighs and pushes his hand through his hair. Locks of thick dark hair fall back into his face.

"I didn't have a pool or a horse or a big house growing up. But I did have the reservoir. That's why I brought you out here. I wanted you to see it."

"Okay," I say, choosing my words carefully. "Wait. Are we on a date?"

"Yeah, maybe. I don't know. I just thought you could use a break. I've always liked coming out here and so I thought, what the hell, let's see if Apollonia wants to go, too."

"Thanks," I say. I sit on a rock, the sunbaked surface warming my butt. "It's beautiful out here." The reservoir is secluded and I can't see any power lines. If I keep my back to the cell tower high above our heads on one of the hills, I can pretend that we're living in the past.

I find myself wanting to share something special with Billy in return. "You know that cemetery at Jessam Crossing?"

"Sure," Billy says. He's standing at the edge of the water.

"My boss thinks it might have been a Black settlement after the Civil War," I blurt.

"Really?" Billy says. He bends and unlaces his boots. His tan line ends at his ankle. His feet are long and white and look like fish that have gone belly-up in a lake.

"Yeah." I find myself telling him everything Tasha and I have discovered so far, minus the scraps I heard at Arnold Weber's grave. Billy lets his boots drop to the sand and by the end of my story, he's watching me with a serene expression.

"What?" I say at the end.

"You light up when you're excited about something. It's nice."

I cross my legs self-consciously. "Thanks," I say.

Billy watches me for moment. Then he reaches for the hem of his t-shirt and pulls it over his head. Anything else I might have said flies out of my head as I take a quick survey of his chest and back, which are lightly muscled and tan like the rest of him.

"You going in?"

"Yeah. Let me go change," I say, my throat dry.

I walk along the lakeshore until it disappears beyond the bend. There's a copse of trees on the shore and I quickly pull off my clothes and slide into my suit. The fresh air on my skin is arousing and I give myself a stern lecture about not falling for the guy who is using me—and violating the newly dead—for his own gain, no matter how nice he's been lately. My mind replies with an image of Billy holding me in St. Nicholas cemetery and I'm torn between grinning and scowling when I return to the shore.

I wade into the water. The sand is soft and squishes between my toes. I can't remember the last time I swam in a place that wasn't heavily chlorinated. I shove my hair underneath the swim cap and propel myself into the water. I've missed swimming. I love the feeling of power and freedom that comes with sliding through the water. My heart lurches. I won't be able to be on the swim team next year if I don't get my work done.

I push the thought away and keep swimming.

I've done two laps across the narrowest channel when I realize Billy is keeping pace beside me. He's changed into green swim trunks. He's elegant in the water, his strokes smooth and efficient. I remember seeing him play baseball once, before he dropped out of school. Henrietta was a huge sports nut so she must have dragged me to the game. I was bored but I do remember marveling over Billy's movements. He was strong, of course, with his broad shoulders and muscled calves, but he was also graceful, moving through the air like a dancer. I laugh at this image, of what Billy would say if I told him, and I take a mouthful of water.

"You okay?" Billy asks, treading water beside me.

"Got distracted," I say after I can talk again.

We swim for another half hour, not talking, just doing laps. At some point Billy heads out toward the middle of the lake. Eventually I'm tired and I flip onto my back. I float for a little bit and then let the waves carry me to shore. I stretch out my towel and lie down on it. I lie in the sun, my muscles warm and relaxed from the swim.

Then, as if I don't have a care in the world, I fall asleep.

When I open my eyes Billy is sitting next to me, looking over the lake.

"What were you burning that night at the high school?" he asks without preamble.

I arch my neck, gazing at the sky. There are puffs of wispy clouds dotting the blue dome. "What makes you think I wasn't just trying to burn down the school?"

"I saw you drag the wood away from the shed. You didn't go far enough."

"No shit."

He has a stick in his hand and he traces patterns in the sand. "What were you burning?"

I sigh and stretch my arms overhead. "My adoption papers."

A whippoorwill calls from the marshes and the waves lap the shore.

"Why?" Billy finally asks.

"I was mad. Adoption does that to people sometimes."

"What happened to your real mom?"

"My mom is my real mom," I say, almost by rote. I prop myself up on my elbows. "You mean my birthmom."

"Your birthmom, then."

"She died."

The words hang in the air between us. I lie back down on my towel.

"When?"

"March."

"So that's what happened."

"Huh?"

"I figured something must have happened. Girls like you don't set fire to school property and run halfway to Arizona for no reason."

"How did you know about Arizona?" I ask, my forehead wrinkling as I look up at him and the sun hits my eyes.

"I, uh, got picked up last spring. Had too much to drink and got behind the wheel. It was stupid. First and last time," Billy says, glancing at me. "I could hear the police scanner from my cell."

"You knew I drove to Arizona?" I ask, sitting up.

"I didn't know why. And you didn't get all the way there, did you?"

"No."

"You want to go now?" Billy asks, gesturing at the truck parked behind us. He looks at me expectantly and I get the sense that if I said yes, we'd be heading west in minutes.

"You're serious, aren't you?"

"As serious as I ever am," he says. "You want to go?"

"Not today," I say with a grin. "But thanks."

"Suit yourself." I feel his shoulders shrug next to me. Our arms are almost but not quite touching. His next question pushes that awareness from my mind. "How did she die?"

"Cancer."

"Huh," Billy says.

"Like your mom," I add, although he was probably already thinking it. "They weren't even supposed to tell me that much."

"They?"

"The adoption agency. I have sisters, too. Half sisters in Arizona. They didn't want to see me."

"Why were you going to Arizona, then?" Billy starts asking. "Oh," he says. "You were going to her grave. To hear what she had to say."

"Yep."

"Why'd she give you up?"

I half-laugh as I roll my head. "Aren't you full of inappropriate questions?"

"Was it inappropriate? I was just wondering."

"I don't know much. The papers say she knew she couldn't support another kid. And we don't use the phrase 'give up.' She made an adoption plan for me. Look, can we talk about something else?"

"Sure." He lies on his back, cradling his head in his hands. His elbow brushes my hair and he leaves it there. "Could be worse, I suppose," he says at last. "We could have been pioneers."

"What?"

"At the last cemetery we were at. The one with Weber. I saw one grave where the mom was eighteen. She and the baby died the same day. Back in 1884, I think."

"Yeah, that happens."

"There was another one where the parents had ten kids and eight of them died before they were teenagers. There was a boy who died in August and a girl who died in October."

I'm surprised he noticed. "There's a section in God's Acre where the parents lost four kids in one week. I asked Tasha about it. She said it was probably an epidemic that swept through town. Diphtheria or something."

"You hear anything at those graves?"

I wait a moment and then decide to tell him. "The babies were calling for their mother."

The words hover between us in the bright air.

"That's too bad," Billy says at last.

"Yeah, it is," I agree. At the shoreline, a small turtle lopes into the tall grasses. A fish jumps midway across the lake and a heron takes flight. "Well, this is an uplifting conversation," I joke at last. My right leg is close enough to Billy's left leg that I can feel the heat radiating off his skin. We are a breath away from touching there, too, but I can't quite bridge the gap.

"Polly," he starts.

"This is nice," I say. "Thanks for bringing me out here."

"Do you think what I'm doing is wrong?"

"Stealing from the dead? Yes."

"It's illegal, sure, but is it morally wrong?"

I roll onto my stomach and let the sun warm my shoulders. "I don't see how you can talk yourself out of this one, Billy."

"The way I see it, once you're dead, you're gone. Even though you can obviously hear something, you're not hearing the actual person, right? It's not like you're talking to a ghost."

"I guess," I say.

"So if you can't take the money with you, why shouldn't some of it go to me?"

"Funerals cost money. Settling estates takes time. Plus, some people are probably counting on that money," I say, rolling back over and propping myself up on my elbows.

"For what? Adding a sun porch to the house? Taking that extra vacation to Cabo?"

"Paying off debts, putting kids through college," I counter. "Now the money's gone."

"I don't take all of it," Billy says. "I haven't cleaned out anyone's bank account. Just a few thousand here or there."

"It's still going to get tracked," I say. "Even if you don't clear it out entirely, someone's eventually going to notice that Ida Mae made a withdrawal from her checking account four days after she died."

"It's less obvious than taking all of it," Billy says. "And I covered my tracks as best I could. But I'm not entirely heartless. I'm just taking what I need."

"Aren't you the gentleman?" I say, taunting him softly. His eyes snap to mine and I see something purposeful in them.

"You're a part of this, too," he reminds me. "You can hardly go taking the high road."

Suddenly the mood is broken. I sit up, brushing sand from my legs.

"We're not going to settle this today. Can you just take me home?" I say.

Billy gets to his feet and holds out his hand to me. "For what it's worth, Polly, the blackmail . . . it's not personal."

I get to my feet unaided and walk to the truck. As he drives me home, we don't say a word.

There are two suitcases in the entryway when I walk into the house. Both are falling apart at the seams, held together by colorful straps and duct tape. They are made of smooth leather and one has a wobbly handle.

"Dad?" I ask, wandering through the living room.

Both of my parents emerge from the kitchen. "Polly!" my dad says, wrapping me in a hug. His plaid shirt smells like peppermint.

"I thought you weren't coming home until next week," I say.

Mom and Dad exchange the briefest of looks. "I wanted to surprise you," Dad says.

I glance between them, my happiness evaporating. "You came home because you're worried I'm losing it."

Dad sighs and runs his hand through his thinning hair. "We're worried about your wellbeing," he says.

"We thought it might be better if we were all together for a while," Mom says, laying her hand on my arm. I shake it off.

"You don't trust me," I say.

"That's not true," Mom protests. "But we are worried you're not getting your schoolwork done."

I drop onto the couch. "I told you I'd show you a rough draft of my essay by the end of the week."

"And how's that going?" Mom asks.

I toe the oriental rug. Everything is falling apart around me, but I remember the relief I felt telling Billy the truth about what happened at the pool. "Not great," I admit. The pressure in my chest eases slightly.

"That's what we thought," Mom says, not unkindly. She sits next to me on the sofa.

"Your mother and I believe in protecting your privacy," Dad says. "And we want you to succeed. But half the summer is already gone. We're worried you're not going to finish before senior year."

"Mr. Belkin called us today," Mom says. "He said your teachers report you haven't turned anything in."

"Oh," I say. Mom is nice enough not to point out that I'd told her a few days ago that I'd finished a bunch of things.

"We think you might need some help," Dad says.

It's silent in the living room except for the ticking of the grandfather clock in the corner.

"I do, too," I finally say. "I think I need to take the next year off and not finish high school right away."

I didn't even know I had that thought until I said it. But the more I think about it, the more I know it's the right thing for me. I can't imagine going back to school and pretending everything is fine and I'm normal.

My parents don't feel the same way. Mom's eyes grow wide and Dad keeps opening and closing his mouth, but no words come out.

"Not finish high school right away? I know you didn't just say that to a professor, Polly," he finally says. He is half joking but there is a warning in his voice.

My mind flits to Billy and I push his face out of my thoughts.

"I'm not saying I'd never go back. But even if I didn't, it's not the worst fate, is it? Maybe I just need to live a bit?"

"You can live a bit, just not without a high school diploma," Dad says, glancing at Mom, who nods. "Your mom and I don't like putting our foot down but we will insist that you finish high school. We're not letting you waste an entire year of your life."

"So mourning my birthmom is a waste?" The words slip out and my parents freeze for a moment.

"Oh, sweetheart," Mom says then, putting her arm around me. "Your dad wasn't saying that."

My dad sits on the other side of me and puts his arm around both of us. "You must miss her. What she was to you. What she would have been. It makes sense that your birthmom dies and you get upset."

Upset is the understatement of the year.

"When you came home, your dad and I promised to give you the life that your birthmom wanted for you," Mom says. "We could give you opportunities and chances that you would never have had in Arizona." She cups my face. "And it breaks my heart when I see you squander those opportunities. And I think it would break Althea's heart, too."

"You're pulling birthmother guilt on me?" I say, but with no emotion behind it.

Mom sighs. "I'm not trying to pull anything on you. We only had a few minutes with your birthmom in the hospital. We already knew she wanted a closed adoption but the social worker explained that she thought she might want to meet you when you were grown. I remember being happy about that. You'd be able to meet her someday and maybe talk to her about everything. I was glad you'd have that chance."

"Then she died."

I can hear my dad sniffling. He awkwardly pulls a Kleenex from his pocket with one hand and swipes his eyes.

"And then she died," Mom says. "And it took away a lot of possibilities. Oh, I'm not saying this right. I'm not trying to guilt you or make it seem like you should be grateful your dad and I can give you opportunities that your birthmom couldn't. But there's loss the other way, too, my love. You lost a life with your biological family. And I will always be sad about that."

My parents have always talked about adoption with me, especially when I was younger. They'd answer my questions about how we became a family and why I looked different than them. But lately we haven't talked about it much, even with Althea's death. I've never heard my mom talk like this before.

I'm starting to feel suffocated. "I'm fine," I say, breaking free of their embrace. I stand up and walk across the room to the bookshelves. I trail my finger along the beat-up spines of spy novels. "Really, I am. But I just can't picture myself sitting in a classroom next year."

"Maybe we can talk about options with Mr. Milford," Mom says, glancing at Dad.

"Who's Mr. Milford?" I ask.

"He's a tutor at Abeline Academy over in Long Branch. Runs a summer tutoring program. Mr. Belkin gave us the contact info and suggested we sign you up." Dad takes a breath. "So we did."

I gape at them. "You signed me up for a tutoring session without asking me?"

"Mr. Belkin made it clear that if you don't finish your work, you'll have to repeat junior year," Dad says.

"That means two more years at high school instead of just one," Mom says.

"I can still fucking count, Mom."

"Language, Polly," Mom warns.

I roll my eyes.

Dad rises to his feet. "We just want you to go over tomorrow to see what it's like. If you hate it, you don't have to stay. But if you don't do the session at Abeline, you'll have to answer to Mom and me every day." He's trying to make a joke, but it comes out stilted and I realize how serious my parents are.

"Can't we at least talk about other options?" I ask. But I've made a tactical mistake.

"We'll talk about it if you promise to go to Abeline for one day," Mom says.

I'm defeated. "Okay. I'll go for one day."

All of the tension eases from the room. There's a flurry of hugs and smiles from my parents before they retreat to the kitchen. I'm left staring at the empty fireplace, wondering what I'm in for.

Mom drives me to Long Branch in her gray Mercedes the next morning. We don't talk much on the drive but it's a comfortable silence. It's not until we pull into the outskirts of Long Branch that I ask the question that's been pressing against my brain for what seems like years.

"Why is this so important to you?"

"Why is what so important to me?"

"Me finishing school."

Mom sighs. The car slows as she pulls through double iron gates. "I'm not having this conversation with you right here, Polly. There's not much security in life without an education."

"You're only saying that because you and dad both have degrees."

Her nostrils flare as she looks at me. "I'm saying that because it's true. Try getting a job without a high school diploma, let alone a college degree. I love you, Polly, and I would do anything for you. But if you fuck this up, I will not let you live in your bedroom for the rest of your life."

It's the swearing that gets me out of the car.

"I'll pick you up before lunch. We'll talk about this later," she says, leaning over her seat to talk to me through the window.

I shoulder my backpack and walk up the steps of Abeline Academy. Abeline is a private school and a hockey powerhouse. It's only twenty minutes from Monroe but I don't know anyone who goes here. It's mainly rich white kids from the southern Twin Cities suburbs.

I pass through several archways and a courtyard before I reach solid oak doors. The school must sink more of its money into the exterior, because the inside is less impressive, with scuffed wooden floors and squeaky doors. I check the sheet the school emailed Mom and find the room number. I shuffle down the hallway past whitewashed walls and glass display cases to the only door that's standing ajar. The whole place smells like wood cleaner.

"Miss Stone, nice of you to join us," a man I assume is Mr. Milford says, turning from the blackboard as I walk into the room. There's no air conditioning and the room is stuffy, but he's wearing a blazer. His dark hair is slicked back from his face. When I read his name in the email, I pictured a reedy old man with tweed blazers and argyle socks. Except for the blazer, Mr. Milford looks like he could be an accountant or software engineer. I wonder if he's even forty. With his dark eyes and olive complexion, he looks a little like Billy.

"Take a seat."

There are a dozen or so other kids in the class. No one pays me much attention as I walk in. Most of them are unpacking messenger bags and laptops.

I drop my bag at a desk near the window. The boy next to me, a white kid with a farmer's tan, is asleep with his head down on his biology textbook.

"I will be checking in with each of you today to revisit your goals and progress," Mr. Milford tells the class. "In the meantime, keep working on your to do lists."

I glance around the room. The other kids are opening books and flipping open laptops. I wasn't sure what to bring, so I have most of my books crammed into my backpack. I dig around in my bag and pull out my calculus book. Mr. Milford is grinning and giving a white kid across the way a high five. The boy next to me snores. He's still snoring fifteen minutes later when Mr. Milford slides into the desk in front of me.

"Now, Miss Stone. Apollonia, is it?"

"Yeah."

"Have you ever done tutoring before?"

"I've usually been the tutor," I say.

Mr. Milford's smile is kind and a little amused. "Well, maybe you'll find this experience useful for when you next tutor a student. So let me run through a few things. You're behind in your work. It's my job to facilitate you completing that work. It is not my job to make you do that work or to stand over you until you finish it. That's up to you. I provide the space, the time, and hopefully, some clarification."

"What kind of clarification?" I ask. This is starting to sound squishy.

"Why are you doing this?"

The boy next to me gives a bigger snort and I jump. Mr. Milford grins.

"Tomorrow you might want to sit on the other side of the room."

"It's okay that he's just sleeping like that?"

"Kevin's holding down two jobs and helping his dad with the farm. He wants to be pre-med so he's prepping for AP Biology. If he needs to sleep in order to accomplish those goals, who am I to stop him?"

"So it's okay if I sleep in class?"

"Okay is up to you. If you decide that you're here to sleep, I'm not going to get in your way."

"Did my mom talk to you? Because I'm sure she would not be okay with me doing that."

He laughs, revealing perfectly white teeth that overlap a little on the bottom. "I don't handle the registration. The office does that. I'm sure they told your mom what they tell all the parents. Your child will get the attention she or he needs to complete their work." He clears his throat. "So let me ask you again, Apollonia. Why are you here?"

Answers crowd my brain but I can't say any of them to Mr. Milford: "I'm here because I went off the deep end after my birthmom died, almost burned down the school, and am being blackmailed by a guy I'm into to steal secrets from dead people who oh, by the way, I can talk to."

Instead I tell him that I'm behind in my work and I'm supposed to finish it so I don't have to repeat junior year.

"Is that really why you're here?"

"Um, yeah?" I suspect he's playing some kind of game but I don't understand the rules.

"Really? Deep down?"

I shrug and he lets me off the hook. "I'm a big believer in individual motivation. I can't tell you to finish your work. I could, but it wouldn't do much. You'd resent me, you'd resent the work even more than you probably already do, and it's unlikely you'd finish. Even if you did, you wouldn't learn anything except more resentment. I need you to figure out why you want to finish your work and then use that motivation to do it."

"What if I don't want to finish my work?"

"Then you won't finish it," he says. "You'll deal with the consequences of that decision and life will go on. It's up to you."

I poke the edge of my math book. "I don't like calculus."

"Then start with something else. Maybe a list of why you are here."

He taps the desk and strides to a boy sitting a few rows behind me. Soon they're murmuring something about the Harlem Renaissance and Langston Hughes.

I take out a notebook and flip to a clean page. I write "Why I'm Here" on the top and underline it. To my surprise, bullet points start spilling onto the page:

- Mom and Dad are making me
- I got suspended from my job at the pool
- Tasha would want me to do this
- Henrietta isn't my friend anymore
- Darcy never really was my friend
- I wasn't in love with Chase but I just pretended to be in love with him because everyone expected it, including Chase
- My dad is gone all the time at his lab
- Harrison would be mad at me if I didn't finish high school
- Billy
- Althea

I don't write anything else next to those last two names. I'm still staring at the page when Mr. Milford circles back fifteen minutes later.

"How's the list?"

"Okay," I say, draping my arm over it. He grins.

"I don't need to see it. In fact, it's better if you don't show me or anyone, not unless you want to. Did you find some good reasons?"

"I found some reasons. Not sure if they're good or not."

"That's fine, too. Do they make you want to do some work, though?"

I shrug. "I guess. I'm here for the rest of the morning, anyway."

"That's true. So what do you want to work on? Not calculus."

"I have to read *Middlemarch*."

"Do you want to do that now?"

"I mean, yeah," I say, but an idea occurs to me. "But if I work on my timeline for world history, I'd be done with that class." For the first time, the idea of finishing a class sounds almost appealing.

"You could do either one. Which one sounds more exciting?"

"Neither."

"Which one sounds more interesting to you right now."

"Um, we can use our laptops?"

"Yes. Abeline has wifi."

"Timeline, I guess."

"Good. Start working on that and I'll be back to check on you."

The rest of morning goes quickly. Kevin, the guy next to me, wakes up after forty-five minutes. He gives me a polite nod and starts quizzing himself with biology flashcards. I return the nod and jot down a few more significant dates from the Ottoman Empire. By lunchtime I have the entire timeline sketched out.

Mr. Milford stops me as I'm leaving at noon.

"How was your first day, Apollonia?"

"Good. I finished a rough draft of the timeline."

"Good for you. Tonight I want you to read the list of reasons again. If it inspires you, I want you to do one more hour of work, but no more than one hour. And if it doesn't inspire you, don't do anything. I'll see you Monday."

"Thanks," I say.

Mom's waiting for me in the parking lot. "How was it?"

"Okay, I guess. I worked on my timeline."

"That's excellent! Have you made a decision about next week?"

"Um, I guess I can go back once more, at least." I say this in part to make Mom happy and in part because I don't feel like a fight. I'm surprised to realize that I don't fully mind the idea of going back, either. It was nice to get some work done.

She kisses my cheek. "Glad to hear it. Now let's get some lunch."

CHAPTER

TWELVE

When I get home I text Tasha to see if I can stop by the archives to do some work, but she writes back almost immediately and says she's up at the Minnesota History Center doing some research and that the archives are closed. I think about going to Jessam Crossing and seeing Harrison, but then I remember that I wanted to add something to my timeline. I take my computer to the screen porch and soon the afternoon is gone. I revise the timeline and then read three chapters of *Middlemarch*. I'm so engrossed that I'm completely discombobulated when Mom calls me for dinner.

"You having a good day, honey?" Mom asks as we sit down to grilled veggie pasta.

"Yeah," I say, diving into the food. I'm dimly aware of my parents talking about the latest city council meeting and plans for the summer but mainly I'm thinking about how normal this is, us having family dinner, me doing homework, my parents talking about life. It makes me sad for some reason.

For dessert there's blueberry cobbler and then I head to my room. "I want to get some more things done," I tell my parents, hugging each of them before heading upstairs. I pretend not to notice their huge smiles of relief.

But my room is warm and I find I can't face the pile of homework that

143

still waits for me. Sure, I got some work done today, but I still have so much to do. I flop onto my bed and stare at the ceiling. After a while it's too dark to see the fairy map and I light the candle next to my bed, bumping Henrietta's elephant. The air conditioning never works quite right, so I get up to open the window.

That's when I find the note shoved beneath the screen, like it was placed there by someone who climbed the side of the house to reach me. I try to remember the last time I opened this window. Yesterday, I think, or maybe the day before. I grasp the note with trembling fingers.

It's written on yellow legal paper, the words scrawled in black ink:

"I must talk to you. A."

It's dated with today's date. The note flutters to the floor and I'm reaching for my phone before I can even think through a clear plan.

Something's wrong. Help.

The response comes a minute later. I send instructions and then spend the next fifteen huddling on my bed with the curtains drawn. I jump when the knock comes at the window.

"What happened?" Billy asks as he clambers through the window into my room. He maneuvers himself quietly to the floor.

I hold out the note with shaking fingers.

"Who's A.?"

"His name is Alatar. He's a death singer. I think he followed me here."

"What do you mean?"

"I posted a question on the death singers page and Alatar texted me with a response. Except he never really answered my question. And then I found the note. I think he's here." My voice shakes.

"What the fuck," Billy swears, loudly enough that I shush him, even as I'm pleased by his reaction.

"My parents can't know you're here."

"You didn't tell them about this?"

"They'd freak."

"Like you're freaking?" he says with a small grin. His expression calms me.

"The guy stuck this in my window," I counter.

"That was an asshole thing to do," Billy says, going to the window. "Means he had to have climbed up like I did."

"He would have seen into my room," I say, clasping my elbows and sinking onto my bed.

"I didn't see anyone outside."

"Where'd you park?"

"I pulled the truck off the road about a quarter mile down the road. That little clearing near the old farm site. I didn't see anybody. When do you think he left it?"

"I was gone most of the morning and I worked on the porch this afternoon, but I was here until about an hour ago. He might have left it when I was out. Or maybe when I was at dinner." I shiver. Billy sits on the bed but he's too far away to touch me, even if he wanted to.

"Why is Alatar contacting you?"

"He has information about something . . . about something I can do."

"Like hearing the dead? If he's a death singer, how's that news?"

"It's more than that," I say, picking at the quilt covering my bed. "It's about Harri—" I stumble on the name. "About Harrison," I finish.

"Who's Harrison?"

I shake my head and Billy's face grows dim. "Boyfriend?"

"No," I say, laughing in spite of myself. "Harrison is buried at Jessam Crossing."

"Okay?"

"I can talk to him."

Billy frowns. "What do you mean, talk to him?"

"It's not like the others. I'm not just hearing his final thoughts. I mean I can have a conversation with him."

Billy is quiet for a long moment. Then he stretches out his legs and settles back against the headboard, his boots hanging off the edge of my mattress.

"So he's like a ghost," he says.

"Yes. That's what he is. Or at least what he seems to be. Not that I know how ghosts usually are. I mean I don't really believe in ghosts, which is weird and all because of what I can do. But if you asked me if I believed in ghosts I'd say no, even though I live in this old house and old houses are supposedly haunted, aren't they?"

"You're babbling."

"I can't help it. It just feels so awful to have this guy, this strange guy who tracked down my phone number and now my address and—oh God." I turn to Billy, my eyes wide with horror.

"What is it?"

"I didn't include my address in my death singer's profile. I didn't have to include it as part of my application or anything. There was a spot but I didn't do it. You're supposed to be eighteen to be a member so I omitted as much as I could just so they couldn't look me up."

"You've got a local area code."

"Huh?"

"Your cell. He probably used the area code to figure out where you lived. He'd have gotten to this part of the state, at least."

"How did he figure out I was in Monroe?"

"I don't know. But once he figured Monroe, it wouldn't have been hard to find you. It's a small enough town."

I shiver again and this time Billy scoots over to me. In a motion as natural as if we have been doing it all our lives, he drapes an afghan over me and draws me back to lean against his chest. I can feel the rise and fall of his breathing. In some ways it's even more intimate than kissing. I freeze for a moment at the realization that I'm in Billy's arms. His breath hitches. I tell myself to relax, and soon my body molds into the shape of his.

"So this Harrison," Billy prompts after a moment.

I nod and tell him everything. I describe how Harrison doesn't know much about his life or Jessam Crossing. I tell him what Alatar has said in his messages, that it's dangerous.

"Dangerous how?" Billy asks.

"Honestly, I don't know. I've only talked to Harrison a few times, but I never felt unsafe."

"You think he'll come back tonight?" Billy's voice rumbles through his chest. I can feel the vibrations in my toes.

"That's what I worry about."

"I'll stay for as long as you like."

I nod and we are silent for a long time, listening to the house settle around us. My parents put the dishes away down in the kitchen, their murmured conversations reaching us through the vents. I lean my head against Billy's shoulder. His skin is warm through the shirt and he smells like laundry detergent and pine sap.

"So this is Apollonia Stone's bedroom," he says after awhile.

"What do you think?" I ask, looking around the room and pretending I've never seen it before. The old mixes with the new. A frilly lamp next to a stack of *Essence* magazine. Tubes of lip gloss clutter a dresser painted white with pink hearts.

"That your homework?" he asks, nodding in the direction of the desk.

"Yeah. That's everything I have to finish before they let me do senior year. I did some today. My parents are making me," I say by way of explanation. I tell him a little about Abeline Academy.

"Good," he says.

"A part of me wants to skip the rest and not finish," I yawn.

"Drop out?"

"Maybe."

Billy sighs and shifts away from me slightly. I lift my head from his shoulder, the side of my face suddenly cold.

"Is this the part where you give me the big speech about not dropping out? Or the big speech about how I should take my future into my hands and conventions be damned? Which one is it?"

"Neither. Do what you want, Polly. Drop out, don't drop out."

"That's it?"

"You wanted wise advice from the guy who dropped out of high school and can't pay his bills except by blackmailing the girl he likes into stealing secrets from dead people?"

"The girl he likes?"

"Sorry, that slipped out," Billy says, running a hand through his hair. Dark locks flop back against his forehead.

"It's okay," I say, my smile soft.

Billy stares at me. His gaze is intense. My heart skips a beat.

"I don't understand why you feel like you're stuck in Monroe for the rest of your life," I say, breaking the moment.

"What am I going to do, Polly?" he asks, his mood darkening. "I mean honestly. What can I do? Work some minimum wage job? Never afford a decent house or insurance?"

"You could get your GED," I suggest. "Try some community college. Maybe talk to a career counselor and figure out what you want to study. There are books you can read about vocation and stuff."

Billy snorts. "All of that costs money."

"Which you're getting, thanks to me."

"I know," Billy says, shrugging off the afghan. He rises and starts pacing around my room. For a tall guy, he is quiet and I don't think my parents can tell there's someone in the room with me, even though my floorboards are squeaky. "I've made maybe four grand in the past few weeks."

"That's good," I say, squashing the annoying voice in my head that reminds me all of that money was stolen.

"That's not enough," he says.

"Then we'll get more," I reply, rising up on my knees. "We'll keep going back to cemeteries. We'll get you the money." I can hardly believe what I'm saying but I know deep down that I want to help Billy, no matter what photographs he has of me.

"No," Billy says. He stops pacing and faces me, his arms crossed over his chest. "I'm not going to take any more money from you or the dead people. We're done with that."

"We are?" I squeak. "But why? You need more money."

"I'll figure it out."

"I'll help." I'm not sure what might have happened in that moment if I hadn't heard the stairs creak. "My parents are coming upstairs. You mind hiding in the closet?"

Billy gives me a searching look and then shakes his head. By the time I've said goodnight to my parents and closed the door, Billy has emerged from the closet. We look at each other across the span of the room.

"You want me to stay?"

There are all kinds of reasons why I should say no but instead I look at Billy's face in the shadows and I say yes.

"Just to sleep," I quickly amend, which makes Billy laugh gently.

"I didn't assume anything else," he says.

We have a few awkward moments where I duck into the bathroom to change into my pajamas and can't decide if I should ditch my bra or not. I opt for a tank and shorts. When I return to my room, Billy has taken off his boots and is lying on my bed. I lie down next to him and after a breath of hesitation, he pulls me into his arms.

"Tell me more about Harrison," he says, his voice rumbling in his chest.

"I was scared as shit when I first realized I could talk to him," I say, relaxing into the curve of his body.

"So that's what you were doing that day. You told me you were supposed to be mapping the cemetery and then you just sat in that one spot."

"I'm surprised you even remember it."

"I remember everything about you, Apollonia." He brushes my curls out of my face. My body tenses. His hand pauses for a moment and then rests on my neck. His fingers are warm. Words flash through my mind, things I'd like to say to him, things I'm not sure should be shared. A part of me desperately wants to be with him, but the rational part of my mind reminds me that we both have so many problems that nothing good could come of it right now.

It's almost like he can feel the confusion radiating off me. "Go to sleep now," he says at last. I nod against his chest. In a few moments his breathing has deepened and his body relaxed into sleep. I lie awake for a long time, thinking about everything I want and all the things I can't have.

THIRTEEN

Alatar never shows up at my house that night. I sleep deeply and Billy wakes me up as the early morning sun slants into my room.

"Hey, I should go. I've got a few things I gotta do at the farm," he says, bending over me. He's already got his boots on. "You going to be okay?"

"Yeah, I'll be fine," I say.

"You let me know if Alatar contacts you."

"I will."

He has one leg out the window when I stop him. "Thanks for coming over. I appreciate it."

"No problem," he says. He's about to drop to the ground when I blurt out, "Want to help me again today?"

"Sure. Meet me at the cottonwood tree in two hours?"

"Absolutely," I say, mentally kicking myself for saying something so lame. Billy's face breaks into a wide smile and then there is a thud as he drops to the ground. I catch a glimpse of his white t-shirt flashing between the trees before he's gone. I'm grinning as I look out the window. The day is bright and sunny. I don't go back to Abeline Academy until Monday and I'm going to see Billy in a few hours. My parents will probably want me to do some homework. I sigh as I look at the stack of books. Then I think about the list Mr. Milford had me write yesterday. I pull out my tablet and read through it again.

The first few reasons make sense. I'm doing tutoring because my parents are making me do it and because I got suspended from the pool, so I have some time on my hands. It feels good to see them written down in black ink. It's not like they were secrets, but now they can no longer hide in the recesses of my brain. Then I look at the rest of the reasons and they start to pull me down a rabbit hole.

I do want Tasha to be proud of me, there's no question about that. And Harrison would want me to finish high school, too. I'm not sure how I know that, but that just seems like the kind of guy he is. I gloss over the one about my dad being gone too much, even though it pulls at the hole in my chest. I know he's not choosing his work over me, but sometimes it feels like it. I focus instead on the ones about the past few years. I stare at the bullet points until the pattern emerges. I tossed over my best friend in favor of shallow idiots.

I throw the tablet back onto my desk and sprawl across my bed. The pillow smells faintly of Billy, a mix of campfire smoke and spice, plus a whiff of detergent.

"Darcy's not an idiot," I explain to my ceiling. "Chase is kind of a douche, though. And I royally fucked things up with Henrietta."

I roll onto my stomach and bury my nose in the pillow.

"Would Dorothea Brooke be mooning around like this?" I ask myself, pushing the pillow away. It occurs to me that I don't know the answer, since I haven't finished Middlemarch, so I head downstairs, grab a bowl of cereal, and take my book to the porch. I pause only to send a few texts to make arrangements for this afternoon.

Two hours later I'm waiting for Billy underneath the cottonwood tree. A huge smile spreads across my face as I think about him. My smile freezes when I catch sight of something in the woods across the road. A flash of green too bright to be foliage and moving too fast to be a trick of the wind. I stare at the spot, a chill creeping down my back. Nothing changes, even though I'm still staring at the spot when Billy pulls up a few minutes later.

"What is it?" he asks, seeing my face.

"I thought I saw something in the woods."

"Alatar?"

"Maybe."

"Is he still there?" he asks, craning his neck.

I put my hand on his arm, the gesture second nature. "No. Even if it is him, what can he do to us?"

Billy smiles and captures my hand, although he has to let go almost immediately to put the truck into gear. He swings the truck around and starts heading down the bluff. We rattle over the gravel road, the canopy of leaves arching over us. It has been weeks since it rained and the leaves are starting to look faded.

"Where are we going?" Billy asks.

I clear my throat. "I thought Jessam Crossing."

He doesn't ask why. Twenty minutes later we've parked at the pull-off and are hiking into the Crossing. It took longer than usual to get here because Billy deliberately took several wrong turns.

"Want to throw him off our trail in case he's following us," he said by way of explanation.

"Jesus, Billy, this isn't *Mission: Impossible*," I quip, quoting what he said to me last week when we were at Bluff Hill. He grins but I can't tell if he remembers. Billy is taking this Alatar thing seriously, though. He parks the truck a few hundred yards farther from where we normally park, behind a copse of trees so it's less visible from the highway.

"I want you to meet Harrison," I say once we reach the site of the settlement.

Billy takes a deep breath and glances over my shoulder at the cemetery. "Maybe later. "

"You don't want to meet him?"

"I think you need to talk to him alone. You go ahead. I'll keep a lookout." My heart drops but he bends down and rests his forehead against mine. For a second I think he's going to kiss me but instead he murmurs, "Cemeteries aren't really my thing." I wonder if he's thinking about his mom. I don't even know where she's buried. "But stay safe."

"I will."

Billy saunters away toward the edge of the clearing and I climb the hill to Harrison's grave.

He's singing again when I get there. I giggle once I realize he's singing *Always Look on the Bright Side of Life* from Monty Python.

"Hey, Harrison," I say, dropping to the ground. Like usual, the shadows beneath the tree shift and I can make out the shape of a young man.

Apollonia. Glad you're back.

"Me, too. Billy's here with me. I told him about you."

Did you now?

"He's down in the clearing. He said he'd meet you later. I . . . um, I had to tell him because of Alatar," I say, telling him about Alatar's messages and the note he left in my window.

I don't like any of it, Harrison says when I finish. *Did he say why talking to me was dangerous?*

"No. You've never seemed dangerous to me. Are you?" I ask, half joking.

Not that I can tell, Harrison laughs back. *Being dead and still able to talk to you notwithstanding, of course.*

I roll a few strings of grass between my fingertips. "What do you think I should do?"

Maybe you should clear out of town for a few days.

His answer surprises me. "If Alatar is following me, what's to say he won't follow me somewhere else?" " I say, crossing my legs. The dark red imprint of grass mars my ankle.

You think he's here now?

I glance over my shoulder at the dense forest creeping down the bluff on the other side of Jessam Crossing. I don't see anything moving in the woods except for a faint stirring of leaves on the trees and Billy pacing the perimeter. The breeze makes its way across the field, blowing the scent of manure off the fields on the other side of the hills. Billy lifts his hand when he sees me looking and I wave back.

"No," I say.

I still think you should go away.

"Not possible. My parents would freak if I left. Where would I go, anyway?"

You don't have a grandma or an aunt you could go visit?

"Nope. My parents were both only children and their parents all died before I was born."

Sounds lonely.

"Nah, I never thought of it that way," I say, although I'm lying. Memories flash through my head of all the bus rides home from school at the start of a holiday weekend and hearing my classmates talk about all the countless aunts and uncles and cousins they were going to see. Of course back then I always had Henrietta.

We sit in silence for a few moments. I study the tree line. There's a flicker of a shadow near the field. I stare at the spot but don't see anything that looks like a mentally unstable death singer.

"What about you? You think you had a big family?"

I like to imagine that I had people. Maybe some in Minnesota and some in Chicago or New York. Maybe we'd take the train to see them once a year.

"Did any of them come visit you? Any of your actual family? That you could tell?"

A woman visited a few years ago, Harrison says. *I didn't quite catch the connection, but I think she was descended from some of the people buried to my right.*

She had a little one with her as well, a little boy who tore around the field with a plastic rocket. She was doing some research on her family. At least that's what I picked up from what she was telling her son. He was more interested in racing. I hoped I might be related to them, though. That kid was really sweet.

He sighs. The long grass stirs.

I like the idea of having relatives out there somewhere.

"I'm sorry to say that there weren't any more Cards in Monroe," I say, telling him information I've been reluctant to share. "I've looked in all the census records through 1930. No Cards."

There's a pause. Then, *I see.*

"And I can't trace anyone who's buried at the cemetery to you, either. The last marked grave, aside from yours, is from 1900. You hadn't even been born yet, but then after you died, you were buried here."

You have any theories about that?

"Tasha thinks you're an anomaly, too. She wondered why there was a twenty-five-year gap between your death and the previous newest grave."

Huh. I wonder if it had something to do with that fire.

The wind dies down. I shift closer to Harrison's shadow. "What fire?"

He pauses. *I guess I didn't mention that memory.*

"Have you been holding out on me, Harrison Card?" I'm aware of how ridiculous this sounds, getting angry at a dead guy.

Hey now, don't get all worked up. I maybe haven't told you everything I remember.

I sit back, hurt. "You don't owe me an explanation, I guess. But I thought we were friends."

We are.

"Then why didn't you say anything about a fire?"

Harrison sighs. *Look, I like you, Apollonia Stone. I have no reason to distrust you. But I also don't know you well. I like talking with you, but I also have a right to my own secrets.*

"I guess," I say. Then, aware of how sullen I sound, I apologize. "You're right, Harrison. I'm sorry."

It's okay. I just . . . the church fire. His voice stumbles. *I don't have a clear memory. Just a sense of heat. And anger.*

"Anger?"

Yes.

"Do you think you died in the fire?"

Don't know. Hope not.

There's movement out of the corner of my eye. Billy emerges around the bend and stands at the base of the hill. All kinds of things are clicking into place.

"Okay. I want to go explore some of this. Check some things at the archives. Is that okay?"

I can't stop you from doing research, sweetheart. He sounds resigned but he also called me "sweetheart," which is a good sign that he's not too pissed at me.

"I need talk to Tasha. I'll be back soon." I gather my stuff and head down the hill, Harrison's faint goodbye at my back. I hope I have some news for him by the time I return. The only question is if he'll want to hear it.

FOURTEEN

an you take me to the archives next?" I ask Billy as we walk back to his truck.

"They're open on a Saturday?"

"Tasha's there right now. I texted her this morning and said I wanted to ask her a few things about Jessam Crossing."

"Sure," Billy says. I'm walking closer to him than I usually do. Our fingers brush and drift apart. Oh, screw it, I think, and I reach for his hand. His fingers close warm over mine and it feels like I've dipped my hand into a vat of happiness that is now traveling up my arm.

"Did you see anything?" I ask.

"No sign of Alatar or anyone else."

"Harrison thinks I should leave town."

"What'd you tell him?" Billy asks, and I'm struck by how natural he makes it sound, as if it's no big deal.

"I don't have anywhere to go and I can't just take off. My parents would mobilize the National Guard. And I can't tell them about Alatar or anything, either." Billy doesn't say anything except to squeeze my hand a little. "Harrison said there was a fire at Jessam Crossing."

"Yeah?"

"He doesn't know when. Or what burned. Might have been the church."

"Well, that clears things up."

"Still, a fire at a church in a Black settlement that later disappears. It's a little creepy." I shiver, the familiar bluffs suddenly seeming hostile.

"But no one's gonna do that now. Right?"

"I hope not, but you never know," I say. "And things still suck. Look at Trayvon Martin."

"The kid in Florida?"

"He died—he was murdered—because some racist felt threatened."

Billy tugged on my hand, pulling me up short. He turned to face me. "Has anything like that ever happened to you?"

I'm surprised by the intensity of his words. "Why?"

"Because I'll take them out for you if I have to."

We're at the truck now and there's a moment where the sun bounces off the mirror into my eyes and then I'm sobbing. Billy is there, folding me into his arms. He doesn't say anything. Eventually I stop crying.

"Sorry," I say, stepping out of his embrace. I've left damp splotches on his shirt.

"Don't be."

I take a shaky breath. "Whoa, not sure where that came from. Usually it's the adoption stuff that makes me upset."

"Why that and not the racism?"

The words spill out of my mouth. "It's because the racism stuff is worse and I try not to think about it."

Billy is silent for a moment, as if he's weighing how to proceed.

"Tell me some of the adoption stuff," he said.

Ah, he's going with distraction. I'll play along.

"Okay, well, it usually doesn't bother me that much. But it does get old when I'm out with my parents and strangers ask really personal questions about how we fit together."

"That happens?" Billy takes my hand and we walk toward the truck.

"Yeah. Mom says they used to get lots of questions from strangers when I was a baby. People don't think they're being rude but it's actually really annoying. Mom remembers going into a grocery store one time up north. This guy asked if I was her daughter. When she said yes, he said I was a cute kid."

Billy frowns as he opens the door. "I don't get it."

"Why did he bother asking Mom about me? He didn't stop anybody else and ask if the kid they were with belonged to them."

"Yeah, I can see how that would be annoying," Billy says as he slides behind the wheel.

"Sometimes people want to share adoption stories and tell you about how their niece adopted from the Congo or someplace, but even then, it's still weird. Like what am I going to say, 'Good for you!' or 'I'll be sure to look up your niece's child at our next adopted-people meeting.'"

Billy laughs. "You should totally have adopted-people meetings."

"We do! My parents used to bring me to a group in the Cities. It was for transracial families."

"Was it any fun?"

"Sometimes. It was nice to play with other kids who looked like me. Then everyone's kids got older and the meetings kinda fell apart."

"Monroe's getting more diverse."

"Still pretty white, though." I settle my feet on the dash and start telling Billy about when Henrietta and I had our magical kingdoms in the forest. I'm tired of talking about racism and adoption and besides, I like making Billy laugh. During the ride back to town I pretend we are a normal couple with a future together.

When we reach Ash Lawn Park, Billy pulls into an empty parking space.

"You want me to go in with you?"

"Depends," I say. "Do you want to meet Tasha?"

"Sure," he says, and turns the key.

We hold hands on the way into the library. The circulation worker I usually chat with is behind the desk. She starts to say hi but her face darkens when she sees Billy. She nods curtly and goes back to organizing books on a cart.

"That was weird," I comment as I lead Billy to the top of the stairs.

"Not really," he says, his fingers tightening around mine. The muscles in his face are rigid.

I want to ask him why but then we hear voices rising from the archives. I pull Billy halfway down the stairs and duck my head to see the basement. There's a middle-aged white man standing with his back to us, wearing a short-sleeved shirt and khaki pants. A messenger bag is draped over his shoulders.

"I understand your concern, Tasha," he's saying. "But the city can't undertake that kind of expense at this time."

"And I'm telling you, Mike, that the cost at this point is negligible. If we have enough proof, which I think we do, that Jessam Crossing is historically significant, we can't ignore it."

"All you have are a few documents in a box and a cemetery record. We've been considering the site for five years now and nothing's turned up."

"Nothing's turned up because the records aren't complete," Tasha says. I have never heard the edge in her voice that I hear now. "Historical records are by nature incomplete. If the settlement was abandoned by 1900, that makes it even harder to track down. But I'm telling you the same thing I told the mayor. The patterns are there if you know what to look for. And I just started looking. I'm positive there's more to be found."

The guy sighs and runs his hand through his thinning hair. "I'm not sure what to tell you. You've got the mayor stirred up but the city is satisfied with what we've uncovered. We're going ahead with the development."

"If nothing else, Jessam Crossing could be a tourist attraction," Tasha says, her voice tighter than I've ever heard it. "A way to explore the African American heritage of this area and of the state itself. And it costs the city nothing to explore it further. Just delay the decision for a few more months."

"Tell you what," the guy says, shifting the messenger bag to his other shoulder. "Go ahead and pull together whatever documents you can find about Jessam Crossing before the next council meeting. Let them decide."

"But that's in three days."

"Development of the site can't wait."

"Can't it?" Tasha says.

"Great. Good talk," Mike says, interrupting her. "See you Tuesday night at the meeting."

The guy gives Billy and me a brief nod as he bounds past us on the stairs. I recognize him from the newspaper, although I forget his last name. I don't like the scraggly goatee he's trying to grow.

"Who was that?" I ask Tasha.

"How long were you there?" she replies, taking in both me and Billy.

"Just caught the end of it."

"Mike Maloney. City manager."

She's standing with her arms crossed over her silk blouse, her lips pursed as she eyes the stairs where Mike disappeared.

"Um, Tasha, this is Billy," I say, gesturing to the boy standing beside me. Tasha snaps out of her reverie and shakes Billy's hand.

"I'm Tasha Washington. Nice to meet you, Billy."

"You too, ma'am," he says, which makes Tasha laugh.

"He's, um, he's been helping me with the cemetery," I say.

"Oh?" Tasha says, her upraised eyebrows the only thing hinting at the fact that she knows there's more to the situation than I'm saying. "Are you interested in local history, Billy?"

"Lately," he says. "Polly's told me some of your theories about Jessam Crossing."

"Theories that might come to nothing if Mike Maloney has anything to say about it. Now I need to pull together everything I have and bring it to the city council on Tuesday night."

"Can we help?"

Tasha regards me for a moment. "If you like. Let's see, we've got all of your records from the cemetery and the census data proving that everyone buried in the Jessam Crossing cemetery was Black. We have that scrap from the store ledger, the church records book, and most importantly, the newspaper clipping alluding to a Black colony at Jessam Crossing." She crosses to the front desk and starts flipping through a folder. "I've done a lot of work tracking down property records and trying to identify who actually owns Jessam Crossing."

"And?"

"And it's inconclusive. So far. Mainly because there are a bunch of records that are missing. But nowhere have I found anything indicating that the city owns it outright. That might be enough to slow down the council."

"Missing records?" I ask, a chill creeping down my spine as I remember the conversation I heard at Arnold Weber's grave, the comment about "She can't use what she can't find." But I don't know how to convey that information to Tasha without telling her how I know.

"There are a few decades' worth of property records that seem to be missing. Mainly the area that includes Jessam Crossing during the late 1800s."

"That's weird."

"Maybe not. The municipal building got hit by lightning in the seventies and there was a big fire. They're saying some of the property records got destroyed in the fire."

"Do you believe them?" Billy asks.

Tasha frowns. "I don't have any cause not to believe them. But it's still a little strange, especially since I toured the building soon after I moved here, mainly to find out about their records, and no one mentioned anything about records being lost in the fire. Still, it does happen."

"What about a fire at Jessam Crossing?" I say, the words slipping out of my mouth before I even knew they were lining up to be spoken. I could kick myself.

"A fire?"

"Well . . . um," I stutter.

"Polly and I were wondering if that's why the buildings aren't there anymore," Billy jumps in. "My uncle's got a barn that stood for eighty years before he let it collapse. We were thinking Jessam Crossing buildings might still be there unless they got destroyed somehow."

"Maybe," Tasha says, chewing her lip. "It's possible the elements took care of them, but I suppose it's worth looking into."

"Can we do that before Tuesday?" I ask.

"Sure. Maybe check the *Monroe Morning Call* on microfilm. I went through it looking for references to Jessam Crossing but it's possible I missed something."

I start heading for the microfilm machines when I remember Billy. "You don't have to stay. Unless you want to."

"I'll stay," he says.

Tasha has already sprung into action, sorting through more folders. "Great. Mainly what we have to do is get everything in order to show to the council. Polly, would you keep typing up your notes on the people buried in the cemetery? And Billy, I can get you set up on the microfilm machine if you don't mind reading through old papers."

"Not at all."

For over an hour we're hard at work. I'm typing up my notes and Tasha is getting things set in a PowerPoint presentation to show the council. It feels like we're a bunch of lawyers in a court show, trying to decide how best to present opening arguments. In a way, I guess we are.

Billy finds the article about the fire midway into the second hour.

"I almost missed it," he says, pointing at the screen. The article is tucked beneath the thirty-seventh installment of a lurid tale about two sisters who are being wooed by a wicked man. Tasha tells us this was common in newspapers of the time.

We are quiet as we read the story. It's two lines long and says that on the night of October 1, 1924, the Ebenezer Baptist Church burned to the ground under suspicious circumstances. It notes that the church was the former home to a small Negro congregation but that the building had been abandoned decades earlier.

"Well, goddamn," Tasha breathes. "Keep looking to see if there's anything more about the fire, okay?"

Billy nods and returns his attention to the machine. I drop back into my chair at one of the reading room tables, the census records swimming before my eyes. Holy shit, Harrison was right.

"You okay?" Billy is kneeling in front of me, his hands on mine.

"Where's Tasha?" I ask, glancing around the empty room.

"She went into that room behind the desk. Said she was looking for something."

"There was a fire four days before Harrison died."

"Yeah, I caught that, too. Seriously, are you okay?"

I give my head a shake and my curls fly. "Yeah, fine. Thanks for checking."

Tasha returns with the Jessam Crossing box and Billy rises to his feet. If she saw us holding hands, she doesn't say anything about it. "The last date in the church records is 1900. I suppose it could have been a coincidence that the church burned when it did. Might have been lightning. But it always raises my attention when a Black church burns, especially since the paper not only points that out, it points out that the fire occurred under suspicious circumstances." She pauses. "Especially when the KKK was on the rise again."

"The Klan? I thought they were only in the South."

"Sadly, no. They had a brief resurgence in the 1920s." Tasha purses her lips and tilts her head as she looks at the church book. "Hm. Anyway. The Klan in Minnesota wasn't quite like it was in the South after the end of the Civil War, but they were related. It was a national movement, tied to the end of World War I. There were a lot of immigrants coming from Eastern Europe, not to mention Blacks moving up from the South. There was a lot of social upheaval. The white people who already lived here felt threatened, like something was being taken away from them."

She glances at me and I nod almost imperceptibly. My mind flashes to our Knowledge Bowl competitions, how Melanie Nelson threw a fit when she didn't make the top team, tossing her blonde hair and implying that I only got my spot due to some kind of diversity quota, even though I'd beaten her by fifteen points on the written test. I wonder how often Tasha has had her presence questioned. Probably a lot.

"Anyway, the Klan stood for an America that was pro-white, pro-Christian, anti-Jew, anti-immigrant, anti-Black. It's not an unfamiliar creed, sadly. They were organized into local chapters and groups, which held rallies and parades." Tasha's voice took on a faraway tone. "Some of them took it further, committing acts of terrorism and murder."

"Jesus," Billy said.

"You know about the Duluth lynchings?" Tasha asks us.

"I . . . um, yeah," I say, remembering the uncomfortable stop my parents and I made on vacation a few years ago. We got out of the car on a busy street, seagulls screeching overhead. The three of us stared at the memorial for the three Black men who had been falsely accused of rape, dragged from prison and lynched.

"It wasn't the Klan, but it was during the same time," Tasha explains. "June 14, 1920. There was a circus in town. A white girl claimed she had been raped by six of the workers. All of them were Black. They were taken to the police station, and a mob broke in, not that it was difficult since the police had been ordered not to use their guns. Three of the men were lynched. Elias Clayton. Elmer Jackson. Isaac McGhie."

"Jesus," Billy says again.

"Yeah," Tasha says.

"What about the Klan rallies?" I ask, finally breaking the silence. "Were there any around here?"

Tasha sends Billy back to the microfilm and twenty minutes later we're looking at newspaper articles about a big Klan rally in Monroe in September of 1924. Klansmen and their families came from all over southeastern Minnesota and the paper boasts that there were over 2,000 people in attendance. The Klan had a big march right down Dolly Madison Avenue, their heads bared because there was a law saying parade marchers couldn't be hooded, according to Tasha. Their wives rode in cars at the back of the parade, waving as they all marched to the fairgrounds.

I'd always thought the practice of naming streets in Monroe after First Ladies was kind of charming. Right before they got the vote, a bunch of Monroe suffragists lobbied the town elders – many of whom were their husbands – to change the names, making the point that the only way women could enter politics was through marriage.

Now, as I stared at the photos, I wonder if some of those same men and women marched in the Klan parade.

"Chilling, isn't it?" Tasha asks.

"Yeah," I say, noticing the post office in the background of one of the pictures. It's the same building I've visited countless times with my parents, the same street I've walked down all my life.

"Look at this," Billy says, pointing to the screen. There, in a grainy photograph, is a large cross engulfed in flames. It's perched above the city skyline, midway up the bluff that leads to my house.

I feel like I want to throw up.

"Maybe we should take a break," Tasha says, laying a hand on my shoulder. "Sometimes this hits too close to home. Anyway, I have all that I need for the council meeting, enough to at least pause the city going forward with the development," she says. "Thank you for all your help. You going to be okay, Polly?

"Yeah, I just need a little air."

"Call me if you want to talk more," she said.

"I will," I say. Then Billy takes my hand and leads me up the stairs into the bright light of day.

CHAPTER

FIFTEEN

ou okay?" Billy is asking me as we walk down the steps of the library. Behind me I hear someone call my name.

"Polly. Polly!" A hand reaches for my arm. I flinch and jerk free before it registers that the voice and the hand grabbing my arm belong to Darcy and not some freaky guy named Alatar.

Darcy stares at me with rounded eyes. "Whoa, you okay, Pol?"

"Yeah, fine," I say, glancing at Billy, who's watching me with concern. "You scared me."

"I was shouting at you from the parking lot. Didn't you hear me? All those ladies with the strollers did," she says with a chagrined laugh.

"What's up?" I ask.

She fidgets with a silver ring on her finger. "Can I talk to you?" Her eyes dart to Billy. "Alone? Just for a few minutes."

"I guess," I say. "Wait for me?" I ask Billy.

"I'll be in the truck," he says, squeezing my shoulder as he leaves. Darcy frowns at his retreating back and then walks with me across the square to the ice cream parlor on Abigail Fillmore Avenue. She has me sit on one of the rickety white iron chairs before heading to the counter.

"Peppermint chip, right?"

"Sure."

She returns to the table a few moments later with a cup of peppermint chip and one of frozen strawberry yogurt. The scent of sugar and vanilla swirls in the air and I dip my spoon into the ice cream.

"Missed you at the houseboat party," she says.

"I saw the pictures on Instagram. Looks like it was fun." I wasn't lying. I had scrolled through the photos briefly, noticing only that I wasn't sad that I'd missed it.

"It was," she says. "You want to hear about it?"

"Um, sure."

Darcy nods and proceeds to tell me about everyone who hooked up and what everyone was wearing. I let it wash over me as I scrape away at my lump of ice cream. My thoughts are still on Jessam Crossing and the Klan rally ninety years ago.

"So, um, Polly, what was up with that guy at the pool? The one you yelled at?" she asks, bringing me back to the present moment.

"Is that why you wanted to talk to me?"

"Well, that was part of the reason."

"I thought he was being creepy. I guess I was wrong."

"Is that all?"

I set my spoon on the sticky table. "Go ahead," I say.

"Go ahead what?"

"You want to ask me about cemeteries. And whether or not I think I can hear dead people."

"Oh, no. No I don't," Darcy says, shaking her head so that a curtain of blond hair covers her face. "If you want to hang out in cemeteries, that's your business. And I don't really think you can hear dead people," she says, glancing at me though her hair. She means it to be reassuring, so why does it feel like rejection?

"Well, is there anything else?" I ask, ready to leave.

"Are you still grounded?"

"Yeah. For the rest of the summer," I say, settling back into my chair. The air conditioning hums around us.

Darcy lays her hand on my arm. "Polly, what's going on? What did you do to get grounded?"

I lean back in my chair, watching Darcy dab at her frozen yogurt. She'll probably only eat a quarter of it before throwing it in the garbage.

I consider what I'm about to say, and imagine what would happen if I finally tell someone the truth. Before I can decide, the words burst from my mouth. "I almost burned the school down and then I ran away to Arizona."

She stares at me for a moment. Then a sound that's a cross between a laugh and a cough explodes from her mouth. She sits back and slides her hand from my arm.

"Good one, Pol."

I shrug.

Darcy tilts her head. "You're shitting me, right? You're not the one who set fire to the shed."

I slurp my ice cream and don't answer her.

"Wait, does that explain why you've been hanging around Billy Meyer?"

My spoon slips from my fingers to the floor as I grab Darcy's hand. "Billy had nothing to do with the fire. It wasn't him. So don't go around saying it was."

Darcy stares at me. "Okay," she finally says.

I go to the counter to get another spoon. My hands are shaking when I return.

"What's so wrong about Billy Meyer anyway?" I ask when I return to my seat.

Darcy watches me carefully. "Nothing, I guess. I mean, he's a dropout and stuff. Doesn't have much going for him. Chase said—" She freezes.

"Ah, Chase," I murmur.

"Um, yeah. Chase," she blushes. "Um, well . . . we've been hooking up."

So this is what she wanted to talk to me about.

"Hooking up?" I probe.

"Yeah. After work a few times. Once at the houseboat party."

"The houseboat party."

Yogurt catches in Darcy's throat and she coughs so hard that I have to get up again to get her a cup of water.

"Polly, I'm sorry about everything. I didn't mean to hook up with your ex, especially at the party when I knew you weren't going to be there." Darcy folds her hands in her lap. She's wearing white shorts that make her legs look super tanned. I scrape the last trickle of peppermint from the bottom of my cup.

"I mean, I'm just really sorry," she whispers.

"You know what?" I say, looking her full in the face. "I don't really care."

I see the hurt in her eyes, although I'm not sure what put it there. "You don't care that I hooked up with your ex-boyfriend?"

"Not really. I broke up with Chase a long time ago, and I never should have been with him in the first place. So have at it."

Darcy stares at me. "I thought we were friends," she whispers.

Suddenly I understand why she looks so hurt. "You're mad that I'm not angry you hooked up with Chase?"

"I betrayed the girl code," she says.

I sigh, suddenly feeling very tired. "Darcy, you didn't betray me. I've been . . . going through some stuff and that's why I've been so distracted lately. I know I haven't been a good friend. It has nothing to do with you. I'm sorry."

Darcy gives a little hiccup of surprise. "I haven't been a great friend, either. You've changed and I haven't asked about it. You want to talk about whatever's going on?" She pauses, giving me an opening to tell her everything.

"I'll be fine," I say, declining the invitation. "Just some stuff at home."

"Okay."

I can tell it's not enough. "Maybe we can see a movie soon," I offer.

"I'd like that," Darcy says. She leans across the table. "Did you really set fire to the school?"

I nod and put my empty ice cream cup down. "It was an accident. But please don't say anything to anybody. Not yet."

"I won't," Darcy promises. "But what are you going to do?"

The question has weighed on me for months. "I'm going to make it right," I finally say. I find myself thinking of Billy, who told me last night that he doesn't want me to use my gifts to steal from the dead anymore. "I don't know how yet. Please don't tell Chase or anyone," I repeat.

Darcy rolls her eyes. "Especially not Chase. Dude can't keep a secret."

I laugh. "Then why are you with him?"

She shrugs. "I don't know. He's hot. Not a great reason," she says, laughing at herself. "Hey, you want to go to the mall or something?"

"Nah, I've got plans," I say, glancing out the window. I can see Billy's truck idling from here.

Darcy gives a low whistle. "You really like him, don't you?"

"What? I . . . um . . . well."

"Enough said," Darcy says. She sighs. "Just, be careful, Polly."

"What do you mean?"

Darcy glances at the truck, too. "He's just . . . he dropped out of high school and used to sell pot. How's that going to work next year when you're at college?"

I bite back my objection that I probably won't be going to college next year so it doesn't matter. "I'll figure it out when I get there."

Darcy nods. "Okay," she says, checking her phone. She looks like she's going to say more, but she's flipping through her messages. "I gotta go," she says. "Maybe coffee next week?"

"Sure," I say. She gives me a quick hug and then she's gone. It occurs to me that this might be the last time I have a personal conversation with Darcy. I see now that she's a nice person, but we have nothing in common. I need friends who accept me as I am, and I was always pretending with her.

Feeling relieved, I toss my cup in the garbage and leave.

———

"How was your ice cream?" Billy asks as I climb into the truck.

"Illuminating," I say, and then I slide across the seat and take a breath. I smell cedar and the faint scent of motor oil. It's the most amazing thing I've ever smelled. My eyes meet Billy's and I see the question in his eyes. I take another breath and bridge the gap.

My mouth brushes his. His lips soften and I hear the faintest groan in the back of his throat. His hand settles on my waist and then he's kissing me back.

When I was fourteen, my parents and I spent a week on the North Shore of Minnesota. On the recommendation of a ranger at Tettegouche State Park, we drove up a narrow, steep road to the top of Palisade Head. When we got out of the car, we tumbled down the short trail to the edge of the cliff. The entirety of Lake Superior spread below us, waves slowly churning against the rocky shore far beneath our feet. A wind blew the hair out of my face and seagulls screeched overhead. The vastness of the lake and sky was dizzying. I felt exhilarated and completely overwhelmed.

I feel the same way kissing Billy Meyer.

I don't know how long we stay like that, my hands in his hair and his fingers clutching my back. At some point one of us bumps the horn.

The sound is like a foghorn, low and loud. I jump back in time to see a group of junior high kids applauding us from the sidewalk.

We both laugh.

"Let's get out of here," Billy says, flipping the kids off with a grin. I slide back to my side of the truck and let Billy drive me away.

"Turn here," I say, pointing left at the intersection. I'm back on my side of the cab now, although our fingers are touching on the seat. Billy has to take his hand back to turn the wheel, but he returns his hand to mine as we drive up the bluff.

"Your house?" he asks, his mouth quirking in amusement.

"No," I say. "Somewhere better."

I direct him to a turnoff. He parks the truck a quarter of a mile from my house and we catch one of the footpaths that skirt my parents' property and takes us farther up the bluff.

"Where are we?" Billy asks as we walk into the clearing where the Sigrudsons lie.

Underneath the canopy of trees, I unlatch the gate. The Sigrudsons murmur pleasantly at my arrival. I turn to face Billy.

"We're at the back of my parents' property. These are my Sigrudsons. They built the original farmhouse and when they died, they were buried here. I've known them for ages."

Billy follows me into the tiny cemetery. I take him to every stone and introduce him, explaining who each one is. I tell them what they are saying as I lead him around the graveyard. His face, open when we arrived, grows steadily somber. He frowns as we complete the tour, and my heart plummets. Did I make a mistake bringing him here?

"I used to come out here all the time with Henrietta," I start to blather. "We used to have picnics and make flower chains and play tag. We got really into mermaids one year and draped blue bed sheets on the stones to pretend we were underwater. And another year—"

"Polly," Billy says. He puts his arm around my shoulder and presses his lips to my hair.

"What is it?" I ask, my voice already wobbling. I don't want to hear what he might say.

"Thank you for bringing me here," he says. He starts to say something else, but stops.

My body goes rigid against his. "Say it," I say.

He shakes his head. "I don't want to. Not here. I don't want you to have that memory here."

He put both arms around me, holding me tight until I relax against him again, my arms slinking up around his shoulders. I am crying, hard, angry tears that soak Billy's shirt.

"I'm going to make you say it," I say.

Billy sighs, the final gasp of wind before the thunderstorm starts. "I like you, Polly. A hell of a lot."

"Uh huh," I sniffle.

"But this shouldn't happen," he whispers. I collapse against him. Soon his arms feel like a trap, so I push against his chest.

"Why not?" I demand, putting space between us.

"I'm no good for you," he says. "I have no future, no prospects, no money, except what I stole. How is that going to work?" he asks, echoing what Darcy said only an hour ago.

"So you just give up?" I demand. "Pretend this isn't happening? That nothing's between us? I never figured you to be a coward, Billy Meyer."

Billy flinches but doesn't rise to the bait. I open my mouth to lay into him again, when he interrupts me.

"I'm leaving," he says.

"What?" I ask, the word catching in my throat. The wind stirs the tree-tops, undulating the branches. I really do feel like I'm underwater, drowning.

"One of my buddies is giving me some of his camping gear. I'm loading it into my truck and driving away."

"Where . . . when?" The words tumble out of my mouth.

"I could leave now," he says. "Tonight if I want. Head west. Maybe see what Wyoming is like. Or maybe see if my truck can make it to Alaska."

"I don't understand," I say, my mouth moving uselessly as my heart breaks. "What about the money?"

"I can't pay off my dad's debts but I have enough to skip town. So that's what I'm going to do."

"When did you decide this?" I ask, my voice shaking.

Billy's look tears through the air between us. "I was always leaving, Polly. You knew that."

"I thought you'd at least stay until . . . until whatever's going on with Alatar is done." I hug my arms to my abdomen, trying to cover my wound.

A squirrel scolds us from a high branch, making me jump.

"Goddamn squirrel," Billy mutters. He pushes his hand through his hair, his white t-shirt straining against his chest. "Damn it, Polly. I thought it would be easier if I just left."

"Easier for you, maybe," I mutter.

"No," he says as he cups my elbows. "Easier for you."

I'm crying again. Billy folds me in his arms and I nestle my head against his shoulder.

"I wasn't going to leave until we dealt with Alatar," Billy says, his voice rumbling in my ear. "I thought we could stay friends until I left, though. Just friends."

"So I shouldn't have kissed you?"

Billy's arms tighten around me. "I'm glad you did. Especially since all I want to do is keep kissing you." His voice trails off. "Although it might complicate things even more."

"This sucks," I finally say, making Billy laugh.

"It does," he agrees. "Maybe one day we'll cross paths again."

"Maybe," I say, even though we're probably both lying. For a second the world opens up and I picture striding across the stage in a graduation gown, then heading off to college, maybe at a place with lots of other kids like me. My heart breaks again when it realizes Billy isn't in the picture.

We stand like that for a long time, not talking, not kissing, just holding each other. Eventually, we break apart.

"I'll walk you to your truck," I say.

Billy shakes his head. "Why don't I walk you to your house. Just in case Alatar is lurking around here somewhere."

His words send a shiver down my spine. I hope the Sigrudsons were the only witnesses.

"Weird to think they burned a cross on this bluff," I comment as I lead him down the footpath to my house.

"Didn't think you'd want to come back here."

I shrug. "It's still my bluff. I'm not going to let a bunch of asshole white guys from the 1920s ruin it for me."

Billy puts his arm around my shoulder. "That's my girl."

He walks me to the edge of my yard. I catch his arm before he goes.

"Can we . . . can we pretend that you're not leaving?" I ask, my voice catching. Billy's face folds in concern, but I cling to his arm. I'm begging, and I hate that I'm begging, but I also know I will regret it forever if I don't say what I'm about to say.

"Please. Let's just pretend. For the next few days, until you really leave, that you might instead be staying."

Billy sighs and his breath stirs the curls around my face. "Polly," he says.

"Please," I interrupt.

He reaches for me, and for a second I think his eyes are full of tears.

"It will just make things harder, you know," he says against my hair.

"I know," I say. "But I don't care."

He leans down and kisses me hard. "Okay," he says when he releases me. "Okay."

CHAPTER
SIXTEEN

My emotions are rioting. When I get home that night, I can't even look at the piles of books on my desk. All of my motivations from the Abeline list disappear. Who cares about homework when Billy is leaving and a crazy guy is stalking me? Instead I stay up way too late listening to nineties hip hop before passing out with my earbuds in my ears around two a.m.

When I wake up the next morning, I find another note from Alatar in the window. He wants to meet. Maybe it's the way things ended with Billy or the fact that Alatar left the note when I was sleeping, but the scrap of paper enrages me. I clomp down the stairs into the backyard. I stride past the corral and walk into the woods.

"You want to talk to me, Alatar? Then come out and talk to me!" I shout. I'm vaguely aware of how ridiculous I must look and sound, but I feel a little like a warrior princess, so I channel that image.

"You can't come onto my lands and threaten me and mine!" I add. Okay, this time I sound like I'm quoting dialogue from a bad Western. I fold my arms across my chest and glare at the undergrowth.

I stand there for fifteen minutes, the mosquitoes buzzing around my shoulders, until I get the feeling that it really is just me in the woods, yelling at invisible monsters.

I compose a quick text on my way back to the house. When I get a reply, I send another and then tell my parents Tasha needs some help at the archives, and they agree to let me leave the house. I don't feel good using Tasha as an excuse, but I need to see Alatar.

An hour later I'm at The Price You Pay Diner on the edge of town. Just like when I was here with Tasha, I get a lot of looks when I come in from the few farmers hunched over their coffee cups. As always, I'm not sure if they're staring because of the color of my skin or because I'm not a regular. I ignore the looks and slide into a booth at the back, choosing the side where the red velour isn't torn. After I order, the waitress brings me a cup of hot water and a saucer filled with crumpled tea bags.

Billy arrives a minute later. The men glance at him and turn back to their coffee without much of a second look. The murmur of conversation doesn't dip even a little.

"Hey," Billy says, I stand up and let him slide into the booth next to me. I take his hand. It's another hot day but they have the air conditioner cranked and I'm grateful for the heat of Billy's body. I nudge closer, my muscles remembering how it felt to kiss him. I know he's leaving, but I decide not to think about that right now.

"Hey," I answer, dipping a tea bag in my cup and watching the water turn green. "You want food?"

"Not hungry. So what's the plan?"

"I don't really have one. But after I got this, I wanted to meet him. Confront him head on."

I slide the second note over the table.

"This guy doesn't know when to stop."

"He is persistent," I agree.

The door clangs once more and this time the whole diner comes to a halt as Alatar walks in. I'm assuming it's Alatar, at least, and the way he fixates on me confirms it. He's wearing a dusty blazer over black jeans. His face is tanned and a little leathery, like he's been out in the sun too long. His pointy cowboy boots slap the tile as he strides toward us. The men at the counter swivel to watch him pass, frowning as they catch sight of the gold chains at his neck and the mane of frizzy brown and gray hair.

"Apollonia," he says as he drops into the booth. "Who's your friend?"

"This is Billy."

"Ah, reinforcements," he comments. His face transforms as a huge smile breaks over it. "You know me as Alatar, although my name's actually Declan. It is lovely to meet you."

"Wish I could say the same."

His forehead creases. "You don't want to meet with me? But you're the one who texted me."

I can't figure it out. He looks genuinely confused.

"She only did that after you kept stalking her. You think this is appropriate?" Billy asks, holding Alatar's note between two fingers. Declan's note, I guess. For a second, Billy sounds like my dad. I bite back a giggle. Oh great, I'm becoming unhinged.

"You didn't return my texts or my messages. I only wanted to talk to you, Apollonia." He fumbles with a pill bottle and shakes two pills into his hand, downing them with the water our waitress sets on the table. I wait until she leaves before interrogating him.

"You left messages tucked into my windowsill. Which means you had to climb up the side of the house and figure out which room was mine." The thought makes my stomach turn. "And how did you know you didn't get the wrong room? What if my parents had seen that note?"

Declan shrugs, making his curls sway around his chiseled face. He grins. "I've been in enough teenage girls' rooms to know what one looks like."

For a second I think I'm going to gag. Declan's face goes pale and he puts out a hand. "That came out wrong. I have a daughter. That's what I meant."

"You have a daughter?" Even Billy sounds surprised.

"Of course. She's all grown up now. Works as an office manager at a snack food company in Queens. I see her from time to time. We were estranged after her mother and I divorced, but she's agreed to see me again on a limited basis."

"That tracks," Billy murmurs to me.

"I really am sorry for invading your privacy," Declan says to me. "I just needed to make sure you were responding suitably to the threat you're under."

"The threat?"

"From your ostara."

"My what?" I demand, my voice squeaking.

"Ostara. It's the word for what you're describing."

"I don't understand," I say. It dawns on me that my fingertips are wet from dangling in the tepid water of my mug. I remove the teabag and plop it onto a paper napkin. Ripples of tea turn the napkin a sodden gray.

"It's simple," Declan says. "I will explain. You and I are death singers. We receive the final song of the dead." His eyes flicker to Billy and he tilts his head. "Sorry, do you know about this? I assume since Apollonia trusts you that you—"

"I know about death singing," Billy says.

This makes Declan smile. "Good. I know we emphasize secrecy among the death singers, but it's nice when you have someone in your life that you trust."

I shift on the bench, not meeting Billy's eyes. He is motionless next to me. I wonder if he's thinking about what happened yesterday by the Sigrudsons, too.

"I don't always think of what we do as singing," I say, my voice hesitant. "The last words of the dead aren't always very . . . very songlike," I say, for want of a better word.

Declan looks at me like I've grown another head. "Of course those are songs!" he cries, slapping his hands on the table. My tea sloshes over the rim of my cup. A few of the farmers glance over at us. "We're just hearing the last lines. The song of the grave is the song of life! Even the most mundane ending is still an expression of life. And we get to experience the last moments of the song before it fades away for good. Isn't that wonderful?"

He reaches across the table and takes my hands. His skin is dry and warm. Billy's eyes are locked on our hands and I know without a doubt that he's ready to murder Declan if he tries to hurt me. I slowly pull my hands away. Declan doesn't seem to notice.

"So these ostaras," I begin.

"Ostara was a goddess of the dawn," Declan explains. "A symbol of rebirth and new life. It's fitting we use her name to describe the dead who are still awake."

I shiver, thinking about what it would be like to be dead but awake. Harrison has told me time moves differently for him, so it's not like he's just been stuck in a box for ninety years, but still.

"The thought disturbs you?" Declan asks, peering at me from over his tented hands.

"It's a long time to be aware of death, is all," I comment.

Declan's brow creases. "Yes, it is."

"Are there a lot of them?" I ask. "Ostaras?" The word is foreign in my mouth. "I asked on the forums and you're the only one who knows anything about it."

"Ostaras are rare. Just as rare as the death singers who can hear them. Most people die and that's the end of the song, except for the repetition. But for some people . . . they keep singing. Making new songs." He twirls a drink-ing straw between his fingers.

"Why?"

He shrugs. "I suspect the ostara have unfinished business and are particu-larly stubborn about letting it go. They appear to be anchored here, more than the rest of the dead. Like ghosts." He gazes at me with piercing eyes. "Maybe the few of us who can hear them have similar unfinished business. And sim-ilar stubbornness."

I look away, wondering if Harrison and I are bound by some kind of common thread.

"Tell me about your ostara," Declan says, his eyes glued to my face.

I shift on the booth, twisting my hands in my lap. "Harrison died in 1924," I begin. "He's Black, like me. He's not sure how he died or why he's buried at Jessam Crossing. He likes the river, wishes he could see it." My voice warms as I think about our conversations. "He's got a good sense of humor and weird taste in music."

Declan frowns as I speak, lines growing deeper around his mouth.

"You like him," he says.

"What? No, not like that," I protest, keenly aware of Billy breathing next to me. "He's . . . he's my friend," I say. "And I don't see what difference it makes."

"It makes all the difference," Declan says.

"Then please tell me," I say, sitting forward in the booth. "You've encoun-tered one."

"Two," Declan says. His face grows dim. "One I was able to help. The other . . ."

"The other what?" I press.

Declan is shaking his head, his curls bouncing all over the place. "I helped one but the other . . . The other ruined me." His voice trails off and he stares at the chipped table.

"What happened?" I ask, my voice low.

Declan presses the heel of his hand against his eye, making the copper bracelets on his wrist clink. When he looks back at us, his eyes are red. "I haven't always been like this, you know," he says, gesturing vaguely at himself. "I was successful, once. I had a house. A family. Degrees. Enviable professional accomplishments."

He waves the waitress over and asks for a cup of coffee, waiting for the half-filled mug to arrive before continuing.

"I had one secret, of course, one that no one knew. Not even my wife."

"Death singing?" I ask.

"I tried telling her once. She thought I was crazy. So I kept it a secret, for her sake. I stayed out of cemeteries, for the most part. My gifts didn't repulse me, but I worried about slipping up, making a mistake. So I stayed away." He clears his throat. "Until I encountered my first ostara."

He sighs and toys with a sugar packet between his nicotine-stained fingers.

"She was one of my daughter's classmates. A little girl who was killed in a car accident. When I took my daughter to the funeral, I discovered the girl was still . . . awake."

"What happened?" I ask.

A smile flashes across Declan's face, brief but affectionate. "I talked to her. She was confused. So was I. She couldn't remember what had happened. She missed her family. I suspect her confusion was her anchor. So I went home and did some research. Then I did some more research. I have an extensive collection of death singer manuscripts," he explains. "Perhaps some day I could show you?"

"Maybe," I reply, knowing I'm never going anywhere with Declan. "So what happened with the girl?"

"The codex explained there was only one thing to do with ostaras." He sips his coffee and I want to bat it out of his hand if it will make him tell us faster.

"What?" I demand.

Declan sets down his cup and dries his mouth on his jacket sleeve.

"Free them," he says.

Billy shifts on the bench next to me, his long legs brushing mine.

"Free them how?" I ask.

"How do you connect with any of the dead?" Declan asks.

"Amplification," I say. "Wait. That's how?"

Declan nods his head, setting his curls swinging. "It's simple. Easier than amplifying one of the regular dead, actually. You don't need anything that belongs to them. All you need is their permission." He takes another sip of coffee. "So with this girl—Emily—I asked if she wanted to go home. She said yes. I amplified her, and she was free."

I narrow my eyes at Declan. "Just like that?"

"Well, it was different than normal amplification. I amplified her, sank into her mind. It was as if we stood together on a train platform. She held my hand and we watched her short life pass us by. Even the car wreck," he says, his face clouding. "That part was unpleasant. But Emily remembered what happened. The knowledge freed her. Then she gave me a hug and faded away. All that was left when I returned was her final thought." His face folds in compassion. "She was asking for a piece of gum."

I lean across the table. "If it's as simple as amplifying them, why did you say it was so dangerous?"

Declan's face pales and he glances over his shoulder as if an army of the dead is advancing on the diner. We're getting open stares from the farmers.

Billy's voice breaks the spell. "It was the other one, wasn't it?" he asks. "You said there were two. The first was the little girl. And the second?"

"The second is the one that went wrong," Declan whispers. Then he shudders so hard that the table shakes and I lose the rest of my tea.

"Tell us what happened," I say as Billy drops a handful of napkins on the puddle.

Declan goes even whiter and his hands are still on the table. "She is nothing I talk about."

"You came all this way but you don't want to talk about it," I say.

Declan flinches. "It is not something I discuss," he repeats. Then he raises his eyes to mine and I see fear in them. "I warn you, but I do not discuss what happened to me. And for what little good I did Emily, it was all undone by Willow."

"Willow? Her name was Willow?" I ask.

"She cost me everything," Declan says. "I fell into her clutches and I was destroyed."

Billy grips my hand underneath the table. I grip his just as hard.

"Was she a child, too?" I ask.

He shakes his head, trembling.

"What did she do?"

Declan says nothing. Eventually he speaks, his voice a monotone. "This is the warning, Apollonia Stone. Even though you can free the ostaras, you should not. Leave them be. They are not your responsibility. This is what I learned from Willow."

We wait to see if he'll tell us more. When he continues to sit with his head downcast, I know we won't learn anything new. "Okay. We're going to go. Thank you for the information," I say, dropping a few dollar bills on the table to cover the cost of the tea and coffee.

Declan's hand covers mine. His eyes no longer carry the glimmer of fear.

"Be careful, Apollonia. This is why I came to warn you. Do not amplify him. No matter what you do. No matter how strong you think you are. It is too dangerous. Stay away. Let the ostara take care of themselves."

"Is that it?" I ask after Declan falls silent. He nods and I slide out of the booth.

"You've said what you had to say," Billy tells Declan, standing over him. "Now you'll leave her alone, right?"

"Of course," Declan says. "I will be in the area for the next few days, however. I'm at the Motel 6 if you have need of me."

"Why stay?"

Declan frowns for a moment. "Cheaper to fly on a weekday."

Outside, the heat smothers us like a wet quilt. Billy wanders to the edge of the parking lot and I follow. I check over my shoulder but Declan hasn't followed us out of the diner. I can still see him in the booth, hunched over the table. I wonder for a second if he's drinking the rest of my tea. The thought grosses me out.

"Clearly he's disturbed," I say.

"He is," Billy agrees, "but could he be telling the truth?"

"About Harrison?"

"You're the one who can talk to Harrison. What do you think?"

"I don't know. I suppose it would be different if we could see Declan's library," I muse, hardly believing I'm contemplating a visit. "But that's not going to happen."

"You do have another source of information," Billy says.

"Who? Harrison?"

Billy shrugs. "It's worth a shot. Tell Harrison what Declan said, see what he thinks."

I kick the ground, like what Astrid does when she's upset. I let the dust settle around my feet. "Maybe."

Billy takes a step toward me. "Polly," he says, his voice low. "You have to tell him. Didn't you hear what Declan said? About the girl? She remembered how she died. And that freed her."

"You think I'm supposed to free Harrison," I say, my words flat. Before, when Harrison talked about staying or going, it was hypothetical. Now he might actually be able to leave. No matter what Declan says, I'll help him if he wants to go. But the thought of Harrison being gone forever leaves me hollow.

"I don't know," Billy says, squinting into the sky. "Declan says it's dangerous. But he freed the other one."

"Maybe you're only supposed to free one ostara," I muse. "And the danger is amplifying more than one."

"Could be," Billy says, although he doesn't sound convinced. "Declan doesn't seem to know fully. But don't you think Harrison deserves to know his options?"

I glance at Declan's silhouette. He hasn't moved from the booth and he's definitely drinking my tea. "Okay," I say. I shield my eyes against the sun. "Will you come with me? I mean, you've been through most of this so far. Maybe you want to see it how it turns out?"

"Yeah, okay. Meet you there." He brushes the curve of my cheek with his hand. I turn my head and kiss his fingertips. I slide behind the wheel, my heart pounding in my cheeks.

———

Jessam Crossing is a ten-minute drive from the diner. I spend half the trip watching the road and the other half watching Billy in my rearview mirror. He has impressive posture when he drives, his head level and his shoulders straight. Despite everything that happened with Declan, and everything that happened in the clearing yesterday, all I want to do is pull the car over and throw myself into Billy's arms. Which is pretty much what I do when we get to the parking area near the trail to the Crossing.

"You okay?" Billy asks even as he draws me close.

"Yeah. Just a little shaken from Declan."

"Understandable," Billy says, his chest rising and falling beneath my cheek.

"Whatever happened to him, with that woman he was talking about, made him genuinely scared."

He takes my hand and we head off toward Jessam Crossing. "I gotta admit, Polly, of all the things I thought I'd be doing with someone like you, trying to decode a conspiracy of people who can talk to the dead wasn't one of them."

"What do you mean, someone like me?" I come to a halt along the path. The grasses are long and brush my shoulders when the wind blows.

"Huh?"

"You said someone like me. What does that mean?"

Billy shrugs and drops his head. "It's not like we were ever going to hang out together in school, Pol. Our social circles didn't exactly overlap."

"I didn't think you cared about that kind of thing."

"I don't. Not really." He shrugs again. "Well, that's probably a lie."

"So we wouldn't have been together in high school. We're together now," I say. "At least until you leave."

Billy regards me with those dark eyes. "At least until I leave," he repeats.

Neither of us says anything more as we walk up the hill toward the cemetery.

We find Harrison singing some Mavis Staples as we arrive.

"I've got someone here with me, Harrison," I say. The shadows under the cottonwood tree shiver and for a second I catch a glimpse of an amused smile.

Lemme guess. Your boyfriend. The mysterious Billy.

I shoot a glance at Billy, who's sitting next to Harrison's stone. "Yeah, he is kinda mysterious, I guess." I wink at Billy and get a slow grin and a shake of the head in return. I don't have it in me to explain to Harrison that Billy isn't mine forever.

"Is he nearby?" Billy asks in a low voice.

"Near the tree," I murmur. Billy's eyes creep past my shoulder. "Can you see him?"

Billy shakes his head no.

Tell him it's an honor to meet him, Harrison says.

I relay the message to Billy.

"Tell him the honor is mine," he says. I don't have to repeat the message because Harrison can hear Billy as well as he hears me. It's an odd thought. "Now tell him about Declan," he says.

Declan?

"Alatar," I say. "Well, his name's really Declan."

What's that guy up to?

I twirl a strand of dry grass between my fingers. I really should bring Harrison flowers.

"Well, he said you are an ostara," I begin, explaining to Harrison what Declan said about the dawn goddess and what he learned from his library. "And he's encountered two ostaras in the past. One he helped. The other . . . the other ruined him."

Ruined him how?

"He wouldn't say. But he warned me to stay away from you."

Yet here you are, Harrison says. I can hear the laughter in his voice.

"Here we are," I say.

"Tell him the rest," Billy prompts.

The rest? Harrison asks.

"Well, um. Declan helped the first ostara by amplifying her. He slid into her mind and together they watched her life pass by. She had . . . she had forgotten how she died. When she remembered, she was free."

For a long time, the only sound we hear is the chorus of frogs singing in the marshes and the whippoorwills answering in the rushes. A breeze steals over the hillside, stirring the leaves in the huge cottonwood tree above us.

Harrison coughs. And asks, *Free how?*

"She wasn't aware anymore. Just her final thought. Like all the other dead."

Where did she go?

"Wherever any of us go," I say, finding Billy's hand across the top of Harrison's grave. His fingers are warm in mine.

Huh. But you kept saying this Declan guy was telling you how dangerous the ostaras are.

"Yeah, well, that's the issue. Declan said that when he tried to help the other ostara, it ruined him. He wouldn't tell us how, but he made it sound like before he worked with her, he had a job, a family. And now he has nothing."

There's another long pause. *And Declan thinks if you try to amplify me, it will ruin you.*

"Yep. Although again, he was scant on details. But the bigger issue is that if I amplify you, you'd be gone. Free."

Free. Huh.

"Do you want to be free?"

We've talked about this already. Better the devil you know than the one you don't. Not that I think I'm heading for the fires of hell or anything, but I'd rather be here than elsewhere.

"Okay," I say, relaying what Harrison said to Billy. Then I start to tell them about the plan that had been forming in my mind on the way over. "What if I can give you a choice?" I ask.

How? Harrison asks, just as Billy asks me the same thing.

"Harrison, what if Jessam Crossing is the key to your death? And what if I can find out what happened to you? Maybe if we tell you how you died, you'd have a choice. You'd know how you died. You could stay or go. And it wouldn't be dangerous the way Declan made it sound. What do you think?"

I speak in a rush, not daring to look at Billy. When I glance at him, his expression is thoughtful, like he's working out a complex and elegant math problem.

But how are you going to do that? Harrison asks. *You told me you did some research already.*

"I have another idea," I say.

CHAPTER

SEVENTEEN

Midway through my Monday session at Abeline Academy, while doodling in the margins of my physics notes, I finalize my plan. I fumble for my phone, knocking a pile of books off my desk. Kevin, who had been sleeping next to me, gives a start and sits up, rubbing his eyes.

"Sorry," I mouth.

"It's okay," he says, stretching his shoulders and reaching for his flashcards.

"Everything okay, Miss Stone?" Mr. Milford asks from across the room. It occurs to me that he asks in a concerned way, not in the way that most teachers ask, as if you're doing something wrong.

"Fine. Just had a burst of inspiration," I say. In another classroom, this would have garnered some odd looks, but here no one bats an eye. We're all focused on our tasks and getting our work done. I wonder if this is what college will be like, at least during the times when no one is partying.

I text Tasha to tell her I'll be at the archives this afternoon, and then I watch the clock hands crawl. After ten agonizing minutes, I work on some calculus. I still don't like calculus but the distraction is oddly comforting.

Finally it's time to leave. I'm halfway to the door when Mr. Milford stops me.

"How was your second day, Miss Stone?"

"Good," I say, adjusting my backpack over my shoulder. I hope he stops talking so I can get to the archives.

"I wanted to touch base with you. Mr. Belkin has been in contact with me. You have a lot of work to finish, but I think if you keep working hard, you'll get there."

"Okay," I say, not wanting to tell him that my motivation for finishing anything has slipped over the weekend. Declan's revelations and Billy breaking my heart make schoolwork seem irrelevant. "The list has been helpful. The one with the reasons why I'm here."

Mr. Milford's eyes crease in a smile. "Excellent. And that's why I stopped you. I want you to add one more reflection piece to your goals. I want you to ask yourself a question over the next few days and see what comes up."

"Sure."

"The question you need to ask yourself, is what do you want most out of your life?"

The words flow unbidden into my mind: *I want to be me.* The words surprise me with their raw truth. Aren't I already me? I wonder, although deep down I know I'm miles away from who I want to be.

"You don't need to have an answer right away, or even share it with anyone," Mr. Milford is saying. "You're a bright student, Apollonia. I'm confident you'll dig yourself out of the hole you're in. And I don't have to tell you that getting a good education is key."

"Not everyone has the chance," I say, my mind flitting to a cramped apartment in Arizona and then to Billy stealing from the dead to pay for a chance to dig out of the hole he's in.

"That's true. But you do."

"And calculus helps how?" I demand.

He laughs. "Calculus helps us build bridges and skyscrapers. Maybe that's not your calling. Maybe it bores you to tears. But maybe it inspires a sense of awe and appreciation. At the very least, passing calculus means you'll pass high school, which makes you one of the people who does have a chance. And maybe you'll use your opportunities to help others. Don't waste it."

"Okay, sure," I say. A part of me means it, while another part of me just wants to get to the archives. What I'm about to do isn't very ethical.

I say goodbye to Mr. Milford and jump into my car. I push the old car to its limits, which aren't very high, on the way back to Monroe.

———

I'm out of breath by the time I race down the archives stairs.

"You in a rush, Apollonia?" Tasha asks, smoothing the edges of her paisley scarf. She's wearing a tan sleeveless blouse and a floaty black skirt. I am suddenly aware of the ragged cutoffs and faded t-shirt I'm wearing. I didn't even bother to shower this morning.

"I think I left my backpack here," I blurt.

"You mean the one on your shoulder?"

The weight of the backpack bumps against me as I half turn. "Oh yeah. I mean my sweatshirt. I think I left it here the other day."

"Well, I didn't see it out here," she says, gesturing to the reading room. "Maybe it's in the back."

"I'll go check," I say, dashing into the back before Tasha can follow me. I find the Jessam Crossing box where it always is, on the fourth shelf in the second bay. I pull out the church ledger and hold it in my hands. I draw a breath, glance at the door, and then drop the ledger into my backpack.

Now, I've never been comfortable with Billy stealing money from the dead. That's illegal and unethical. And what I've just done is also illegal and unethical. And Tasha needs to bring the ledger to the city council to show them how Jessam Crossing is important. But if this helps Harrison, it's worth it. Besides, I'm only borrowing it anyway. I'll bring it back before the council meeting tomorrow.

"Find it?" Tasha asks when I emerge.

"No. Must have left it somewhere else." I can't quite meet her eye.

"I've got an extra sweatshirt if you're cold." She gestures to the chair, where I see a Howard University shirt draped over the back.

"You went to Howard, huh."

"Sure did."

"That's an HBCU."

"Yep," she says with pride.

"I was thinking about going to one of those before . . . well, before every-thing happened."

"Before what happened, Apollonia?" Tasha asks, her voice level. "You want to talk about it?"

"I, um, I hit a rough patch. I got upset about a lot of things and kinda wigged out. But I'm better now. Getting there, at least." I try to ignore the weight of the ledger as it bumps against my spine.

"Glad to hear it. And I'm happy to tell you about my experience at How-ard. I had a great time and got a great education. It was also nice to be around other Black people," she ventures.

"Yeah, that part would be nice," I allow. "It'd be different from Monroe, at least."

"That's the truth," Tasha laughs.

I should get going but the questions pour out of me. "Was it hard mov-ing here? It's getting more diverse but there still aren't a lot of other African Americans around."

"It has its challenges," Tasha says. "I have to drive to St. Paul to get my hair done. And I have to order the lotion I use online since Russ's doesn't carry it. I get tired of people looking up at me whenever I walk into a restaurant, although I'm suspecting that's a small town thing in general. Still, I can't help feeling like they pause a little longer when they see I'm a Black woman."

"Happens to me all the time."

"You should check out a few HBCUs," Tasha says, tilting her head to study me. "I think you'd appreciate the experience."

"Thanks. I'll check it out." I'm eager to change the conversation. "How are things going with Jessam Crossing and the city?"

"Still gathering information. I should be set for the council meeting tomorrow night, thanks to you and Billy."

"Oh, sure," I say, edging to the door. The backpack feels like it weighs a million pounds and I'm sure Tasha can see the guilt written all over my face.

"You sure you're okay, Polly?"

"What? Yeah, I'm fine. Didn't get enough sleep last night." This is the truth, at least.

"So do you want to do some work now or do you have other plans?"

"Um, I've got some errands to run. I'll be in tomorrow, though."

"See you then, Polly. And if you like, I can tell you more about Howard sometime and college in general."

"Yeah, I'd like that. Good luck with the meeting."

As I head up the stairs to the main floor of the library, I have a weird feeling that I may not be back to talk to Tasha again.

"Chill out, Polly," I tell myself, then I spill out the front door into the heat of a Monroe summer.

Billy is waiting for me at Jessam Crossing when I arrive. I park behind his truck and sigh as I step into his arms. The backpack falls at my feet with a thud.

"Oops," I say, detangling myself from Billy to scoop up the backpack.

"What've you got in there?" Billy asks as I rummage around and pull out the ledger.

"Church ledger from Ebenezer Baptist. It's the one that was at Jessam Crossing. I borrowed it from the archives."

"Borrowed?" Billy asks, his eyebrows quirking.

"I'm going to put it back," I say with a wry grin. "Now let's go see Harrison."

"This plan of yours. How safe is it?" Billy asks as we amble toward the cemetery. He shortens his stride so I can keep up with him.

"As safe as any other time I've amplified."

"Huh."

"So it's a good thing I have a plan." I flash Billy a bright, false smile. He takes my hand and says nothing.

When we reach the cemetery, I can hear a few murmured whispers and Harrison's bright tenor singing an ABBA song. Honestly, that guy has the oddest taste in music.

You here to figure out how I died? Harrison asks as I kneel by his grave. I glance around but I can't quite see him today.

"Yep. I brought a church ledger from Ebenezer Baptist to see if I can amplify some of the other graves."

How's that going to help? You said that everyone else here died decades before me.

I don't have a great answer to this. "You're right. But we're out of other options, so maybe one of these graves can give me clues about Jessam Crossing and what happened here. Then I can go back to the archives and do more research. Maybe find out how you died. That way you'd have the knowledge of what happened. And maybe knowing would be enough to give you a choice about whether to stay or go. I know it's a long shot, but the only other option—"

Is to amplify me.

A breeze rushes through the trees on the bluff across from us, but it hasn't hit us yet. We're still cast in stillness.

"Have you changed your mind?" I ask, my voice gravelly.

A sigh comes on the wind. *Why don't you see what you can learn from the others first.*

"Okay," I say, opening the ledger.

That nice archivist know you have the ledger?

"Um, no. Not exactly. I'm going to return it, though, and it's not supposed to rain or anything, so it should be fine."

Uh huh.

"Don't you criticize me, too," I say, which draws a chuckle from Billy.

Where are you going to start?

"I found an entry for somebody named Matthias Jackson, who died in 1898. His stone is on the top of the ridge."

You going to do it now?

"No time like the present."

You said it, sister. Good luck.

Billy gives Harrison's stone a friendly pat when he stands up.

"You need me to do anything?"

"Nope. Same routine as before."

Billy mutters something I don't catch and stands with his feet braced at the top of Mr. Jackson's grave.

"I'll grab you or something if it looks like things are getting weird."

"And how are you going to know if things are getting weird?"

"I know you, Polly. I'll be able to tell."

His words take my breath away. I force myself to start breathing again. After my heart slows, I sit at the edge of Matthias Jackson's grave, the church book open against my thighs. I rest my fingertips on his name, at the spot where his hand might have rested once. Truth is, I have no way of knowing if Matthias Jackson ever signed the book or if the names were recorded by someone else. The handwriting is different throughout the book, so it's possible Matthias touched this very page.

I push aside my doubts, close my eyes, and reach for the dead man.

There's nothing. Not at first, at least. I shift my knees in the grass and concentrate harder, ignoring even the mosquitoes whining in my ear.

The words float up from the ground: *Should have packed the suitcase.*

Huh. I listen harder and hear the same phrase repeated, and then once more. Matthias Jackson hasn't faded away completely yet. This has promise. I press my fingers harder against the paper, dimly aware that I'm getting oil from my skin on the paper, which Tasha says will destroy the paper in time. Oh well.

I feel myself slip away from my body and toward the words about the suitcase. It's like other times when I've amplified the dead, but everything is moving slowly, like those dreams where you're trying to run but your feet are stuck in a bucket of Jell-O.

Should have packed the suitcase. Should have packed the suitcase.

The words wrap themselves around my consciousness and I know I'm close. I press my fingers so hard against the page that the spine of the book cuts into my thighs. I wonder if it will leave a mark.

Here we go, I think.

Then, nothing. My eyes flick open and I am a girl crouched at the side of an old grave with a book in my lap. The sun blazes in my eyes.

"What happened?" Billy asks.

"Nothing. I got close, I mean. I could hear his words and it felt like how it usually does when I'm about to amplify someone. But then, nothing."

"Nothing?"

"It was like running into a wall where you thought a door would be. Or like when you take out your earbuds in a library. Nothing."

"You want to try again?"

"Yeah."

I sink into concentration again, my hands on the book, but the same thing happens again. Or rather, nothing happens again. We try another grave, a Mrs. Reginald Johnson. She's listed in the book, too, although she died in 1878. She's singing, a scrap of "Amazing Grace." I latch onto the song and am about to slide into her memories, when the same thing happens. I'm shut out.

"Anything else you can try?" Billy asks once I return. He's standing at my side now, his fingers flexed to grab me if the dead try to take over my mind. The situation is so absurd it makes me want to laugh, although I'm too bummed by my failure to give in.

"Let's try a few more."

I visit six more graves, people in the book and people not in the book. People who died in the 1890s and a few who died in the 1880s. I even find an unmarked grave by following a heavy sigh, but the results are the same. I'm not able to amplify them.

We give the news to Harrison.

Were you surprised?

"Not really. It's only worked in the past when I had something that belonged to them. This time I only had scraps of their handwriting. Or maybe they didn't even sign. Still, I'd hoped this would work."

I hoped so, too, for your sake.

"I guess we're out of luck," I say.

Why do you want to help me, Apollonia? I'm just a dead guy in the ground. Devilishly handsome, I'm sure, but still, I'm dead. Nothing's going to change.

I laugh at his joke and try to answer. "I guess the fact that you'll never change makes me sad. I keep thinking about you being out here all alone after I'm gone."

Gone? Where are you going?

"Well, college, maybe," I say, sneaking a glance at Billy, who is watching me with a solemn expression. "I mean, I'll come back to visit, but some day I'll . . . die myself," I say, stumbling on the words. "What if you never find another death singer? And you're just out here by yourself forever? All alone?"

A wave of loneliness comes over me, so powerful that I have to press my hands into my stomach to keep from sobbing. Billy starts to move toward me, but I shake my head. If he touches me I will dissolve.

Despite my best efforts, a sob escapes.

You've had a rough time of things, haven't you, Apollonia Stone?

"Yeah," I say, wiping tears from my eyes.

What happened, Apollonia?

"I . . . People keep leaving me," I whisper, even though it's not quite right. I try again. "People leave because of me."

The morning stills and then stops. In the momentary pause, all of the grief I've been holding for the past seventeen years comes slamming down on me.

"That's not true," Billy is saying, reaching for me. The breeze stirs and for a second I feel the breath of another hand in my hair.

"It is true," I say. "People leave because of me. My birthmom. My birth sisters. Henrietta." I don't say the last name that's risen to my lips. It's too hard to talk about Billy when he's sitting next to me, holding my hand.

Harrison's sigh is a ripple in the wind.

You know that's not true, Apollonia Stone. You don't know what your birthmom was thinking when she let you go. You were a tiny, helpless baby. Your relationship with your birth family . . . that's got nothing to do with you. And how do you know she wasn't missing you and thinking about you these past years?

I've heard this language before, from my parents, from the adoption support group we used to attend, even from the family therapist we visited for a few years when I was in middle school. But no matter what they've said, I've always believed deep down that it had something to do with me.

"But—" I start to protest.

If there's one thing I've learned in my years, darlin', it's that nobody's got the control they think they do.

"I messed up my friendship with Henrietta," I say.

So fix it, Harrison says.

"I know," I whisper.

But it's hard to do that when you're just so angry.

I let his words hang in the air for a moment.

"Angry?" I finally ask. "I'm not sure I'm angry. I mean, yeah, sometimes. Lots of things piss me off. And I have to deal with shit that white people don't. But . . . " My voice trails off. I am angry about all of those things. But deep down I realize that my anger has been a mask for my grief.

Billy is giving me a quizzical look. I shake my head, trying to indicate that I'll fill him in later. Something is tugging at my mind.

"Wait. Harrison. You're angry, aren't you?" I press my hand on top of his grave. "That's what's keeping you here, isn't it?"

There is a pause. And then the world changes. The response is a howl of rage so deep and ragged that it takes everything in me to keep my hands pressed to the earth, trying to offer any support I can. Tears run down my face and my arms tremble. I would give anything to be able to make it stop for Harrison's sake.

Eventually the howl ends and the only sound left is someone murmuring Harrison's name. It takes me a moment to realize the voice is mine.

"Harrison, what can I do?"

When his voice comes, it is distant and rusty. *It hurts. I didn't realize how much it hurts.*

"How much what hurts? Are you in pain now?"

There's a sigh and a sound like sniffling. I can picture dark eyes filled with tears, although perhaps I'm just picturing my own.

When Harrison speaks, his voice sounds older. Sadder.

All these years I've been here, listening to the world around me. I've been dead for so long. And yet I am so goddamn angry.

"Is that what's holding you here?"

I don't know, Apollonia. Probably. Maybe.

"What are you angry about?"

He doesn't answer right away. When he does speak, he sounds like he's talking to himself more than to me.

I've been a ghost for ninety years. I learn a few new songs, talk to a pretty girl, but otherwise I float through time, pretending everything is okay. Holding onto a few scraps of my memories but having no idea about the rest of my life. Pretending I'm not being crushed. Maybe that's what I needed for these past years, but not anymore.

I get on my knees and lean over his grave.

"Harrison, what are you saying?"

He lets out a whoosh of air.

I want you to amplify me.

EIGHTEEN

Billy objects to the plan as soon as I tell him. I wait until we're driving back to town before telling him what Harrison said. Harrison wanted some time alone before I amplify him, so we're giving him some space.

"Are you forgetting everything Declan said?" Billy exclaims as he pulls into the parking lot at Riverside Park. "How dangerous it is? The risk?"

"He helped the first ostara," I point out. "And that went well."

"But what about the second? The one who ruined him?"

"Don't forget—you're the one who insisted I tell Harrison his options."

Billy's head drops, his dark hair covering his eyes. "I know. I just hoped he wouldn't take you up on it."

"Billy, do you really think Harrison will hurt me?" I ask, laying a hand on his arm. His eyes fall to where our bodies touch and I can feel his muscles trembling.

"No," he says at last, the tension leaving his body. "I don't think Harrison would try to hurt you. Not deliberately. But you don't know what it will be like. What if something happens no matter what you and Harrison intend? And what if you get hurt?"

"There are a lot of unanswered questions," I concede. "But Declan did free his first one. Emily. So maybe each death singer gets one ostara to help. And Harrison is mine."

Billy can't argue with this logic. Mainly because we're both grasping at threads, knowing there's a whole tapestry we're not able to see. At this point, we could make countless arguments about whether or not to amplify Harrison. All I know is that deep down, it's the right thing to do.

"Come on," I say. "Let's go for a walk."

We get out of the car and meander the paths next to the Mississippi. Even though I used to spend hours each day in the summer along the river with Henrietta, lately I've forgotten that the river is here. There's a nice stretch in the park with trails and a playground, but the rest of the riverfront is industrial. It's the antique stores and craft fairs that bring tourists to Monroe in the summer more than the water.

A barge slides downstream toward New Orleans and the Gulf of Mexico, its orange sides thick and dented. We perch on top of a picnic table on the edge of the park. I rest my feet on the bench and watch the river swirl past. A woman pushes a double stroller along the path near us. She tears up pieces of bread and hands them to her toddlers, who laugh riotously as ducks waddle up to them. I watch the woman's face. She doesn't smile once. I wonder if she ever smiles or if she's just having a bad day. I wonder if my birthmom ever smiled.

"What was it that made Harrison change his mind?" Billy asks.

"Me, I guess. Telling him about everything that's fucked up in my life. He . . . he's angry. And he wants to be free."

"You told him everything that's messed up in your life," Billy repeats, surprising me by not asking more about Harrison's anger.

"Uh huh. Why?"

Billy turns his face toward the river. "You didn't tell him about me leaving."

"I couldn't," I say, curling in on myself.

"Why?"

I open and close my mouth twice before I answer. "I didn't want Harrison's last few hours to be spent listening to me sob." I keep my words light, but Billy still flinches.

"I'm sorry for all of this, Polly," he says, dragging his hand through his hair. "I dragged you into this mess. It's all my fault."

I take his hand. "You may have dragged me into some of it, but I did my fair share of screwing things up. Even before you saw me that night." I'm smiling and crying at the same time. "So don't go taking all the credit for the mess."

Billy's smile is sad and his hand is warm around mine. For a while we sit and watch the river. The woman with the toddlers passes us again, talking on her phone. Her children are asleep in the stroller.

"You know I'm not leaving because of you," Billy says. "It's not your fault."

I lean my head against his shoulder. His shirt is warm from the sun and the muscles bunching beneath the fabric.

"I know," I say.

"And your . . . your birth family,» he begins.

"I'll figure it out," I say. "Do some journaling. Maybe do some therapy."

We sit for a while longer in comfortable silence.

"You think this is going to work?" he asks eventually.

"No idea."

"What if it works and Harrison is free?" he asks. "How would you feel about that?"

I take a deep breath to stifle the grief ballooning in my chest. "I'll miss him," I say. "But he shouldn't be stuck in that cemetery forever. And now maybe he'll get a chance to see what else is out there."

I check my phone. "We should get going." I slide off the picnic table, Billy at my heels.

"What if nothing's out there?" Billy asks as we walk back to the parking lot.

"Then nothing's out there," I shrug.

"I didn't know if Harrison changed your views of things. That maybe something exists after this."

"Is that what you want?" I ask, pausing next to Billy's truck. The front is crusted with dead bugs. "To believe in an afterlife?"

"Don't you?"

"Sure. But I don't see how we'll ever know for sure, not until we die. All the religions in the world talk about this. They all have answers to what happens after you die. But no one really knows. All we have are questions. So that's the cool part about dying."

"What is?"

"You get to go find the answers."

Billy looks across the narrow park to the river beyond. The wind ruffles his hair. I can tell he's thinking, but all he says is, "C'mon, let's go."

———

A hot wind is blowing off the bluff when we return to Jessam Crossing. Strands of hair stick to my face. Billy reaches out wordlessly and brushes them away, his fingers gentle on my face. I blink back the tears filling my eyes and force myself to pretend he's not leaving.

Harrison isn't making a sound when we approach his grave. It's the first time I've been to see him that he's not singing.

That you, Apollonia? he asks as we draw near. His voice sounds a little faint.

"Yeah. Billy's here, too."

"Harrison," Billy says, ducking his head in the way I've seen men do at the gas station.

Say hi from me.

"He says hi. You sound nervous, Harrison."

At the end of this, I might be gone entirely. Can't blame a guy for being a little anxious.

"We're not even sure this is going to work," I say, hunkering down on the grass. The blades poke my thigh and I wonder why we keep forgetting to bring a blanket. "We might be walking out of here in a half hour and nothing's changed."

So how does this work?

"Well, usually I have something that belongs to the person. I concentrate on the item and that lets my mind merge with the dead person's."

But you don't have anything of mine.

"According to Declan, it's not necessary. All I need is your permission." I fill my lungs with air and puff my cheeks as I blow out the breath. The gesture relaxes me but I'm still fidgeting with the grass near my ankles, shredding it between my fingers.

"What can I do?" Billy asks.

"Just be with me," I say, glancing up into his face. His eyes are serious as he presses a hand to my shoulder. His hand falls away and I turn to Harrison.

"Ready?"

As ready as I'll ever be.

I don't think about saying goodbye to Harrison yet, because Declan made it sound like he was with the little girl he amplified while she was remembering her death. Still, I feel like the occasion calls for something formal. "Harrison J. Card, do you give me permission to amplify you?"

There's a moment before he answers. Then I hear his whisper: Yes.

I lean forward and place my palms on his grave. It's been so long since he was buried that the grave has blended seamlessly with the earth surrounding it. Like most graves, were it not for the headstone, you would never know anyone was here.

"I'm going to reach toward your mind. I have no idea if you'll sense it or not. But here we go."

I close my eyes and let my mind expand.

I find Harrison right away, the tendrils of his mind reaching toward me. Unlike the others, his mind is both in the ground and above it. I picture looping a finger around a curl of thought as if we were walking along a sidewalk and I took his hand. I stay with the image and sounds emerge in my mind, shoe leather against a wooden sidewalk. I feel a tug around my hand and I look down to see brown fingers tangled around my own. I raise my eyes but the image fades and I never see the eyes of the person holding my hand.

I seek the consciousness that even now is drawing away from me. I don't understand the resistance. I reach out with my mind, this time latching onto the hard plane of Harrison's presence. There's a buckle, a jolt like one of Astrid's rare protests when I climb on her back. Like I do with Astrid, I channel relaxation into my touch. Harrison's mind relaxes.

This time I feel hot sun beating down on my face as I hoist a crate into a barge. Men swarm around me, heaving their own burdens, and the smell of sawdust lingers in the air. I brace my hands on my knees, relieving the ache in my shoulders, feeling the muscles bunch in my thighs. I realize then that the body is not my own.

There's a stronger buck and I'm thrown out of Harrison's memories. I surge forward, wrapping my arms around the retreating imprint of his mind.

This time there's the smell of something burning. This time, the contact is far, far worse than before. A blanket of smoke smothers my mouth and there's an unbearable pressure around my neck. I can't breathe. My arms are bound. The wind gusts, blowing cinders into my nose and against my cheek. Tiny sparks flare across my cheeks. For a moment I wonder if I've ended up in the hell that Henrietta told me about. I try to open my eyes. That's when the screaming starts.

I get thrown from Harrison's mind and I catapult back to my own body. I can still hear screaming. I'm splayed on the ground, dirt caked beneath my fingernails, when I realize the screaming is mine. Hands reach for me and then lift me high. My screams echo through the evening air, but they are not the only screams. The louder, worse screams come from all around me. The only thing I know is that my screams will never be loud enough to drown out Harrison's.

I don't remember much. A door slams and I hear voices. There are muttered curse words and Billy's voice, urgent. I'm lying on something soft, my head tilted toward the sky. I'm dimly aware that I'm no longer screaming. I open my eyes and see a tiny plane slide across the black canvas of the sky, red lights flashing.

When did it get to be night?

I blink and the plane disappears. The edge of the sky looks like the inside of a seashell, soft bands of pink fading to purple and blue. The crickets are singing, replacing the whine of the cicadas.

The dome light of the truck shines in my eyes. Then a shadow spills across my face. "How long was she with him?"

"Not that long. Ten minutes?"

Hands cup my head. "Don't touch my hair," I murmur.

"What did she say?"

"Can you help her?" This voice is Billy's, tinged with an anxiety I've never heard before.

"If she wants it," the other voice responds.

"You really are an asshole."

"That may be true, but for now I'm your only hope."

The shadow crosses my face again and I open my eyes. "Declan."

"That's a good sign," he murmurs. He's still holding my head, and even though yesterday I never would have let him touch me, his hands feel

necessary, as if they're keeping my skull from exploding. He's chanting something underneath his breath, a low monotone. I can't make out the words.
After a while I stop caring and let myself float.

"That should do it," Declan says, hours or minutes later.

I open my eyes again. Declan has released my head. I see Billy's drawn
face over his shoulder.

"Feeling better?" Declan asks as I leverage myself to a sitting position.

"Um, yeah, kind of. How did you get here?"

"I followed you," he says without a shred of embarrassment. "I've been
following you since you left the diner. I assumed you would not listen to me.
I was right."

I wince as I shake my head and press my hand to my forehead.

"You'll have quite the headache for a few days," Declan continues. "But
you should be fine. As for the other one . . ." his voice trails off as he looks up
the hill toward the cemetery.

Memories of what happened crash through me. "Harrison."

"He's in much worse shape than you. I can hear him screaming from here."

"Why are we just sitting here, then? Why don't you go help him?" I stumble to my feet and Billy catches me.

"What makes you think I can help him?"

"You have to help him! You know about the ostaras."

"Knowledge that you did not heed, I'd like to point out."

"It worked once, you said! With your daughter's friend."

"But it did not work the second time," he says.

"What happened?"

Declan's face pales, then hardens. "You've seen the danger. You've seen
how they can destroy us."

"I haven't seen anything!" I cry. "All I know is that I tried to reach Harrison but he wouldn't let me in."

"He fought against you," Declan muses. "Interesting. Did you see any-thing?"

Images of the fire came back to me. I sniff the air, certain I can smell smoke. "I saw flames. My hands were tied. Oh God, is that how he died?"

"Perhaps," Declan says without moving.

We can both still hear the screaming.

I snap. "He's in trouble. And goddamn it, Declan, you are going to help me fix him!" I spin on my heel and start marching up the hill.

"How bad is Harrison?" Billy asks, catching up to me.

"He's screaming," I say. "Worse than I was. Much worse." I don't dare look over my shoulder. "Is he coming?"

"He's thinking about it," Billy says, squeezing my hand. "You sure about this?"

"Harrison is in pain," I say, wincing because I can still hear him shrieking. "He's been in pain for hours. And if Declan won't help, I'll do it myself."

I fall on my knees when we reach the grave. "Harrison, I'm so sorry. Harrison," I sob, my words lost to the screams coming from the ground. "I'm going to help you. I'll fix this, I promise."

I curl my fingers into the hard earth by Harrison's stone, my tears splatter-ing the smooth surface. I reach again and again for his mind, but I'm shaking and his screams are awful.

"Not like that," the voice says at my shoulder. Pointy cowboy boots enter my line of vision. Declan has joined me.

"How, then?"

"Harrison," Declan says, his raspy voice measured and slow. "My name is Declan. I'm here with Apollonia. We're here to help you." He drops to his knees next to Harrison and motions for me to do the same.

Harrison's screaming slows and then stops, only to be replaced by a wave of whimpers. He sounds like a scared little boy woken by a thunderstorm, wondering why no one is coming to help him. Somehow the whimpers are worse than the screams.

I face Declan across the grave. Billy hovers at my shoulder. I give him a weak smile to let him know I'm glad he's here.

"Harrison," I whisper. "Are you still there?"

There's only the sound of whimpering.

"You saw a fire?" Declan asks.

"Yes. Earlier I saw him loading a crate onto a boat."

"You saw him or you were him?" he asks, his face marring.

"I was him. Both with the crate and also in the fire. Before that there was one more image of walking down a sidewalk holding hands. But I was me in that one."

"The fire's the one we need to focus on," Declan says. "I will keep you as safe as I can, but there is still danger. Do you understand?"

"Yeah, fine," I sputter. "Let's just do this."

He holds out a callused hand, which I take. His skin is warm and his hand is firm, like a rock on a lakeshore that's been baking in the sun.

"Let's go."

That's the only warning I get before we plunge into Harrison's mind.

CHAPTER

NINETEEN

I love the river at night. That's when it's easiest to hear it. Most people don't know this, but the river is talking to us all the time. Usually it doesn't have profound things to say, mainly updates from upstream. Stories of eddies and backwaters, the deadheads lurking under the surface waiting to snag the flat bottom of a steamboat. Sometimes it tells tales of faraway places, of headwaters rolling over boulders in pine forests, of the tribes who camped by the stream, the fur traders who portaged and trapped their way to status. It talks about Fort Snelling, the Dakota who awaited exile from Minnesota, Harriet and Dred Scott who tried to leverage their time on free soil into actual freedom. I read a lot, too. So maybe I learned some of this from the books I purloined from the discard bin outside the Monroe Public Library. But I learn the truth of matters from the river.

That's why I came out here tonight, to learn the truth of matters. I've been here for a few years and am already feeling that itch I have to keep moving and see what else is out there. My mom tells me that there isn't a lot out there for a boy with my skin color. She's right, but I don't want to believe her. Sure, things are rough. Dangerous, even, but why would I be put on this earth if not to find something better than what the world wants to offer me?

Nellie agrees with me.

I smile when I think about her, even though it's dark and no one can see me. She's gone already, ran back to Monroe to be home before her daddy got off work. I offered to go with her but she said she'd been running through these woods since she could walk and she wasn't going to let any old fear of the dark scare her away. It's not the dark that scares me but the creatures lurking within it. So that's why I followed her all the way home until I saw her duck through her front door under the porch light. I had more thinking to do, which is why I rambled all the way back to Jessam Crossing, even though it's a fair hike from Monroe.

I stretch out on my back underneath the old oak tree. Nellie and I usually meet in the cemetery. She thinks it's strange but I think it's romantic.

"You find the oddest things romantic, Harrison Card," she told me the first time we met here. It was the time I waited for hours, convinced she wouldn't come. Maybe I'd made it all up, her eyes finding me in the lobby before *Shuffle Along,* the shy smile after the performance. The risk I took, pressing a note into her hand. Then I saw her cotton dress flapping as she came through the grass. Even though she was wearing a red print dress, she looked like a bride coming through the meadow, the grasses parting as she approached. Now that's a romantic image, but I didn't share it with her for a few months. Didn't want to completely scare her off.

"I guess that's not so odd," she said after I told her.

"Glad you agree," I said, right before I kissed her. That was two weeks ago when I told her my plans. Tonight she agreed to go with me.

"Are you sure?" she asked, her eyes wary.

"You don't want to go?" All my hopes hung on her answer.

"Of course I do. I just . . . I worry."

"For you?"

She gave me an exasperated look. "For both of us. But for you, especially. Being with me could get you killed."

I took her in my arms then. "Don't you worry about that," I said, feigning confidence I didn't feel.

"All right then. You wore me down with your charm, Harrison Card," she said, sighing against my lips.

"As long as I wore you down with something, Nellie Andover," I agreed.

There aren't a lot of places we can go, a Black boy and a white girl. Most places won't let us get married. We'll find a place, though, something all our own. We'll head east. Chicago and then New York City. And if that doesn't work, I'll save up enough money and we'll board a steamer ship for Europe. The war's been over for a few years and so has the flu epidemic. There might be something for us there.

I'm pondering our future, staring up at the inky darkness, when the world explodes. There's light and heat and a blinding terribleness that fills me with fear.

The flare came from the bottom of the hill. I scramble to my feet and run toward it, probably out of some kind of old instinct to help. I don't get far before I realize the church is on fire.

The heat from the fire scorches my face and I feel like the skin is peeling. I stumble blindly away from the heat, holding my arms over my eyes. I trip over something and fall onto my hip. A hand clamps over my wrist and I'm dragged to my feet.

"Look what we have here," a voice snarls in my ear.

"This is the Card kid," another voice says. I flinch as a finger prods me in the ribs. "Recognize him from the docks."

"Yeah, I do, too. We should make sure he knows what happened. Someone dropped a cigarette butt in the grass. Been so dry lately, no wonder the church went up in smoke."

I recognize the voice of the man who speaks. I've heard his hoarse growl down at the docks, barking orders at his crew. I don't remember his name but

I could pick him out of a crowd if I had to. I blink and paw at my face with my free hand. The hoarse man gives me a shake.

"Why, if I didn't know any better, I'd say he did it himself. Isn't that true, boy?"

"Nnnn . . . no sir,» I stutter. He gives me another shake.

"You didn't set this fire, boy? You sure about that?"

I know what's expected of me, but I hate how scared my voice sounds. "The fire . . . it was an accident, sir. That's all."

Hoarse Voice grunts and gives me another shake. "That's right. That's all that happened. The fire was an accident. And was anyone else here?"

"No, sir." My words come fast now.

"How do we know this kid won't turn us in?" the other man asks.

"Because we know who he is," Hoarse Voice says. "We know who he is and where he lives. Ain't you got people, boy?"

He shakes my arm again and I consider lying, but that would probably make the situation worse. "I . . . I have people, sir."

"Who are your people, boy?"

"I won't tell anyone about the fire. I swear."

"I asked who your people were, boy?"

The tip of a knife arches toward my throat. "The Lattimores," I stutter, spitting out my stepfather's name. "On Abigail Adams Avenue." I hate myself for giving them up but the men already know who I am. They can figure out who my people are.

"You got that high yellow mama, don't you? Cleans at the hotel, doesn't she?"

"Yes, sir."

"And you got some half sisters, don't you? Young, pretty things. One of them's a little dark but maybe I'll give her to George here."

My knees are shaking and a murder of crows claws the inside of my stomach. "I swear I won't say anything," I repeat.

There's a pause when they consider my words. I can hear the flicker of fire, the whoosh of air that blows a billow of smoke straight toward us. I cough and so do the men. In the distance I hear a shout.

"Shit," Hoarse Voice says, dropping my arm.

"We gotta get out of here, Leroy."

"Don't say my fucking name, George."

I know the other man, too. He owns the general store in Monroe. The wind blows another billow of smoke at us and we choke on the ash. I take advantage of the chaos to run as fast as I can. Behind me I hear the men shout but I'm gone, running through the cemetery, up the hill, where they won't think to look for me. There's only one main road connecting Jessam Crossing with Monroe, but I know a half dozen routes through the wetlands and a few through the bluffs. I run for a while and then I hide underneath a cottonwood tree, rubbing my eyes. Then I silently but thoroughly curse myself out.

My mom does an even more thorough job when I get home. My sisters are already asleep in the back bedroom but Mom's waiting up for me in the parlor, her hair up and a shawl wrapped around her shoulders.

"What were you thinking?" she asks, bending me over the wash basin. She's dabbing at the peeling skin on my face.

"I don't know."

"I raised you better than that. What on earth made you sneak out of the house on a Tuesday night and go all the way to Jessam Crossing. Was it a girl?"

"No, nothing like that."

"Then what was it?"

I shrug, spinning through possibilities in my mind. "I needed to think, is all."

"You needed to think."

"It gets crowded in here. Sometimes I like to get out of the house and do some thinking. That's all. I wasn't up to anything."

"Then why do your clothes reek of smoke?"

I'm tempted to tell her I was sneaking cigarettes, a crime that would normally lead to a thorough tongue-lashing, but I suspect she'd be happy to hear the smoke was only from cigarettes. I can't fool her, though. Arson and cigarettes don't smell a bit like each other.

"Mom, the church. It's on fire."

"What church?" she asks, just as we hear the first peal of bells from the fire engines. They fade as they head toward the Crossing. My mom's face drops. "Not Ebenezer." No one used the church anymore, but our neighbor, Alice Jackson, used to tell us stories about going to church there as a young girl.

"There were two men, maybe more. They burned it. At least I think they did."

"How do you know that?"

"They saw me."

Mother's knees buckle and she grasps the back of a kitchen chair. "They saw you. Do they know who you are?"

"Yes, ma'am."

This time my mom drops into the chair. She props her head on her hands. "I was afraid something like this would happen after that goddamn rally." I've never heard her swear before. "You need to leave."

"And go where?"

"Chicago. To be with your father's people."

"Chicago," I say, feeling optimistic despite what just happened. I could go to Chicago with Nellie and we could disappear into the crowds for a while.

"It's better than Alabama with my family, isn't it? Or Florida with your stepfather's?" She stares at the table for a long moment and then snaps to her feet. "You need to get rid of those clothes. Take them off and leave them by the stove. I'll burn them. We need to air out the house, too." She bustles around, making more plans to cover the smell of smoke in the house and to send me away.

"You listening to me, Harrison?"

"Yes, ma'am."

She stands before me and for a moment I hope she'll give me a hug or at least cup my cheek. She keeps her hands at her side, however.

"When you were born, I swore I would do everything in my power to protect you. That's my job and that's what I'm doing. Now go change your clothes."

"Yes, ma'am."

Mom and I don't say anything more about it the next day, although my sisters are curious why I'm being sent away to Chicago. My mother brushes away their questions with a simple, "It's time your brother learned something about his people."

They accept her answer, although they shoot me inquisitive looks as they hurry out the door to school.

News about the fire travels quickly through Monroe. The church burned completely to the ground. Nothing was saved. The local paper runs a paragraph about it, buried on page six. All it says is that the old Ebenezer Baptist Church burned to the ground on Tuesday night, due to unknown circumstances. The paper notes that the church was one of the oldest Negro churches in the state, although it had been abandoned for years, and that the police have determined that no foul play was involved. No one is surprised by this, my sisters report when they come home. I'm not allowed out of the house. Mom tells my neighbors that I've come down with an autumn flu. She then lets drop that she's considering sending me to Chicago to recuperate.

The neighbors agree with her, agree that it is probably best I leave town for a bit. In fact, many of them wish they could leave, too, and more than a few ask if a cousin or son could accompany me. More plans are made and soon it seems like half the Black population of Monroe might be following me to Chicago.

"Why does everyone want to get out of town?" I ask my mom that night. She snorts. "I raised you not to ask stupid questions."

I know the recent Ku Klux Klan activity has made her scared. A few weeks ago there was a huge Klan rally in Monroe. Two hundred men in white bed sheets and pointy hats marched down the middle of Dolly Madison Avenue, their feet matching the ominous drum tattoo at the front of the parade. They walked in perfect formation, eyes straight ahead, faces unmasked. The back of the parade was less organized, a flotilla of automobiles carrying the wives of Klan members from all across southern Minnesota. They marched to the fairgrounds on the edge of town and had a big meeting that lasted two days. We could hear the occasional chant and cheer.

"Why are they doing this?" I'd whispered. We were all huddled in the back parlor. No one was leaving the house, Mom had declared.

"They feel like something's being taken from them," Mom said, answering even though I'd meant it as a rhetorical question. "They look around and suddenly they see more and more Black faces in Monroe. And they feel like we're taking what's rightfully theirs. Money. Business. Land. And so they lash out, like a wounded animal backed into a corner."

"It's not right," I said.

She cut me a sharp look. "It's not, but don't you ever forget what they'll do to you if they get a chance."

On the evening of the first day, they burned a huge cross on top of the bluff. We could see it from my house, two thin lines flickering over the dark town. Our neighbors saw it too, and then we all went inside and closed our doors and windows. It wasn't like the old Klan in the South, this new Klan claimed. They weren't lynching anyone. True, my neighbors said, but doesn't it just feel like a matter of time?

I sneak out to Jessam Crossing one last time the night before I'm supposed to leave. I leave a note for Nellie in the rock wall behind the brewery. When I get to the Crossing, I only have to wait for a little while before Nellie arrives soon after dusk.

"Harrison," she says, throwing herself into my arms.

"Hey, baby doll," I say, brushing away the tears streaking down her face. We're hidden by a screen of dogwoods, but it is still dangerous for us to be here, perched on the edge of the cemetery overlooking the ruins of Ebenezer Baptist Church. It's been a few days since the fire and the ruins have finally stopped smoldering.

"You're really going, aren't you?"

"But you're coming with me," I say.

"When? Tomorrow?"

"Yes, tomorrow. Meet me at the train station and we'll ride out of this town tomorrow."

I see the hope in her eyes for a moment as her eyes flicker to the east. "I . . . no."

The word falls out of her mouth like something embarrassing, a wad of phlegm that plops on the ground between our feet.

"What are you talking about?" I ask.

She raises her hands to her face and I notice she's not wearing the dime store ring I got her. It wasn't an engagement ring. More of an engaged to be engaged kind of thing. "I can't leave," she says. "I can't go with you."

"Why the hell not?" I demand, my voice louder than intended.

"I can't leave. I love you, but I can't leave."

"So what, this was just a fling? You thought you'd see what it was like to be with a Negro so you have a story to tell your lily-white grandkids?"

She flinches. "It wasn't just a fling, Harrison. I love you. But what is our life going to look like? Always getting dirty looks, always worried that those looks might turn into something worse."

"We've talked about this, baby. Yeah, it's a risk, but it's worth it for us to be together. You used to think so, too. I don't get it. What changed?"

"The fire," she whispers. My body tenses.

"What about the fire?"

"They're saying it was an accident," Nellie says.

"They're saying that," I allow.

"But it wasn't, was it?"

I sigh and put my arm around her again, lightly tracing patterns against the fabric covering her upper arm. "No, it wasn't an accident. It was some men from the docks. They're part of the Klan."

"How do you know that?" she asks, her voice filled with dread.

"I was here that night."

"No you weren't," she protests. "You followed me home to make sure I was safe."

I smile. "You know about that, do you?"

"Of course I know," she says, nestling against me. "So you weren't here."

"I came back," I say. Nellie is silent. "It was a pretty night," I continue. "Warm. I wanted to think about you, think about our future. I saw the fire. I was running away and the men found me."

"Did they see you?"

"Yeah. I knew them and they knew me."

"That's why you're going to Chicago so suddenly, isn't it?"

I nod. "They threatened me and my family. I have to leave."

"Oh, Harrison," she says, throwing her arms around my neck and sobbing. I hold her close, enjoying the feel of her against me. It might be a long time until I hold her again, although I'm not giving up.

"It will be different in Chicago," I tell her. "You'll see. Just come with me. Or if you can't do that, then wait for me. I'll go there and get settled and then I'll send for you."

She raises her head and kisses me. Our mouths break apart for a moment. "If life were easier, I'd marry you right now."

It's both the bravest and the saddest thing she's ever said. When I hear the rifle cocked behind us, I realize it might be the last thing she ever says.

"Run," I whisper and I shove her as hard as I can.

"What?" she asks, shocked as I cast her out of my arms.

"Run," I say and push her again. There's a chuckle behind me and I feint left to cover Nellie's face from the weak moonlight.

"Go," I shout and then she's gone, a blur of calico quickly swallowed up by the night.

"You don't learn, do you, boy?" Hoarse Voice says, stepping out of the shadows. There's a few laughs and I realize he's got friends with him.

"Let her go."

Hoarse Voice searches the darkness behind me for long, agonizing moments. "Didn't get a good look at her face. But we'll track her down."

For a moment I hear my mother's voice as clear as day, as if she was standing right next to me, whispering in my ear. "Run," she says. Just like what I told Nellie. My feet stay planted to the ground. There are too many of them. I won't win. I don't want to get shot in the back, either. Hoarse Voice doesn't move either for a moment, and we are suspended in time, an eternal dance that has no resolution. Something scurries in the underbrush, a raccoon maybe, or an opossum. Then all hell breaks loose.

The men shout as they race toward me. For a second I think it is all of them, but most stay in the background. I manage to land a few punches on the three or four who tackle me. I think I break somebody's nose. Then one of the men retaliates in kind and my nose snaps as the blow lands square in my face. They drag me to my feet and hold my arms wide. Hoarse Voice approaches, his eyes beady in the moonlight.

"You're trapped now, boy," he sneers. Then he clenches his fist and drives it straight into my abdomen. The air leaves my body and I can't manage any-thing more than a pathetic wheeze. I stay on my feet and at that moment I decide they won't get the better of me.

"That all you got?" I taunt. I shouldn't say anything, should keep my mouth closed, but they're going to beat me up anyway.

"Looks like we caught ourselves an uppity coon!" Hoarse Voice crows. "Time to teach this boy a lesson."

What follows is a parade of punches to my face, back, stomach, anywhere they can reach. When I fall to the ground and spit out two teeth, they begin kicking me.

"Not his head!" Hoarse Voice keeps shouting as boot after boot lands in my kidneys and abdomen. Even at this moment I think they might let me go. It's only when I see the rope dangling from Hoarse Voice's hand that I realize they're going to kill me.

The noose is tight around my neck by the time they drag me to the tree. It's the same tree Nellie and I used to meet under. Pictures of her rise in my mind, followed by images of my mother and sisters, even my daddy, who left us when I was three. Angrily, I push the images away. I keep my toes on the ground as long as possible as they fumble with the rope. It slides off the first branch but then catches on the second. As soon as they pull me from the earth, I know I'm as good as dead. My legs dangle and the rope cuts into my throat.

My screams are still echoing when they come toward me, the grizzled man and the smooth-skinned girl. They step out from behind the dogwoods, their faces scared. They walk through Hoarse Voice and his men as if they are nothing more than ghosts, and indeed the men soon vanish, blown away by the midnight breeze. The grizzled man and the girl reach the tree, their hands raised. The girl wraps her arms around my legs and holds me up. I don't mean to kick but I do. I must hurt her but she only wraps her arms tighter around me and lifts, as if she could launch me into the stars. The man is behind me, untangling the rope. There's a shudder and then I'm free, sinking to the ground, my legs buckling as they lay me down.

"Apollonia?" I ask, the name coming to me unbidden.

She smiles, a sad, crooked grin. "Hi, Harrison."

The man comes to help her and they stretch me out on the ground, arranging my hands over my chest, smoothing my pant legs. They remove the rope from around my neck and I sigh. The man cups my head and leans over my face, murmuring words I can't understand. Apollonia holds my hands, washing me with her tears.

"You're safe now," she says.

"I don't understand what's happening."

The girl looks at the man, who nods at her even as he doesn't break his chanting.

"You're dying, Harrison. This is death."

"Is it?"

"You stayed for a long time," she is saying. Memories come to me as she speaks, of my mind's refusal to leave this place, even though my body expired decades ago. I remember the years passing, scraps of songs and conversations as I waited on my lonely hill. I thought I was waiting for Nellie but maybe I was waiting for this girl.

There's so much I want to tell her. How I thought it was my anger that kept me here, and maybe it did, but even more than that, I was bound by my grief. Grief over what I'd lost, over what was taken from me, over a country that killed me because of the color of my skin. I don't need to run from the grief anymore. What happened to me was terrible. Criminal. But my song isn't finished, not even now. She taught me this.

"You've wondered about death," she continues, touching my face, the tears shining on her own cheeks. "And now you get to go find the answers."

"Death doesn't feel like what I thought it would," I'm finally able to say. I hadn't wanted to go. Now it feels like sinking into the softest feather bed.

"Nothing does," she says with that same sad grin. I try to smile back but I'm just too damned tired. She glances at the man, who is still murmuring to me. He meets her eyes and she must see the answer. She turns back to me. Her hands tighten around mine.

"It's okay, Harrison. You can let go."

And so I do.

CHAPTER

TWENTY

Billy's voice brings me back to the present. "Polly?" he's saying, his voice low and urgent. I sit back on my heels, dropping my hands in my lap. Declan kneels across from me, still murmuring an indistinct chant.

"Polly?" Billy's voice is hesitant as he rests his fingertips on my shoulder. I reach up to tangle my fingers with his.

"It's okay," I say. I glance up and see the tree arching over the grave, the same tree that bore Harrison's swinging body all those years ago. I hate that tree.

"Is he . . .?"

"He's gone," I say. I listen to the grave, hearing nothing at all. "They lynched him," I said. "He saw them burn the church and they didn't like that he was with a white girl. So they lynched him. That's how he died."

Billy's hands tighten around mine.

"You did well," Declan says. He looks terrible, his face haggard and worn.

"What happened to you?"

He knows what I'm asking. "Her name was Willow. She died in 1886. Her baby died on the same day. They're both buried in a forgotten cemetery in Massachusetts. Willow was an ostara."

"What did she do to you?"

"It wasn't what she did to me. It's what I did to her." His face folds in grief.

231

"She wanted to be free, to be with her baby. And I . . ." He looks up at me, supplicant. "I'd fallen in love with her, you see. And I refused to let her go."

"What happened?"

"I became obsessed. Spent all my time in the cemetery, talking to her. I lost my job. My wife. Custody of my daughter. I couldn't let go. And in the end she hated me for it."

"Did you ever free her?" Billy asks.

Declan's shoulders slump. "Eventually. I amplified her and stood with her as we watched her die. She spit in my face before she let go. I didn't blame her."

"So you thought I would hang onto Harrison? That I wouldn't let him go?"

He shrugs. "It's human nature to cling. I wanted to spare you having to make that choice. When I saw your post, I knew I had to come out. I don't want anyone going through this." He sighs and shakes his head. "But you did make the right choice. You did not try to control the things you couldn't control. You freed him. Even though it would cause you grief, you let him go."

I nod, feeling his words deep in my bones. Then I collapse.

———

"I still can't believe you faced my parents the other night," I say, the phone pressed to my ear. I'm wearing jammies and I'm stretched out on my bed, a pot of cooling tea on my bedside table.

"Yeah, well, I figured that dumping you on the stoop and running after I hit the doorbell wasn't classy."

"You're a classy guy, Billy," I say. I barely remember when Billy took me home on Monday night. I remember the porch light and my mother's voice, anxious at first and then calm as she had Billy help me upstairs. "Wait, did you carry me to my room?"

"I did," Billy says, his voice warm. "They didn't let me stay, though."

I laugh. "Too bad." I'm still determined to forget the fact that Billy's leaving.

"How are you feeling?"

"Better. I slept most of the day yesterday so now I'm starving."

"What did you tell your parents?"

"Just that I was out late and got sick. I'm going to talk to them more today."

"What are you going to tell them?"

"The truth," I say. "At least as much as I can."

"You're a very convincing person, Apollonia Stone."

There's silence on the line between us. I twirl a loose thread from my quilt between my fingers.

"Did you get the ledger back to the archives?" I ask.

"Took it back Tuesday morning," Billy said. "Tasha wasn't around so I left it at the front desk with a note that it got swept up in our stuff by accident and that you'd be in touch."

"Thank you," I say. "For that and for bringing me home. And for dealing with my parents. For everything."

"Yeah, well."

"Declan gone?" I ask.

"I swung past the Motel 6 this morning. Front desk said he cleared out early yesterday morning. He been in contact?"

"No. But I wasn't expecting him to. He finished what he had to do and that was that."

"I went to see Harrison, too."

The breath catches in my throat. "You did?"

"It was weird. Being there without you. Even though I never heard him, it sounded quieter."

"What did you do there?"

"Sat for a while. Thought about Harrison. And you."

"I'm glad you went." I pick at my bedspread. "Although I was kinda hoping you'd cut down that tree."

"It's not the tree's fault," Billy says. "But I know what you mean."

I say his name and my voice breaks. He lets me cry on the phone for a while. When I'm done crying, I wipe my eyes and set the phone down to blow my nose.

"So what now?" Billy asks.

"I'm going to see if I can learn anything more about Harrison," I say. "Trace his family. And his killers. I doubt I can bring him any justice, but I'd like to try."

"Maybe you will be an archivist after all. Or a detective."

"Maybe," I say. My future stretches in front of me. I have a lot of amends to make. I'm going to come clean about how I set the school on fire. And I'm going to double down on my homework and try to catch up. But I'll do all of these things later. Right now I want to stay in this bubble with Billy. Even if it only lasts the length of this phone conversation.

"I should see if I can track down the girlfriend, too. Maybe she stayed in the area and there's family."

"What was her name?" Billy asks.

"Nellie Andover," I say.

I hear a cough on Billy's end of the line. "What did you say?"

"Nellie Andover," I repeat.

"Goddamn," Billy mutters.

"What?" I ask, sitting up. "Did you know her?"

"I had a great aunt named Nellie Andover."

"Oh wow. Do you think it's the same one?"

"Could be. She's buried in St. Boniface Cemetery. About twenty miles from town."

I pause. "Maybe we should go visit."

"It's also where my mom's buried."

There's silence on the line. "You want to go today?" I finally ask.

"You think your parents will let you go?"

"No, but it can't hurt to ask."

"I'll swing past and pick you up."

"Okay."

I hang up the phone and stare at the cracks on my ceiling. Is it my imagination or have they moved closer together?

After a few minutes, I get up from the bed and pull on some shorts and a t-shirt. Then I head downstairs. Mom and Dad are sitting on the couch on the screen porch, drinking tea out of purple mugs my mom made years ago.

I perch on the edge of the rocking chair across from them. A gentle breeze blows through the screens, carrying the scent of earth and grass. Wind chimes tinkle overhead. I try to remember this moment, how peaceful it is, especially since I'm about to make my parents even more disappointed in me.

"I have to tell you some things," I say.

My dad puts his mug down on the table. "We figured you did," he says.

"I've really messed up these past few months. I made a lot of mistakes."

"Yes, honey?" my mom prompts.

"I kinda freaked out after Althea died. That's why I took the car and tried to drive to Arizona. I wanted to see her grave. To . . . to see if I could find some closure," I say, omitting the part about how I wanted to hear her final thoughts. My parents don't need to know about me being a death singer. There are some things they just wouldn't understand.

"You know this part already," I say, "although I didn't let you know how upset I was by Althea's death. I tried to push it away, pretend like it didn't matter. I didn't even tell any of my friends what had happened. And what you also don't know is that I went to a party soon after I got back and got really drunk.

Then I took all of my adoption papers to the school. I wanted to burn them."

My parents are watching me very closely, mugs paused halfway to their mouths.

"I put them on the wood they were saving for the bonfire. Except I didn't move the wood far enough from the school and I set the shed on fire. So it was me. I'm the one who almost burned down the school."

Mom and Dad are staring at me, mouths agape.

"There's more," I say. "I pretended everything was fine this summer and that I was getting my work done. I wasn't, as you know. And I got suspended from my job at the pool because I yelled at that guy. I've been lying to everyone the past several months. And I'm done lying. I made so many mistakes, but I'm going to take responsibility for my actions. I hope you can forgive me."

By this time my mom is crying, tears running down her face. In an instant she's off the couch and has pulled me into her arms.

"Oh sweetheart," she murmurs against my shoulder, smoothing my hair with her hand. "My darling girl."

"Well, that explains some things," my dad says. He puts his arms around both of us and we stand like that for a very long time.

The scrape of a boot on the side steps breaks our embrace.

"Sorry, I didn't mean to interrupt," Billy says, standing on the other side of the screen door.

My mom wipes her eyes and goes over to the door. "You're the one who brought Polly back the other night. Billy, isn't it?"

"Yes, ma'am."

Mom pushes open the door. "Come in."

"Mom and Dad, Billy and I need to go do one thing," I say.

"You want to run off again after you just told us . . . what you told us?" Dad asks, his eyes flickering to Billy.

"It's okay. Billy knows about the fire," I say. "He knows about everything."

My dad frowns and starts to say something.

"He didn't have anything to do with the fire," I interrupt. "He's been the one thing keeping me sane these past few weeks." Billy dips his head, refusing to meet my eye. "And I will make amends for everything, I promise. I'll confess to setting the fire and I'll keep going to Abeline for sessions and I'll finish all of my work. And maybe start therapy. I just need to do one more thing right now to tie up some loose ends."

"I can come back later," Billy mutters.

"No," I say, turning to him. "There might not be a later."

He knows what I mean. He's leaving in a few days, maybe sooner. We have to go to the cemetery now.

"Fine," my mom says, surprising all of us. She cups my cheek. "I trust you, Polly. No matter what."

Tears fill my eyes as I rest my forehead against hers. "Thanks, Mom."

"Where are you going and when will you be back?" Dad asks.

"Two hours," I say. "We're going to St. Boniface Cemetery outside of town."

"Is this an archives thing?" my dad asks, relaxing slightly. I suppose he was worried Billy and I were running off to have sex. I try to push the image of having sex with Billy out of my head, even though I've imagined it plenty of times in the past few weeks. I don't want to turn bright red.

"It relates to our archives project," I say. "Billy's been helping Tasha with some of our project, too."

"Tasha mentioned something about that when she called," Dad confirms. "All right. Two hours. See you then."

I give him a hug, too. "Thanks, Dad."

Then I take Billy's hand and we head for his truck.

Billy's quiet on the drive. We don't talk much. With each mile that passes on rolling county lanes, the cold truth of what I told my parents becomes more real. I'm nervous. I never thought about what it might be like to confess to the fire. Maybe I'll end up in prison or something and have to get my GED instead of graduate from high school. Suddenly high school seems like a precious dream that's slipping out of my fingers, which is strange since I've spent months ignoring my work.

"Gotta make one stop," Billy says, interrupting my spiraling thoughts.

"Where are we going?" I ask as he turns onto a gravel road. We bounce down the rutted path before turning onto another, smaller gravel road. Before long we've pulled into a dirt driveway.

"This is where I live," Billy says, a muscle tensing in his cheek.

"This is your farm?"

Billy shakes his head. "My uncle's farm. Wait here, okay?"

Before I have a chance to answer, Billy is out of the truck. Soon his long stride takes him into the house.

The farmyard contains a few outbuildings along with two rusty tractors and several ATVs. The house itself squats in the center of the yard, chipped white paint and sagging front porch almost obscured by scraggly shrubs.

The door of the truck squeaks open and Billy slides behind the wheel.

"So this is it," I say.

"Yeah. My birthright," he says with a snort. "It was never much, even when my dad had it." He looks around the farmyard with tired eyes. "You ready?"

"Sure."

There's a bleary-eyed man peering at us from the barn.

"My uncle," Billy says. The two men stare at each other, then Billy's uncle scratches his ear and disappears into the darkness.

We back out of the driveway in a cloud of dust and drive along arrow-straight gravel roads until we're back at the highway. After another fifteen minutes we arrive at a town, although the word is too generous for this crossroads. There's a bar on one side of us and a metal shed on the other, the yard lined with rusted tractors. What I notice, however, is the church rising against the blue sky across the road. The church is huge, a red brick building with a red roof and white-trimmed bell tower. A flight of stairs leads to the front door and I already feel small, even though I'm all the way across the street. Statues of women stand on the steps, an army of Marys standing guard.

"This is it," Billy says, parking the truck on the flat strip of pavement in front of the church.

The cemetery is right next to the church, surrounded by a wooden fence. A sign arches over the gate: St. Boniface Catholic Cemetery. We sit and look at the cemetery. Neither of us makes a move to get out.

"You ready?" I ask.

Billy nods and opens the door. His feet are heavy as we walk through the gate. We pass a set of curved stone benches that look uncomfortable and a stone plinth dedicated to the memory of the unborn. I walk with Billy down the wide brick path. Trees arch overhead. The cemetery is long and narrow, flattening to farm fields at the boundaries. There's a mix of gravestones, everything from graying columns to shiny granite, as well as simple flat stones laid in the ground.

I hear voices as we pass, old men murmuring in German, old women sighing. I stop near a polished black granite stone, drawn by twin high-pitched shouts. Brothers, aged eleven and eight, died on the same day six years ago. There's a picture on the stone of the two of them standing arm in arm at a Vikings game. As I listen closely, I realize one of them is shouting the other's name.

"I'm so sorry," I whisper, laying a hand on the stone.

Billy waits for me, linking his hand with mine and squeezing my fingers as I wipe tears from my eyes.

"Sorry," I say. "This is supposed to be about you."

"No need. I knew the family. Car crash."

We hold hands as we walk to the end of the path, stopping before a flat stone bearing the name Eleanor Andover Johnson, October 14, 1906–April 5, 1977.

"This is her," Billy says.

"May I?" I ask. Billy nods. I crouch and listen at the grave.

"She's whispering the name John," I say after a few minutes. "That's all."

Billy nods at the stone next to Nellie's, which is inscribed with the name John Johnson. There's a veteran's star on a spike poking up from the ground.

"Her husband. My great-uncle."

"She died thinking about him."

"I'm surprised. From what I've heard, he was kind of a bastard."

He digs in his pocket and pulls out a scrap of fabric trimmed with lace. He hands it to me. The handkerchief is satin and was maybe once ivory. Now it is stained and yellowed with age. "It was her wedding handkerchief. Most of the women in my family carry it when they get married. Can you still use it, even though it wasn't just hers?"

"I can try."

I fold the handkerchief between my fingers and turn back to the grave. I feel nervous and realize I'm afraid of what I might see of Harrison. I know she ran the night he was lynched, but what if she hid in the shrubs and saw the whole thing?

"Stop being such a coward, Apollonia," I murmur to myself. I close my eyes, clutch the cloth in my hands, and reach toward the whisper coming from Nellie's grave.

I wade through Christmases shrouded in cigarette smoke, the moon landing on a grainy television, a damp cabin in Bemidji and a vegetable garden bursting with ripe tomatoes. I see faces of nieces and nephews and I wonder which one is Billy's mom. There are battered paperback copies of romance novels and the collected work of Emily Dickinson. I chase her further back in her mind, my fingers tingling as I go. I learn that she started a correspondence course from the University of Minnesota but never finished it. I learn she loved John enough to marry him. Only at the very end, as the memories blurred, do I see a flash of brown eyes and a familiar quirking smile. Then I'm borne back to the present on a wave of grief.

"She never forgot Harrison," I say as I rise to my feet. Billy loops his arm around my waist and I lean against him. "I don't know more than that."

"Are you going to see him again?"

"Soon. Maybe later today."

We stand in silence for a while, hearing only birdcalls and the rumble of a tractor in a distant field. Eventually Billy speaks. "There's one more," he says.

I know what I'll see as Billy leads me to the back corner of the cemetery. The flat stone is matted with grass clippings. I kneel and brush them away, getting dirt underneath my fingernails as I scrape the last layer away to read the inscription.

"Marlie Marie Meyer February 13, 1960–April 11, 2007. Beloved wife and mother."

"Even the stones lie," Billy murmurs.

"You didn't love her?"

"My dad didn't." His face is drawn, his lips compressed. "Just her name and two dates. That's all that's left of her."

"That's all any of us get, really."

"Some people get more. That guy over there has fresh flowers on his grave and he died in 1962. The one over there has pinwheels and there's a flag with butterflies next to it."

"So bring her some flowers. Or buy her a flag."

Billy shakes his head. "Some day I'll be gone and she'll be forgotten."

I stand up and point to the grave with the flowers. "You know that eventually no one will be around to bring him flowers. Do you see any flowers on the old graves? They probably had people to bring them flowers at one point, and now those people are dead. People die and are forgotten, Billy. Not right away, but eventually the ones who remember die and then they're forgotten in turn. It's the cycle of death, really."

"So you're okay with being forgotten someday."

"Does it matter in the end? I'll be dead, after all. I won't care," I grin through the tears in my eyes.

"And you're okay knowing that people will forget about your birthmom? And Harrison?"

This stops me cold. "No, I'm not okay with that," I say eventually, my voice hoarse. "But that's the way it works. It doesn't erase the fact that they both lived once. Nothing can change that. Just think of all the people who've lived and died over the past hundreds of thousands of years. We don't remember a fraction of them but it doesn't mean they weren't alive once." I purse my lips, a thought flittering around my head. "Maybe it's like a wave in the ocean, rolling in. The wave rises and we come into existence. Then the wave continues to shore and we fade. But that doesn't mean there isn't another wave."

I'm not quite sure where these images are coming from. It's like my subconscious has been unlocked and all of the things I've ever wondered about death are tumbling out.

"Sounds like reincarnation," Billy says.

"Maybe. I don't know. But don't you think it's amazing that we get to be part of the wave, even for a moment?"

"You're getting dangerously close to quoting one of those posters with a cat hanging from a tree: 'Life is short, live each day like it's your last,' et cetera."

I snort. "Do I look an inspirational-poster kind of girl? You know me better than that."

Billy scratches the back of his neck and brushes the hair out of his eyes.

"I do," he says, the words sending a thrill through me. Then he nods at the ground. "Can you tell me what she's saying?"

I drop to my knees in the dry grass and press my hand against the stone, listening. After a moment, I look up at him, the sun in my eyes. He moves so that his shadow falls across my face.

"She's saying 'sunrise,'" I say.

Billy turns away. I sit next to his mother's grave, listening to the cicadas screeching in the mid-afternoon heat.

"She used to say that when I was a kid. Your problems don't seem that bad at sunrise."

"Do you want me to amplify her?"

Billy shakes his head. "Not today."

He helps me to my feet and then pulls me into his arms. "Thank you, Polly," he says against my hair. Then he takes my hand and we walk back to the truck. We don't say much on the ride back to my house.

A curtain falls across the front window as Billy pulls into the driveway. My parents have been watching for me.

"You want to come inside?" I ask.

Billy won't meet my eyes as he shakes his head. "I can't. I have something that I need to do."

"What is it?"

He raises his gaze to me, his eyes haggard. I know what he's going to say before he says it.

"You're leaving," I blurt, my voice cracking.

Billy shakes his head, tears in his own eyes.

"The cops came to my house yesterday. They tracked down some of the transactions. They know it's me. Or at least they're pretty sure it's me."

I bury my face in my hands, my body shaking.

"What's going to happen to you?"

"I'm turning myself in," he says, lifting my head to look into my eyes. "I'm not going to turn you in. I wanted you to know that."

My voice is shaking. "You could, you know. I'm guilty, too."

His grin is sudden and fatigued. "I'm half tempted, as I'd like to hear how you'd explain your involvement to the police. But I'm not going to do it."

"Why not?"

Everything comes to a stop, the breath catching in my throat.

"Because you need to live your life, Polly."

It's not what I was expecting him to say, but it cuts deeply. I'm crying as he gets out of the truck and comes around to my side. He opens the door and helps me down. I reach for him, my arms locking around his solid frame. He holds me tight, his arms locking around me.

"Will I ever see you again?" I ask.

His smile is sad. "I hope so," he says. Then, "Have a good life, Apollonia." He kisses me one last time.

"So this is it?" I whisper against his mouth.

His smile is genuine and sad as he skims my cheek with his fingertips.

"Yeah. This is it."

Then he drops his hands and walks back to his truck. He pulls out of the driveway and our eyes lock for one last moment before he's gone. I stand on the front steps, grief tearing a new hole in my chest. This will be a loss I will carry with me forever. I hold it to my heart, adding it like a bead to the strand of losses I'm already carrying in my pocket. Then I wipe my face and go inside.

phone. Henrietta doesn't pick up, but I leave a message asking her to meet me. She doesn't respond, but I'm still hopeful as I make my way along the trail at the appointed time.

Is it my imagination, or are the Sigrudsons quieter?

"Soon I'll lose you, too," I say, laying my hand on Pethra's grave. "I'll miss you."

The grass around their stones is neatly clipped and the hedges have been trimmed.

"Dad must have been here again," I muse, assuming he was the one keeping the cemetery cleared.

"It wasn't your dad," a voice says.

Hope rises in my chest as I turn to the gate. Henrietta stands awkwardly outside the fence, watching me with wary eyes.

"You came," I say.

"What did you want to say?" she asks, her hands swinging at her side.

I'm tongue-tied as I digest her words. "Wait, you were the one taking care of the Sigrudsons?"

Henrietta purses her lips and nods.

"Why?"

She shrugs, her narrow shoulders shifting under her denim jacket. "They were my family, too."

A sob breaks free and tears start running down my face. Henrietta looks worried and moves toward me, taking my hands. It's the first time we've touched in years.

"Are you okay?" she asks.

I laugh through my tears. "Yes. And no. I have so much to tell you. But I'll get to that." My hands tighten around hers. "But first I want to say that I'm so sorry for how I hurt you at the houseboat party. I was a terrible friend. I didn't stick up for you and I embarrassed you in front of everybody. I threw away our friendship because of my stupid need to be one of the popular kids. I messed up. I hope you can forgive me some day."

Henrietta's hands tighten around mine and I can't tell if she's holding on or trying to get free. I'm not sure she knows, either.

Then her grip relaxes in mine. "Maybe," she says.

It's not everything, but for now, it's enough.

Relief flows through me. "So how are you?" I ask. "Can you stay and talk?"

Henrietta's gaze moves over the neatly tended stones. Hostas wave near the fence and a soft breeze carries the scent of warm earth. Henrietta adjusts her glasses on her nose and nods.

"For a little while," she says. "I'd like that."

She takes my hand and, like we did long years ago, pulls me down to sit among the familiar stones. I'm surrounded once more by my family.

———

The grass is brittle underfoot as I approach Harrison's grave, but this time it's because of frost, not drought. It's early November and all the leaves have fallen from the trees. It will snow tonight, a forecasted dusting that portends the fierce winter to come. I'm wearing jeans and the cold is leaching through my Converse sneakers. I think about Billy. He got put on probation and transferred out of the county. He also has to pay back the money he stole. I've written to him twice but so far he hasn't written back. I'll be in college by the time he's done with his sentence, maybe even studying abroad if I can convince my parents to let me go.

I went back and forth for weeks about confessing to helping Billy, but I didn't for two reasons. One was that I couldn't figure out how to explain my role in the operation without revealing my gifts as a death singer. The second is that Billy was so adamant about not turning me in that I felt I was some-how honoring him by not confessing. I hope I get a chance to see him again someday.

I pause at the base of the cemetery hill. A lot has happened with Jessam Crossing in the past few months. It turns out that someone hid the property records that would have helped prove Jessam Crossing was founded as a Black colony after the Civil War. Tasha only discovered the plot when she got the woman from the county assessor's office involved and they realized that a whole bunch of records had gone missing. After a little digging, they found the missing boxes buried in the back of a closet in Arnold Weber's old office. Mike, the city manager, swore he knew nothing about it and that the records must have just been misplaced. I don't know if Arnold hid the records on his own or if he was working with Mike. I couldn't use Arnold's words from when I amplified him as evidence, though, so nobody got fired over the mess.

Tasha combined what I'd learned from the census data with the property records, which confirmed that a number of Black families owned land in Jessam Crossing, and her own theories, which convinced the city council that Jessam Crossing was worth investigating as a historic site. From what we can tell from census data, the church ledger, and the cemetery, there were only five or six families and a half-dozen single men who lived in Jessam Crossing at its peak. Tasha suspects that when the city diverted the railroad tracks, most of the inhabitants left. It was probably intentional, a way for the city to drive out unwanted neighbors. We've traced several of the names from Jessam Crossing and found that a few original inhabitants moved to Monroe, while most left for Minneapolis or Chicago.

Tasha's also exploring a theory that Jessam Crossing might have connec-tions to the Underground Railroad. She told me this one day at the end of the summer after she came back from a research trip at the Minnesota History Center. She'd found an article that discussed an account by a guy named

Joseph Farr who talked about how his uncle's barbershop in St. Paul served as a stop on the Underground Railroad.

"I didn't know Minnesota had anything to do with the Underground Railroad," I'd said.

"Not many people do. It wasn't part of the system along the east coast, but there were enslaved Africans who escaped up the Mississippi or were accompanying their white owners who were on vacation. Farr and his associates would hide them and shepherd them to freedom. Farr talks about several enslaved Africans who came through Galena, Illinois, and alludes to other stations along the way."

She took out her phone and pulled up a map. "If you look on the map, Jessam Crossing is on the way."

"Holy Jesus."

Tasha laughed. "Exactly. Not that we'd necessarily be able to prove it either way, but it's still cool to contemplate."

Archaeologists spent most of the fall in Jessam Crossing excavating the church foundations and identifying the location of several other buildings. I spent weeks on the microfilm machine, but never found anything that mentioned the lynching of a young Black man, so the tragic death of Harrison J. Card will forever go unknown except by me and Billy. And Declan, I guess. The city is going ahead with the senior housing development, but they're building on farmland halfway up the bluff on the north side of town.

A few days ago I asked Tasha if she was mad that nobody got fired over the cover-up of Jessam Crossing.

"You gotta take your victories where you can," she said.

That's going into my college application essay, along with my attempt at answering some of the questions Mr. Milford posed at Abeline. I'm not sure yet what it fully means to be me, but I'm writing about how college will give me the chance to find out.

The wind whips up and I burrow deeper into my jacket. I've been to Jessam Crossing and the shadow of the cottonwood tree countless times in the past few months, bringing flowers and wind chimes and flags to decorate Harrison's grave. I'd watch the archaeologists at work and dream about the future. Sometimes I'd lie in the grass and cry a little about the past, but in ways that felt cathartic. I learned so much from Harrison. Without him, I wouldn't have discovered the truth about Jessam Crossing. I wouldn't have touched my grief. I wouldn't have thought about what I want most out of life before I die.

Jessam Crossing also holds loss. Billy's gone and it kills me to think that Harrison is gone, too. But deep down I know that loss is a part of life.

I lay the bundle of daisies on the stone as I approach Harrison's grave. It took me a few visits before I realized that his final thoughts weren't, in fact, his final thoughts. I had already heard his final thoughts when I helped him die. So I choose to believe his final thought is a message to me, a little joke, a farewell from a friend. He's singing the chorus of Bob Dylan's "Like a Rolling Stone."

"Hi, Harrison," I say, brushing the inscription on his grave marker. There isn't an answer and I don't expect one. "I just wanted to say thank you. For everything."

I listen for a while as the lyrics loop, as I always do. Then I smile and wipe away the tears. I kiss my fingertips and press them to Harrison's marker. Then I walk down the hill to my car, into the great unknown.

Acknowledgements

As all writers and most readers know, novels don't emerge out of a vacuum, and *Cemetery Songs* is no exception. I have many people to thank. My words can't fully capture my deep gratitude and appreciation.

Thanks to those who helped me with all aspects of my research (even librarians need research help!), including the librarians and staff at the Minnesota History Center, as well as my colleagues Adrianna Darden and Jeff Jenson. Thanks to Jeff in particular for taking the time to walk through my random questions about history and historical records, and for helping me see that the patterns are there if you know where to look.

For those who indulged me by accompanying me on some of my countless cemetery walks, including Blake Couey, Susie & Simon Carlin, Alyssa Auten, and Ben Leonard. I need to thank Alyssa in particular for her boundless enthusiasm, abiding friendship, and her spirit of adventure and inquiry. And special thanks to Ben for his insightful questions and his belief in the project, especially during the early stages.

For those who encouraged and supported me during the time it took to write and revise the novel: Sara Scrimshaw, Jen & Steve Baxa, Erika & Joe Urban, Eva Hendrickson, Andy Davis, Anna Hulseberg, Jeremiah Burnham, Diane & Carter Aikin, my parents, and all who took even a passing interest in my work. Also extra thanks to Nate Freeman, who read the novel at a late stage and helped guide it to shore.

Thanks to Lisa Vega for designing such a gorgeous cover.

Special thanks to Torrie White, extraordinary writer, gifted critic and marvelous beta reader.

To Stewart Huff, friend and comic, who championed my work and so graciously permitted me to use his words about how dying is the chance to go find the answers. Apollonia - and I - owe you a huge debt of gratitude.

To Jordyn Taylor, amazing sensitivity reader, talented publisher and all-around awesome person.

To Meghan Pinson, whose edits made the manuscript stronger, and whose belief in the project made me strong.

To Leila Brammer, who is not only my favorite reader but my favorite person.

To Chris, tireless supporter, biggest cheerleader, excellent beta reader, husband and friend.

To Sam and Jesse, of course. *Cemetery Songs* is for you.

And finally, to Don. He knows why.

RECOMMENDED READING

Transracial Adoption

As a parent, I have especially appreciated the work of Rhonda Roorda and Rita Simon, including *In Their Own Voices: Transracial Adoptees Tell Their Stories* and *In Their Parents' Voices: Reflections on Raising Transracial Adoptees*, both from Columbia University Press. I also recommend *Outsiders Within: Writing on Transracial Adoption*, eds. Jane Jeong Trenka, Julia Chinyere Oparah and Sun Yung Shin, from South End Press.

African Americans in Minnesota

Green, William D. *A Peculiar Imbalance: The Fall and Rise of Racial Equality in Early Minnesota*. Saint Paul, MN: Minnesota Historical Society Press, 2007.

Green, William D. *Degrees of Freedom: The Origins of Civil Rights in Minnesota, 1965-1912*. Minneapolis, MN: University of Minnesota Press, 2020.

Hatel, Elizabeth Dorsey. *The Ku Klux Klan in Minnesota*. Charleston, SC: The History Press, 2013.

Johnson, Frederick L. *Uncertain Lives: African Americans and Their First 150 Years in the Red Wing, Minnesota Area*. Red Wing, MN: Goodhue County Historical Society Press, 2005.

Pluth, Edward J. "A Negro Colony for Todd County." *Minnesota History*. Fall 2009. 312-324.

Swanson, Deborah, ed. "Joseph Farr Remembers the Underground Railroad in St. Paul." *Minnesota History*. Fall 2000. 123-129.

Taylor, David Vassar. *African Americans in Minnesota*. Saint Paul, MN: Minnesota Historical Society Press, 2002.

About the Author

Julie Gilbert's writing adventures have taken her into the nooks and crannies of various archives, the ruins of several forts, and prairie cemeteries too numerous to count. She is the author of the *Dark Waters* series from Stone Arch Books, as well as several titles in the *Girls Survive* series, and a graphic novel about workers' rights in the early twentieth century. Her short fiction, which has appeared in numerous publications, explores topics ranging from airport security lines to adoption to antique wreaths made of hair. Her most recent project is *Cemetery Songs*, a young adult novel exploring adoption, identity, and the mysteries surrounding an abandoned Black settlement in Minnesota. Learn more and connect with Julie at juliegilbertbooks.com.